Buying Time

Legacy Series, Book 1

PAULA KAY

DEDICATION

To my parents, Bob and Sandy.
Thank you for your endless love and support
and for always believing in me.

TABLE OF CONTENTS

CHAPTER 1

Arianna sighed as she and Blu left Douglas's office. Finally she could start planning her trip and get on with everything. "I thought this financial business was never going to be settled. You'd think that Daddy would have had things a little more organized," she said as the two young women made their way across the parking lot.

"Ari, seriously?" Blu said. "What's your big hurry? It's only been four months."

Arianna stopped to turn towards Blu, who'd been walking slightly behind her.

"Really? You wanna go there with me right now?" Arianna glared at her best friend, narrowed eyes hidden behind her designer sunglasses, not bothering to stifle the anger that seemed to come out of nowhere these days.

Blu turned her head away, but not before Arianna saw the tears welling up in her eyes. She could count on one hand the times that she'd seen her best friend cry, and all in the last few months. The petite rocker girl was what Arianna would describe as a little spitfire. Blu was quick to speak her mind and slow to show any vulnerability whatsoever.

Arianna took a deep breath and reached out to pull Blu in for a slight hug. "Hey, I'm sorry. I know the last few months haven't been easy on you either. And I'm totally out of it, if you want to know the truth."

At that, Blu reached over and slid Arianna's sunglasses up onto her thick dark hair, staring intensely at her eyes. "What's up with you? You're really starting to freak me out. I'm so worried about you."

Arianna laughed, dismissing the seriousness of Blu's question, and reached into her Chanel bag for the keys to her convertible. "Not to worry. It's just that I haven't been sleeping well so Doc gave me some new meds to try." She slid the sunglasses back down over her eyes. "I'm fine…really. I probably just shouldn't be driving. Do you mind?" She dangled the keys in front of her friend playfully.

Blu grabbed the keys from her friend. "You know me. I'll pass up the chance to drive a BMW…never."

Arianna smiled as the vision of Blu's old beat-up truck flashed in her mind. "And by the way, hopefully now that I've finally got access to this money, you'll let me treat you to something—and that something *should* be a car that's a little more reliable for you."

Blu hesitated for a few seconds and Arianna waited for her typical response, which was to decline anything that even resembled help or what she called a handout.

"We'll see." Blu reached to turn off the opera music that began blaring the moment she started the car. "And we are not listening to that God-awful music."

"Yeah, we'll see. You can be so damn stubborn. I don't know why you won't let me help you a little," Arianna said.

Blu glanced at her as she pulled the sleek red convertible out into the downtown San Francisco traffic. "Excuse me? *I'm* the stubborn one? *I* need help? You should talk. You're seriously starting to annoy me now. Ever since the accident and—"

"I know, I'm sorry." Arianna's head was pounding and she knew that she only had herself to blame for seemingly pushing all of her friend's buttons this morning. And she knew them well. *God, what's wrong with me?* She glanced at Blu, suddenly desperate to make everything okay between them, to make things normal.

"If it makes you feel any better, this was a big topic of discussion during my session with Doc yesterday." It was a manipulation of sorts on her part, because she rarely offered any information about what was happening in her therapy. From the change in Blu's stern expression, she could tell it had worked.

"What? *I* was the topic?" Blu said.

"Well no, not exactly that. But I have been opening up to her a bit more. She's always wanting to know about my support system, and of course you come up in that discussion, being my best friend and all." Arianna lifted

3

her sunglasses and batted her long black eyelashes at Blu in exaggeration.

Blu laughed. "Why you think your gorgeous Italian looks will ever work on me, I'll never know. And yes, you're stuck with me. Forever."

Arianna glanced at Blu, and then quickly looked out the window as she gathered her words during what seemed to her like an eternity.

"You're the best friend I've ever had, Blu."

Arianna swallowed the lump in her throat, then laughed, trying to lighten the mood, but they drove across the bridge towards her home in silence.

Arianna could still feel the slight tension as Blu pulled the convertible off at the Sausalito exit that would have her home in less than ten minutes. Suddenly she pulled over at the side of the road and turned the engine off. *Not today*, Arianna thought. *I really can't handle another big conversation.* But true to form, Blu was ready to speak her mind.

"You need to think about what you're doing, Ari. The decisions you're making. No one would fault you for needing some time. And you *should* take some time. Right now, you don't need to be traipsing off on this big world trip like you haven't got a care in the world. You know it's not best for you." Blu seemed well past the pleading stage as she looked Arianna square in the eyes. "You trust me to tell you the truth, don't you?"

Arianna nodded and braced herself for another one of Blu's lectures, which had become more and more common over the past few weeks.

"You're not well. You've suffered more loss and shock than anyone I've known. I'm just very concerned that you are not dealing with any of this. Does your doctor know your travel plans?"

"She knows. Yes. We've been talking about it all month. What's my motivation, am I running away, do I understand the possible ramifications, blah, blah, blah. I'm sick of talking about it, quite frankly," Arianna said, not bothering to hide her annoyance.

"You know that's not what—"

"Blu. Please. Just please. Can we talk about it later? I'm so—" She turned a bit towards her friend, trusting that the exhaustion she felt was just as apparent on her face. "—I'm just so tired."

Blu nodded, her mouth tight. "Okay, you win for now. But this discussion isn't over."

"Okay, Mom." Blu visibly winced as Arianna uttered the phrase she must have said hundreds of times since they'd become friends. Immediately Arianna regretted it, but not because of her own feelings. Nobody understood her, and she feared she'd spent way too much time already justifying why her tears had dried up so quickly after the accident. After her initial breakdown, that is.

Damn it. Why can't everyone just leave me alone? What I want isn't so crazy, is it? Anyone who had just inherited tons of money would do the same, wouldn't they? Heck, my parents loved to travel—even they would understand my desire. And really it's the least they could do for me, isn't it? Arianna swallowed the anger that threatened to bubble up to the surface again.

"Let's go back to my place and we'll have Gigi make us a nice cup of coffee. I just need to take a breath and chill for a bit."

"I can't today." Blu picked up her phone to glance at the time. "I'm already running late to pick Jemma up from daycare and I wanna spend a little time with her before I head to work later this afternoon."

"The restaurant? Or the bar?" Arianna asked, prepared to bite her tongue to keep from saying more. She hated how much Blu had to work, and had tried to convince her to accept some help with her bills, but she was the most stubborn person Arianna knew—at least when it came to financial matters. She recognized the defensive look on her friend's face now and silently reminded herself to keep quiet.

"Restaurant tonight, bartending tomorrow night. And I have the day free tomorrow—well, I'll be sewing, but I'll get Jemma for the day anyways," Blu said.

They started making their way up the steep driveway to Arianna's house, which overlooked the bay and city beyond. The view of the Golden Gate Bridge was magnificent here from the large estate where she had grown up, and it never failed to take her breath away.

Blu pulled into the massive garage and handed her the

keys. "Go have a rest. We'll talk later."

"Give J-bean a little squeeze for me and tell her I have a present for her the next time I see her." Arianna had bought the six-year-old the cutest little handbag that matched one of her own, and Jemma was going to love it.

"You spoil her way too much."

Blu's back was to her as she walked away, so Arianna couldn't tell by her face if she was still as angry as she sounded, or if the comment was meant to be light-hearted.

"Hey, Blu." Arianna called after her as she was getting in her own truck outside of the garage. "Thanks for coming with me today. You know I couldn't do any of this without you."

Blu turned her truck around to head down the hill, pulling up next to Arianna with her passenger-side window down.

"You'll be okay." Blu was silent for a few seconds, and Arianna guessed that there was much more she wanted to say. "And you're welcome."

Arianna felt sick to her stomach as she watched Blu drive away. She hated fighting with her; it wasn't something that happened often. She'd call her later to see about going over to her apartment tomorrow. It had been way too long since she'd seen Jemma, and she knew that her friend wouldn't stay angry at her for long. At least she hoped not. She sighed, thinking about how tough Blu could be sometimes as she turned to go into the house.

CHAPTER 2

Before Arianna was at the door, Gigi had it opened and was calling out to her. "Bella, what are you doing out here? Come in. I have a nice cup of tea ready for you. And I want to hear all about the meeting."

She smiled at Gigi's familiar term of endearment. She was way more than a housekeeper to Arianna; she had been a part of the Sinclair household for as long as Ari could remember. It was Gigi who had bandaged her knees and taken her to play dates when she was small. She couldn't remember her mother ever making a plate of cookies or helping her with her homework. It was Gigi who had been the constant in her life.

Arianna brushed a quick kiss across Gigi's cheek, thinking, as she often did, how lovely her skin was. She could only hope to have such beautiful skin herself at age fifty. The thought was in her head before she had even a moment to stop herself. She sighed.

"Thanks, Gi, but I'm so tired right now. Can we chat later? I'm dying for a hot bath and a little nap. Would you mind?" Arianna was used to Gigi taking care of her, and she had been especially attentive to her since the accident.

Gigi looked at her for a moment with the look of concern that Arianna knew all too well these days. "Come here." Gigi reached out her arms to pull her into the comfort of the embrace that Arianna had known all her life. "Everything's going to be okay, bella. You'll see."

Arianna cried the tears she'd been hanging on to all day. She didn't think she had any more tears in her, but they came fast and furious.

"Go on. I'll bring your tea up by the bath and we can chat later." Gigi smoothed Arianna's wild hair and kissed her on the forehead before she turned to make her way back to the kitchen.

Arianna walked through the massive foyer to the great room with its floor-to-ceiling windows and incredible view of the bay. Looking out at the bridge and city that she loved, she felt a panic rising up inside her.

When would it stop? This feeling like she was living someone else's life. Everything had changed. She couldn't count on anything, and if she was being honest with herself, she really didn't want to have to count on anyone either.

At the sound of Gigi's call that the bath was ready, Arianna started up the long staircase. For now, she'd not think about anything. All she wanted was a long soak in the bathtub that had become heaven to her on days like today.

After a nice soak in the tub, Arianna entered her suite

to find that Gigi had turned down her bed and drawn the curtains. Pulling her cashmere robe tighter, she sunk onto her mattress and brought the down comforter up close around her. Sleep. That was what she needed right now. And something for her headache. She rubbed her temples, thinking that the pain seemed a bit worse. She reached into the drawer of her nightstand for the bottle of prescription pills. She had never in her life taken so much medication as she had in the last few months. But she trusted Doc and she knew that the circumstances warranted extreme measures. She was hardly in her right mind these days. Whatever her right mind was anyways. She'd been on an emotional roller coaster. One she couldn't wait to get off. She'd do anything to get off.

Arianna woke up a few hours later feeling refreshed. With a new resolve, she reached for the journal on her nightstand. She just needed to gather her thoughts. She'd been keeping a journal for as long as she could remember, and it had seemed especially important to her these past few months since her parents had died. It was the one place she could truly talk about her feelings. There were thoughts she had a hard time expressing, even in therapy. But it felt good to get it down on paper somehow. Her journal knew the real truth, every fear and dark thought she'd ever had.

Arianna knew that she could be labeled with the "spoiled rich girl" stereotype and, to be honest, she didn't care all that much. It was something she had been discussing during therapy, so her self-awareness was getting better. Life had always been easy for her. The Sinclairs had seen to it that she grew up wanting for nothing. It had been that way for as long as she could remember. Fancy dresses and parties when she was young. Private schools, horseback riding lessons, and summers away at the family beach house in San Diego.

She didn't know exactly when things had changed between her and her parents. But thinking back, and also after logging her recent hours in therapy: once she was old enough to realize it, she started to resent who her parents were in her life. Sure, they said that they did love her, but it always seemed to be about appearances, and it didn't feel like there was any real closeness there.

Doc got her to open up about feeling unloved and thinking that this had partially caused the rebellious stage she had gone through during her teenage years. Well, the fact that she was adopted only compounded the intense feelings. She could say the words now without feeling too much behind the thought.

Arianna stopped writing, closed her journal, and let out a big sigh. *Just keep putting one foot in front of the other. Go through the motions until you get to where you want to be.*

She'd take this trip next month and if she was lucky, she'd meet lots of cute men and spend most of the time partying the nights away. Or she'd shop her way around Europe. For now, she'd just focus on her trip because that's what seemed to make her feel the happiest these days.

Arianna sat on the small sofa in her room, feeling relaxed and hopeful as she sipped her glass of Chianti and listened to her favorite opera playing quietly in the background. "La Boheme." It reminded her of her mother. It had been one of the first operas that her parents had ever taken her to as a child, and she immediately fell in love with the music.

She unfolded the world map that displayed the places that she would go on her trip. She had been working on this for the past two years, and it had become one of her favorite things to do. She'd start in London. It was the only place in Europe that she'd been before with her parents, but she enjoyed it and knew that it would be the perfect jumping-off point for her international adventure.

There were several cities marked throughout Europe, and she hadn't made her final decision yet as to when she would visit each or if she'd even make it to every place on her wish list. She planned to jump on a train and go where she fancied. She'd opted for train travel, rather than the first class flights she was used to, because she felt it would give her the more authentic travel experience that she was craving. On her list of countries that she didn't want to miss in Europe were: Portugal, Spain, Germany, Greece, and Italy. Italy was actually at the top of her list, and out of all the places on this map, it was where her heart led her the most.

After Europe, she'd go to Turkey and India, before heading to Southeast Asia. Thailand was also high on her list of places she wanted to go. She figured that she would rent something spectacular on an island beach there for a few weeks, assuming she was feeling pretty tired from the travel at that point. She sighed as she thought about all of the places still marked on her map: Japan, Australia, New Zealand, Central and South America. When she'd been planning the trip with her father's travel agent, she'd planned on taking six to nine months to do it all. Now— well, she'd have to just play it by ear.

She thought about Gigi and Blu and their reluctance to support her when it came to this trip. She needed for them to be on board with it, but she also understood their concerns. Her whole world had changed—collapsed even, since the time that her father had paid for this ticket for her. She'd changed.

She turned towards the knock on her door, folding the map as she called out. "Come in."

"Ah, *La Boheme*. My favorite." Gigi entered, twirling her way over to Arianna.

Arianna laughed at her sarcasm, because she knew that Gigi barely tolerated the music that she loved. "I think you missed your calling. Ever thought of being a dancer?"

"Not in this lifetime." Gigi laughed too. "I was just wondering if you will be here this evening for dinner?"

"Are you cooking?" Arianna winked, teasing her.

"No. But I can order in from that lovely Italian place that you like so much."

"Sure, that sounds great. Maybe for around seven?"

Gigi nodded as she came around the sofa to sit next to Arianna. "What are you doing, bella?" she said, eyeing the map. "I wish you'd think about—"

"Not now, Gi. Okay? Can we talk about this later, please?" Arianna wasn't quite ready to have the conversation with Gigi again about her trip just yet. "How about another glass of wine outside in the garden? Join me?"

"Yes, I'll meet you outside. The weather is perfect right now and I could use a little fresh air."

"Okay, I'll see you down there in a few minutes," Arianna said. She wanted to jot a few quick notes in her journal before heading downstairs. "Tonight I want to just talk about you, okay? I want to hear all the scoop about what you and your friends have been up to all of these weekend evenings when you're nowhere to be found." Arianna winked.

Gigi laughed but looked as if she wanted to say something more.

"I promise I'll fill you in on the meeting—on everything—tomorrow. When I get back from Blu's. Deal?" Arianna said.

"You win. For now." Gigi laughed as she walked out of the room.

PAULA KAY

CHAPTER 3

Arianna hadn't had a lot of great girlfriends before Blu came into her life. She had been part of the popular crowd at her private high school and pretty much throughout her whole life. Money seemed to do that for you around here. But she didn't have girlfriends to confide in, or anyone that she felt really cared anything about her. She didn't concern herself about any of that when she was younger, but she was now realizing everything that had been missing in her life back then.

Blu came into Arianna's life three years ago when Arianna had popped into the little bar where she worked in the Mission District. She had been out partying with her friends and they were looking for a nightcap, trying with little success to use their fake IDs at one of the smaller spots in the city.

The small bar was quiet that night, with only a handful of people playing darts and another couple of guys at the pool table. While her friends grabbed the other open pool table, Arianna had sat at the bar, ordering a wine from the cool-looking girl who seemed to be in charge that night.

Blu had eyed her with suspicion, and after a last glance around the place slid the glass of wine towards her, promising her that it would be the only thing she'd serve her because she didn't want to lose her job.

Arianna had spent that night talking to Blu well past the time that her friends had all left. Her blond hair with the bright pink streak and her rocker clothes perfectly suited her spunky personality, and Arianna was drawn to her because she was so unlike anyone within her social circle. They began hanging out and Blu became the best friend that Arianna had never had. Well, they hung out as much as Blu could working two jobs and raising Jemma, who had been three years old at the time. Arianna smiled as she thought about sweet Jemma. She loved that little girl, as much as she had tried to resist spending time with her at first.

Arianna pulled into a parking spot near Blu's apartment and walked up to ring the doorbell.

"Come in," she heard from inside.

"What are you up to?" she said as she walked through the living room to the little space that Blu had converted into a work area. Blu sat hunched over her sewing machine completely absorbed in what she was working on. There was one dress form mannequin in the corner near her and big piles of fabric coming out of the basket nearby.

Blu finished what she was sewing, and held it up for

Arianna to see.

"I dunno. What do you think? Too dark for a little girl maybe?"

It looked like another tutu for Jemma, but instead of the pretty pastels that Arianna was used to seeing Jemma in, the skirt was black with one strip of bright blue around the waist. "I don't know. Maybe it's okay if you're getting her ready to perform at a funeral or something." Arianna laughed and then saw the look of distaste on Blu's face.

"Oh, sorry. I didn't mean anything by it." She reached over to give her best friend a hug. "I love it and I'm sure Jemma will too. But what's with the black?" Blu was so excellent with her design and fit; Arianna knew that she gravitated towards black garments a lot with her adult pieces, but typically when it came to the clothes she sewed for Jemma, she stuck to much brighter colors, more suited for kids.

"Oh, I've just been thinking a lot about my signature style. No matter what I do, I can't seem to get away from wanting to do the black pieces; but even I know that I need some color to make them pop a bit."

Arianna loved everything that Blu had ever made for her—and she'd given her quite a few pieces, saying that Arianna was her perfect model. They were edgier pieces than most of Arianna's wardrobe, but she loved that about them and often wore her favorite tops and jackets made by Blu out to the clubs at night. She'd gotten a lot of compliments on them and was constantly begging Blu to get started on her collection.

Arianna had offered to back her with the funding many times, but Blu, being Blu, had not said yes to anything yet—even though Arianna knew what a huge dream designing was to her. She just couldn't seem to get over her stubbornness when it came to accepting help, or more specifically money. Arianna made a mental note to bring it up again and frame it as a business partnership. That might be the thing that would help Blu to go for it. And Arianna did believe in her, so it was a no-brainer, really, for her.

Arianna turned her attention back towards Blu, who was holding up another piece for her to look at. It was a fitted black jacket, and she could see that the inside was lined in the same bright blue as the tutu. She reached for it to try on, looking at her reflection in the full-length mirror that was next to the mannequin. The bright blue was just noticeable around the collar, and Arianna's eyes lit up as she admired the fit and expertise of Blu's work.

"Oh, I love it." She smiled broadly.

"Do you?" Blu said with a hint of disbelief in her voice.

"Are you kidding? It's gorgeous. And very expensive-looking."

"I found this great fabric sale and I had to have it, thinking of you of course." Blu laughed.

"So…for moi?" Arianna teased, knowing the answer before asking the question.

"Of course. I made it with you in mind," Blu said.

"I wish you would make more things for yourself."

"To wear? You know how little I'm going out these days. I really have nowhere to wear it. I have little use for clothes other than my two different work uniforms." Blu laughed.

"Oh, believe me. I know. You work too hard." Arianna looked again at the perfect details of the jacket. "So tell me about the signature style." She was genuinely curious, and she loved to hear Blu talk about her dreams for her collection. Her whole face lit up and it was as if all of her worries disappeared for a time.

"So, you know how I have a hard time getting away from the black?"

Arianna nodded.

"I just decided to go with it, but I wanted to add something to make it a little different. A signature look, if you will. So I thought it would be kinda cool if I used the same color someplace subtle in each of the garments. Thus this blue color. What do you think?"

Arianna reached over to kiss her friend quickly on the cheek. "I think you are a creative genius. And I love it."

"You do?"

"I do, yes." Arianna smiled. "Do you love it?"

Blu nodded. "I do. It's settled, then. I've just created my signature style."

"It's on to the big time," Arianna said.

"Now if I can only find the time to finish about

twelve more pieces." Blu laughed but Arianna knew the truth was that she wouldn't find the time. Not unless something forced her too.

"So I have an idea."

"Oh boy. Should I brace myself?" Blu laughed.

"Probably, because I'm about to ask you to take off work." Arianna laughed, knowing that this was a hard concept for Blu even though she had earned several days that she had yet to use. "How about if you, Jemma, and I go to the beach house next weekend for a few days? I've been craving some time at the beach and you can bring your sewing machine and whatever else you need. I'll book the private plane so we can be pretty flexible with the schedule." Arianna was familiar with the look that she saw on Blu's face. It was a cross between worry and wistfulness.

"I don't know, Ari. It sounds nice but—"

"But what? Come on. I've been dying to get you down to San Diego with me. And you'll love it. I promise. I'll play with Jemma on the beach and you can have lots of time for working on your collection. Or whatever you want to do. Say you'll come. And don't say no because of money. I know you hate it when I offer, but I'll help you if you need it to make up for the days off work. Please." Arianna tried to give Blu her best look of desperation. "It will mean a lot to me because I don't want to go by myself right now."

Blu looked like she'd suddenly had a change of heart.

"Well, I do know that Jemma would love it. She's been begging me to take her to the beach here but it's so darn cold all the time. Okay. Yes. And thank you." She reached over to hug Arianna.

"I'm so happy. This is going to be fun. Now speaking of that little rug rat, where is she?" She was used to Jemma running out to greet her whenever she came over, but so far there had been no sound of her.

"Oh I let her go for a play date with her little friend from daycare."

"Really?" Arianna raised an eyebrow. She knew how protective Blu was, and it was unusual that Jemma would be anywhere, other than with the two sitters that she knew Blu trusted.

"Yes, she was begging me so much when I went to pick her up after work today. The other mother was there and I had a hard time saying no. She took them to the park and normally I would have gone too, but I really wanted to try to get at least this one thing accomplished today with the collection."

"Well, I'm sure she's fine at the park. Honestly, I'm the last one to tell you how to parent, but you could stand to loosen up just a little." She tried to keep it light, but noticed that Blu seemed to be tensing up a bit before responding.

"I know. What I can I say? It's what I do." She laughed. "Anyways, she should be home any minute. Stay and then you can tell her about the beach. She'll be very excited."

"That sounds great." Arianna said.

CHAPTER 4

When Arianna arrived home a few hours later, Gigi had a salad ready for her and it looked gorgeous. She wasn't the best cook, but she could make a few things very well, namely her homemade scones, which Arianna loved, and a salad to compete with any of Arianna's favorite restaurants. Gigi said the key was being early to the farmer's market twice a week. She was a regular, along with her friends, and all of the vendors knew them by name.

"Would you like to eat in the garden? You look as if you could use a little fresh air, bella." Deep frown lines appeared on Gigi's forehead as she asked the question.

"Sure, that would be great. Come sit with me, Gi, will you? Did you have your lunch already?" Arianna said.

"I did. You know me. Like clockwork, with my club sandwich and soap opera." Gigi winked and Arianna smiled in response, because she did know where she could find Gigi come one o'clock each day.

"But let me go grab my cup of tea, and I would love to sit here with you," Gigi said.

While Gigi went back into the kitchen, Arianna spent

a minute collecting her thoughts. *Just say it. Blurt it out.* She was surprised at the amount of anxiety this conversation was causing her. She'd have to remember to bring it up with Doc tomorrow.

Gigi was back with her tea before Arianna had another moment to formulate her words just right in her head.

"You've not told me yet about your meeting with Douglas yesterday. Did it go well, and was he able to finalize everything that you've been waiting for with the will?" Gigi asked.

This questioning from an employee might not have been appropriate in one of her friend's homes. But Gigi really was like family to Arianna, and she knew that Gigi's concern for her was genuine. She didn't care about Arianna's wealth and she deserved to know the truth. And Arianna had confided in Gigi. About everything. It was a special bond that they shared, made all the more stronger, it seemed, after the death of her parents four months ago.

With those thoughts, Arianna did decide to come right out with it. "Gi, the meeting went well and I've now got access to all the money. Douglas did a good job handling everything, just as Daddy knew he would, I suppose. Now there's something else that I want to talk to you about. And please hear me out, okay?"

Arianna paused long enough to notice Gigi repositioning herself in her chair. She knew how fidgety

Gigi got when she was uncomfortable. She had noticed it several times during the worst of the arguments that would break out between Arianna and her parents.

"Go on, Ari. You're making me nervous, but I can't imagine anything worse than what you've already told me these past months." Gigi pulled a tissue out of her pocket as if she was preparing for the worst.

"Oh, I'm sorry." Arianna reached over to give her a quick squeeze before continuing. "You've been amazing. Really. You do know how much I appreciate you, don't you?"

"Arianna, are you getting ready to sack me?" Gigi had a look of shock on her face.

"Good God, no, Gi." Arianna laughed, despite Gigi's obvious discomfort. "That is not going to happen. Ever. This is about me, and I'm just worried as to how you're going to react to it. But I've made up my mind, so there's nothing that you can say to keep me from doing it."

Gigi seemed amused as she motioned for Arianna to continue. "Well, go on. Out with it then."

"I'm going. On my big trip." Arianna's voice was stern as she noted Gigi's expression of disapproval. "Honestly, I'd think that you'd try to understand where I'm coming from with this. You know how long I've been planning it." She was stern on the outside, but in her head she was begging Gigi to give her her blessing for the trip. She didn't like being at odds with her. Their eyes met and held for a beat as Arianna finished her little speech.

"I know but—it's just that so much has happened." Arianna saw the look of genuine concern on Gigi's face, and she understood it.

Arianna's voice softened. "I know." She looked her in the eyes. "But you have to trust me on this, okay? It's something that I need to do."

Gigi sighed and stared at Arianna for a full minute. Arianna was used to Gigi's quiet approach to things that she disapproved of. It was how she had always handled Arianna since she was little. She could remember a time when Gigi had caught her in a lie. When asked by Gigi if she was telling the truth, Arianna just burst into tears. She hated Gigi's disapproval more than any her parents had displayed, and those times had been plentiful for sure. But Arianna was a grown woman now and she could make decisions for herself. She had to be making her own decisions now. She felt a new resolve as she waited for Gigi to speak.

"Ari, my dear. You know how much I love you." Arianna winced visibly at her words and waited for Gigi to continue. "If you are asking my opinion, and I think you are not, it's a big mistake. With the accident, your breakdown and—"

"Gi, please. I don't want to keep going over this," Arianna interrupted. "All of those reasons you're listing are the exact reasons that I need to take this trip. Can you understand that? This is something that I need to do for myself." She willed Gigi to understand.

"*Sì*, bella. I do understand. I want you to be happy. Especially now." A tear made its way down Gigi's cheek as she continued. "But do you think you'll be alright? I want to take care of you here. Where you can be comfortable and have your friends, your doc—"

"I've been talking about it with Doc. She knows what my plans are and she knows that I've made up my mind. I'm feeling so much stronger emotionally and the new medication seems to be helping with my sleep. Good grief, I'm way too young to be headed to the loony bin— but if I stay here, surrounded by doctors and worried friends, that's where I might end up." Arianna laughed in an attempt to lighten the tone of the conversation.

"It's a miracle you're even thinking of getting on a plane after all you've been through." Gigi didn't catch herself before the words came out. "I'm sorry. I shouldn't have said that. You're fine to be flying and I'm sure it will be safe." Gigi looked worried that she had brought up something so sensitive.

"Flying to Europe isn't anything like the small plane my parents were on. I really think I'll be fine with it." Arianna had flown many times with her parents as a child, including the small plane that was piloted by their friend during the accident. She shuddered and closed her eyes for a moment, willing the picture of the small plane going down out of her mind. Yes, a lot had happened, and Arianna didn't feel she had the time for prolonged grieving. She was going on this trip to get away from everything that was stressing her out. Now, if she could only convince Blu to make the trip with her, everything would be perfect. But she'd go alone if she had to. She was ready to be alone for a while.

"Well, do you know how long you'll be gone?" Gigi said.

"No, not really." Arianna did want to ease the worry that she saw on Gigi's face. "But it won't be too long. I'll come back soon. I promise." She reached over, giving her a big hug. "I'll come back here where you can take care of me again, feeding me your delicious home cooking and—"

"Very funny." Gigi laughed at Arianna's teasing about her mediocre cooking abilities. "You just come home," she said quietly.

The phone rang, interrupting Arianna's thoughts and the unfinished conversation the two women were still having. "Let me run and get that and then we'll finish our talk," Gigi said as she got up to make her way to the kitchen.

Arianna had a few moments to collect her thoughts again before Gigi was standing in the doorway, her hand over the mouthpiece of the phone, with a strange look on her face. "Gigi, what is it? Is something wrong?" She got up to make her way across the space between them.

"Bella, it's for you. She says she's your mother. Your birth mother," Gigi said.

CHAPTER 5

Arianna looked at Gigi with panic on her face. *What the hell? My mother?* She couldn't handle this right now, could she? For a moment she thought about having Gigi tell the woman that she had the wrong number, to dismiss the call completely. But even as the thought flitted through her mind, her curiosity was peeked. *My mother?*

Her hand shaking, Arianna took the phone out of Gigi's hand and crossed the distance to the patio chair outside to have a seat. "Hello?" she whispered into the phone.

"Arianna, is it you?"

Arianna was taken aback when she heard the lovely Italian accent.

"It's me, yes. Who is this?" Arianna could barely get the words out and wondered if the woman on the other end had even heard her speak.

"It's—I'm—"

The woman on the other end of the line seemed to be as nervous as Arianna felt.

"I'm your mother, Arianna," she said.

"What do you want?" The question popped out of

her mouth before she could edit herself. "I mean—oh, I don't know what to say. Where are you?" Arianna asked. She felt completely numb with shock and was having a hard time formulating a coherent thought, much less speaking in a way that she thought made any sense.

"I'm sorry. I'm sure this must be a shock to you. I've been debating about when to call. I know about the accident. About your—your parents. I'm so sorry, Arianna."

She was listening to this woman speak on the other end of the phone, but nothing was making any sense.

"What? How? I don't even know your name," Arianna blurted out in a rush.

"*Si*, sorry. My name is Lia. And I'm here. In San Francisco." The line was silent for a few seconds. "Can I see you?" The woman asked, her voice quiet.

Arianna needed some time. Didn't she? She needed lots of time, but things were happening so fast around her, and now this, of all things. She rubbed her temple and noticed the glass of water that Gigi had placed on the table beside her. She needed a drink, but not of water right now. *God, I really need a drink tonight.*

"Arianna, are you still there?" The voice of the woman on the other end of the line was barely a whisper.

Arianna was sure that she heard fear in the voice of this woman that called herself her mother. "Yes, I'm sorry. This is all so—so shocking. When would you want to meet?" Arianna could hardly believe that she was considering it. She could cancel later if she wanted. She'd talk to Doc about it before the meeting. And Blu.

"Any time that is good for you. You tell me when and where and I'll be there, okay?" Lia sounded hopeful, and Arianna felt a rush of emotions all at once.

"Okay." Arianna whispered into the phone. She cleared her throat. "How about this Thursday? I know a nice little cafe in Little Italy. Cafe Villa. Do you know it?"

"*Si*, yes. I know the area well."

She knows it well? Arianna thought.

"Say, eleven o'clock?" Arianna said.

"Yes, eleven will be perfect. Arianna, I've been waiting for this moment for a long time." Arianna imagined the tears coming down this face she'd never seen as the woman choked on the words. The face of her mother. She couldn't help but wonder what this woman looked like. *Is this really happening to me right now?*

Arianna collected herself for what seemed like the hundredth time since she'd gotten on the phone. "Alright then. Let me get a number from you too." *Just in case. In case I can't go through with it*, she told herself.

They exchanged mobile numbers and said goodbye. It was then that Arianna noticed Gigi sitting there beside her, looking a bit pale. She turned to her. "Gi, that was my birth mom. I think it really is her." Arianna felt like she was in shock as she reiterated to Gigi what the woman had told her.

"Bella, yes. I think it is. Are you okay?" said Gigi,

reaching out to pull Arianna in for a slight hug.

Arianna pulled back and took a deep breath. "Yes. I think I'm okay. I don't know. This is way more than I bargained for when I got up this morning. I need to excuse myself. Can we talk more later?" Arianna said.

"*Sí*, yes, of course, bella. Your head must be swimming. Go on. You know where I am if you need me."

"Thanks." Arianna gave her a proper hug now before she went back inside the house. She headed back upstairs to her room. She needed to get Blu on the phone. Blu would help her sort out all of these thoughts in her head.

After trying unsuccessfully to get hold of Blu, Arianna sat down in the chaise lounge in the corner of her bedroom. She looked out the window at the view of the bay and the city skyline, journal in hand, ready to try to make some sense of all the thoughts she was having.

She could hardly believe that she was even writing the words, but she mostly noticed a sense of peace coming over her—which seemed odd, given the drama that had unfolded today. Her mother. She could hardly believe this was happening. She had wanted it. Dreamed about the day, but that was before. She looked up and caught a glimpse of her reflection in the window. When had she started looking so much older and less carefree? She sighed because she knew exactly when her world had changed.

CHAPTER 6

Arianna really needed to talk to someone, and an idea occurred to her. Did Douglas know anything about this? She reached for her phone to call him before she had time to think about what she would say.

He answered on the third ring. "Ari, hi. How are you doing, my dear? I've been meaning to phone you to see if we are still on for lunch tomorrow."

"Yes, for sure. Our usual time before my session. But that's not why I'm calling." Arianna took a moment for a deep breath. "I just got a phone call from a woman who says she's my mother. My birth mother. I was wondering if this is something you know anything about?"

Seconds passed as she waited for a response on the other end of the phone. "Douglas? Are you there?"

"What are you doing right now? Can I come over?" Douglas finally responded into the phone. "I'd rather talk about this in person."

Oh God, Arianna thought. *More surprises?* "I'm home, yes. But honestly, I don't think I can handle much more today." She tried to lighten the mood with a small laugh. "Yes, come over. I'll be here."

"Okay. I'll see you in thirty minutes."

Arianna clicked off the phone, wondering what it was that he wanted to talk to her about. She'd gotten close to her father's best friend since the accident. Douglas had been around for as long as she could remember. And she knew that he genuinely cared for her. Not having any children of his own, she guessed that with her parents gone, he felt a strong sense of responsibility to her; and she did feel a great deal of comfort knowing that he was there.

Douglas had helped so much these past few months. She knew that she wouldn't have gotten through any of it without him. He'd been the one to give her the news that day about the flight going down. He'd made all of the funeral arrangements, and it was Douglas that was there the day she had her breakdown, taking her to the hospital and seeing to it that she got the help that she needed.

She believed that he was always honest with her, and she was counting on him to help her wade through this new information about Lia. About her mother. The thought shocked her back to the present.

Arianna busied herself with tidying her room, something she'd only taken to doing recently, as she'd grown up with Gigi taking care of all of that. But she had to grow up now. She knew this and had been taking the steps to make herself more independent. Although she couldn't imagine a time when she wouldn't have Gigi there for her. It was more about the companionship than her help, really. But she could afford it anyways.

Before she knew it, Gigi was calling her on the intercom to let her know of Douglas's arrival.

Arianna went downstairs to the living room, where Gigi and Douglas were caught up in conversation. She stood quietly for a moment on the staircase, watching them unnoticed. She'd wondered lately about the two of them. Gigi and Douglas. It wasn't a crazy idea, even though they both seemed resigned to being single. She'd have to take it up with them separately and see if there wasn't a little matchmaking to be done there. She smiled at the thought as she entered the living room.

Douglas stood to kiss her on the cheek and Gigi stood up as well. "I'll leave you two. Would you like anything to drink?" Gigi asked.

Douglas and Arianna each requested a water, and Arianna sat down on the plush sofa across from where Douglas was seated in the formal living room. She hated this room. It was the most stuffy of any room in the house. Her mother had never let her play in here as a child. It was a room for entertaining and grown-ups only. *Look at me, all grown-up now.* She stifled the silly thought as her mind turned towards Douglas and the more serious matters at hand.

"So, what is it that's so important for you to take time out of your busy lawyer schedule in the middle of the afternoon?" Arianna said in her teasing way.

"How are you doing?" Douglas said with a look of

unmistakable concern on his face. "I've been a little worried about you. You seemed a little out of it when I saw you yesterday."

"Oh, that. Yes, I'm fine. I was trying a new medication that Doc had given me to help with the lack of sleep I've been having. So yes. I'm fine except for the fact that my birth mother just called me out of the blue. Something which doesn't surprise you, I gather?" She looked pointedly at him as she spoke. "Douglas, what's going on?"

Douglas looked at her intently. "Ari, I do know about Lia. I've known about her for a while."

Arianna felt a sudden rush of emotion. She hated being lied to more than anything, and she'd be shocked if he had been keeping something this important from her. "Go on," she said.

"Your father came to me about a month before the accident. Lia, your birth mom, had contacted him then. She had just moved to the area and, after some good detective work on her part, she found out who you were and wanted to schedule a meeting with your father," Douglas said.

"Wait. You mean to tell me that she's been living here for months? And my father knew about it? This is all so confusing." Arianna rubbed her head and reached for the water that Gigi had placed on the coffee table. "Go on. Don't stop now. Tell me everything you know. Please." She knew that he would be honest with her. It had been the agreement they'd made a few months ago when she finally confided in him about all that she'd been going through herself since the accident. That was really when their friendship had begun.

Douglas took a deep breath. "Your father would not agree to the meeting. He was worried about your mother and how she would handle it. But he did spend a significant amount of time with Lia on the phone. He told her about you. And he asked that she not disrupt your life right now. He gave Lia my phone number, telling her that if she needed to communicate again, she should do so through me." Douglas watched Arianna as she took in the information.

"But I'm a grown woman. Why didn't my father believe that I had a right to make that decision for myself?" Arianna could feel herself bristling with the anger that was always on the surface when it came to her parents, even now, months after their deaths.

Douglas continued. "You're right. And that's what I told your father. And Lia did call me, basically saying the same thing. We had been discussing all of this the weekend that the accident happened. Lia called me right after and I asked her to give you some time. So, it looks like the time ran out for her today." Douglas attempted a slight smile and Arianna couldn't help but share one back, if only for a second.

"Wow. It's all a lot to take in, you know? I mean, it seems like I keep getting hit with one thing after another.

How much more can I take?" Arianna said.

"I know. And I am worried about you. But I've thought about Lia a lot since the accident and I think maybe this is going to be a good thing for you. I don't think it's bad. You've come through a lot and you seem to be coping with everything so much better. I'm sure that you will sort this out in a way that works for you during this time," Douglas said.

Arianna sighed and suddenly felt overcome with fatigue. "I'm sure I'll be fine. I'm meeting Lia on Thursday and I'll be talking to Doc tomorrow, so I should be able to prepare myself." She laughed in spite of the seriousness of the conversation. "I'm sure she'll help me to formulate some goals for the meeting and what I hope to get out of it."

"That's all fine, Ari. But I think it's okay to let your heart lead you too, you know. This could be a really good thing for you now. It might be exactly the thing you need the most."

At that Arianna uncharacteristically burst into tears. Douglas seemed to have that effect on her ever since she'd opened up to him. He pulled her to him and she left herself be comforted. She couldn't help but wonder why her father had never hugged her this way. She knew he'd loved her but he rarely showed any emotion. She was still learning in therapy how much that lack of physical love in her life had affected her.

"I'll be okay. Thank you for coming over. Thank you

for caring about me." She gave Douglas a last squeeze before she got up to walk him to the door.

"I love you Arianna. You're the daughter I never had. Giving me gray hairs and all, lately." They both laughed as they said goodbye.

Arianna excused herself after dinner and went upstairs to get ready for a night out. Since she hadn't been able to reach Blu on the phone earlier, she planned to go by the bar where she was working. She needed a good stiff drink anyways, after the day that she'd had.

After a nice hot bath, she pulled on a pair of her favorite designer jeans and a new top that she'd bought earlier that week. Arianna loved fashion, and it had been her biggest expense out of the hefty allowance her father had been giving her. Right before the accident, she had been looking with her father at apartments in the city. They were all set to buy something that she loved in Pacific Heights, and then the accident happened. She sighed at the thought of how much everything had changed. Now she knew she would stay here in the home she'd grown up in.

She grabbed her handbag, leather jacket, and keys and headed downstairs to say good night to Gigi.

Not finding her in the kitchen, Arianna walked down the hall to Gigi's room and knocked on the door. "Gi, are you awake?"

"*Si*, come in," Gigi said. "I'm just watching one of my

programs." She laughed as she paused it with the remote.

"I'm going out now. I'll see you in the morning, okay?" Gigi looked up, and Arianna knew the look of concern before she could voice the question.

"I'm taking my car, but don't worry. I'll use a cab if I end up drinking. Which quite honestly, I'll probably do tonight." Arianna laughed. "Honest. I'll be fine. Have a good night and enjoy your TV."

"Okay, bella. Have a good night too. And be careful. I know you will be." Gigi smiled and Arianna turned to close the door.

As she stepped outside, she noticed that the night air was unusually warm. *A perfect night for keeping the top down. I could do with some fresh air.*

Driving over the bridge to make her way into the city, Arianna almost felt as if nothing had happened. It would be so nice to feel carefree again. To have nothing to think about except meeting her friends, out for drinks and dancing. She did love to party. It had been the source of many arguments with her parents, and it didn't seem to be any better once she had turned twenty-one this last year.

Tonight she'd forget about everything. Well, maybe after she got Blu all caught up about Lia. She wondered what Blu would have to say about it all. Her best friend was a straight shooter, especially when it came to Arianna. It was what she loved about her the most.

She made her way through the city traffic with the top down and one of her favorite operas blasting. Tonight she definitely needed a drink. She needed to forget her problems for a little while. She felt that familiar feeling of letting go…of not caring…as she pulled into a parking space close by the little bar.

PAULA KAY

CHAPTER 7

Arianna was relieved when she walked into the bar and found it nearly empty. It wasn't great for Blu and her tips, but she had really hoped that they could have a nice long talk.

Blu grinned when she saw Arianna headed towards her. "Well, look who the cat dragged in." She winked and reached for a glass. "What are you drinking, my friend? Your usual red wine?"

Arianna nodded. "You know it. I can't wait to have a sip and talk to you. You wouldn't believe the day I've had."

Blu looked at Arianna with concern on her face. "Sorry, I forgot my phone at home. I was kicking myself because I wanted to check in with you—to see how your chat with Gigi went. Are you okay? Tell me what's going on."

"Blu, you'll never guess who called me today..." Arianna didn't wait for a response from her before continuing. "My mother. My *birth* mother."

"What? That's kind of incredible." Blu looked genuinely shocked at the news. "How did she find you?

Where does she live? Ari, how are you feeling about all this?"

"I don't know. Believe me, I'm still in shock after speaking with her. I don't know a lot, but I do know a few more details after speaking with Douglas this afternoon; he apparently knows quite a bit about her."

"Go on. Tell me everything that you know. I'm so curious," said Blu.

"Well firstly, to answer your question, yes, I'm okay. I was definitely in shock about it and I'm sure that I'm still processing everything, but I'll be meeting with Doc tomorrow. I'm sure it will help, as our sessions lately usually have that effect on me. I'm meeting Lia—that's her name—the name of my mother. Wow. That sounds a bit surreal now that I'm actually saying it out loud," Arianna said.

Blu nodded in agreement. "I'm sure it does. So when are you meeting her?"

"Right. So I'm meeting her on Thursday. For coffee. In Little Italy. I just got a horrible sinking feeling in my stomach when I said that just now. What do you think? I mean, I could cancel and forget about everything." Arianna took a big gulp of her wine as she waited for Blu to respond.

"Well, I would say that the timing is very interesting, isn't it?"

Arianna could always count on Blu to be logical with her viewpoint on things. This is what she was counting on now.

"What do you mean? With the timing being after the accident?" Arianna asked.

"Yes. I mean unless she'd been living under a rock around here, she'd know about the death and wealth of your parents. Look, I'm not saying that she doesn't want to meet you or that your inheritance would have anything to do with her calling you now, but it's something to think about," Blu said.

"Well, here's the thing. When she called me, I thought that too, honestly—once I hung up and was able to collect my thoughts about the conversation—but I need to tell you more—the bit about my conversation with Douglas." Arianna stopped for another swallow of wine.

"So where does he fit into all of this? Go on then," Blu said.

Arianna knew that Blu also had a lot of respect for Douglas. Though she could be slow to warm up to, she was a good judge of character, and Blu had said on more than one occasion to her that she knew Douglas was someone Arianna could count on.

"So, when I called Douglas to ask him about Lia and this phone call that had taken place, he wanted to come right over. Obviously this meant some seriously big information. It turns out that Douglas did know about Lia. And actually Lia had called my father before the accident. So I really don't think it's about the money. That makes me feel a lot better about everything, you know?"

She looked to Blu for some reassurance at this latest bit of news.

"Oh, yes. That makes me feel a lot better about it too. So what happened when she called your father and why did Douglas know about all of this? And why didn't he tell you about it, for that matter?"

Arianna filled Blu in on the rest of the conversation that had taken place with Douglas.

"Ari, this doesn't make a lot of sense to me. And it's making me slightly annoyed at your parents. I mean, it's not like your birth mom even needed your father's permission. You're an adult and you were an adult at that time. He should have left the decision up to you. And why was he so worried about your mom? What's that about?" said Blu.

"I know. I ask myself the same questions and honestly, it's just another thing for me to be angry at my parents about." Arianna sighed. "Can I get another wine, please?" She laughed. "I definitely need to relax a little bit, and after we finish talking about this, I'm not planning to think about it for the rest of the night."

"Sure." Blu grabbed Arianna's glass for a refill. "I get what you're saying about all the anger that's coming up, and I'm glad that you're working through that with your therapist. She'll be able to help you with this also. I'm sure of it. Wanna talk about something else then?"

"Yes, I do actually. How's J-bean?" Arianna could feel her mood instantly shifting when she asked about Jemma.

She had known the child for three years now, and the nickname was a recent one after her discovering Jemma's love for the jelly beans that Arianna had started bringing her whenever she'd see her.

"You know Jemma. She's doing amazing. I hate working so much and having her in daycare for the summer, but she seems to be enjoying it and she doesn't complain much about going."

Arianna noticed a wistful expression on Blu's face and had the familiar thought about how easy it would be to help her out with her finances. But she would tread carefully about that. She knew she'd finally get her to accept something. She had to.

"Hey, I want you to think about something, okay?"

"What's that?" Blu asked.

"You know I'm planning this fantastic trip." Arianna didn't stop for Blu to respond. "I want you and Jemma to come. It's all my treat, and you know that I can easily afford it. You, of anyone that I know, needs a vacation. And I want you to come with me. I really do. Please say yes." Arianna waited for what she was sure would be resistance.

"How long is this actual trip that you're planning?" Blu said.

"I'm still in early stages with it all, but I'm thinking I'll do an open ticket with no exact planned date to return. Hopefully, I can stretch it to a few months at least." Arianna met Blu's gaze and the seconds of silence said everything that they were both thinking in that moment.

"But, Ari, don't you think you should be home—"

"Honestly, I keep having this same argument with everyone. I'll come home. I'll come home when I need to come home. Can you just trust me on that?"

Blu nodded and sighed. "Yes, okay. I will stop bugging you about the trip. You're a grown woman and you've been through a lot. You're still going through a lot. I get it. And I want you to have the best time. As long as you are taking care of yourself while you are away. And not *too* much partying, right?"

Arianna laughed. "Okay, deal. Not *too* much partying. But there *will* be partying. I promise you that. I just need a fun escape plan from my life right now." Arianna looked down at her wineglass and then back up at Blu. "So you'll think about coming then, will you?"

"Well, for sure I can't come for too long, but I might see if I can get a week off, if that would work for you? It's a bit tricky with the two jobs, but I suppose I can give enough notice and work some overtime. The boss at the restaurant has been happy with me lately, so it's possible he'll give me the time even though I don't technically get vacation. Now that we're talking about it, a vacation does sound nice." She smiled at Arianna. "And Jemma would be delighted to go on an adventure with you. She adores you, you know."

Arianna could feel her face light up at Blu's words. "And I adore that little munchkin." She felt a touch of something familiar in her heart. It hurt for a moment, but she was so used to ignoring the feeling that it passed quickly. "And yes, a week would be fine. Whatever you need to do, and I'll arrange everything. We can decide where you'd like to go. I'm thinking Italy might be fun for us together…"

Blu got a dreamy expression on her face. "Oh, Italy. You know that's my dream destination. Okay, I really need to make this happen, Ari. And thank you. So much. Really." She reached across the bar to give Arianna a quick hug. "You're too good to me," Blu said with a smile.

"Are you kidding? You never let me do *anything* for you. And that needs to change, in my opinion. There's no reason for you to need to be working so hard," Arianna said.

Blu turned around to help another customer at the bar, and Arianna took one last sip of her wine as she contemplated her next move of the evening. She thought she might call up some of her clubbing pals to see which spots would be hopping tonight. She could use a good night out dancing and a few more drinks. She'd refrain from anything harder than alcohol. It didn't seem wise to partake of the other these days. Maybe the drugs were behind her now. Then again, why not? She didn't feel that she had much to lose. But she was trying to be responsible. And she did have her appointment with Doc tomorrow. And Douglas. They would both easily be able to see a good hangover on her, and she didn't know if she had it in her to be ready for heavy conversations with so much explaining on her part.

While Arianna waited for Blu to finish up with the customer, she noticed that her head was starting to hurt a bit. Her recent headaches were starting to get to her. She didn't remember ever having felt so exhausted. She sighed. Maybe going out dancing wasn't the best idea after all. She really was starting to get more responsible.

She chatted with Blu awhile longer and had a few glasses of water so that she'd feel comfortable making the thirty-minute drive home. Yes, she needed a good night of sleep. Tomorrow was going to be a big day, and Thursday an even bigger day in terms of her emotions.

Her stomach flipped as she thought about her meeting with her birth mom. Arianna wondered what it would be like to be sitting across from her, looking into the eyes of the woman who had given her up so long ago. She admitted to herself that, despite the anger that always seemed to be on the surface, she was very curious about Lia. Maybe she'd finally get some answers to the questions that she'd had all her life. Questions her parents hadn't been able to answer, or at least had been unwilling to answer for her.

CHAPTER 8

Arianna spent a nice lazy morning curled up with a good book and writing in her journal. Before she knew it, it was time to get ready for her lunch date with Douglas. She'd been meeting him regularly for lunch one day a week before seeing her therapist. His office was downtown not far from that of her therapist so the routine had been an easy one to get into. She smiled as she thought about him. He'd been so good to her and he never broke his lunch commitment, even though she knew his schedule at the law firm was very busy.

She thought about her own father and how he had constantly canceled his plans with her and her mother throughout the years. It certainly had seemed that his family wasn't the most important thing to him, even though that was not how he would have described his priorities. He had worked hard to provide them an amazing lifestyle, but then he'd never been around really. Looking back, through her adult eyes, she imagined that it had been a point of contention between her mother and him.

Arianna carefully picked a designer dress from her

closet. One of her favorites, a deep blue that she'd been told was beautiful with her skin tone. She put on just a dash of make-up—some mascara to darken her already long curled eyelashes and a hint of pale blush. A quick swipe of her favorite lip gloss and she was ready. She grabbed her bag and car keys and headed out to her convertible, very happy with her decision to come home early last night so as not to have to deal with taking a cab into the city.

Arianna enjoyed her drive in. Making her way across the bridge with the top down on her car had always been one of her favorite things to do. She had a lot on her mind these days, and these simple normal things seemed to give her a feeling of peace and a memory of how easy her life had been mere months ago. God. Had it really been just five months ago that she didn't have a care in the world? The only things that she had worried about back then were who to spend the evening partying with and which apartment her father was going to buy for her in the city.

Arianna sighed. This was her life now and she might as well just keep dealing with it. And she was. The best that she knew how. At the stoplight she glanced down at her phone to the address that Douglas had texted her. They were going to try a new restaurant today and she was trying her best not to be late. She hated to keep him waiting for her when his work schedule was so busy.

She pulled up to the valet parking at the little

restaurant in the heart of downtown San Francisco. She loved the hustle and bustle of being there during a workday. She had never thought about a career all that much and she wondered how she would have been as a businesswoman. The only thing she had ever considered doing was her modeling, and she had been doing that since she was a young girl. A local agency scout had spotted her out shopping with her friends one day, and after that she'd had quite a few gigs during her high school years. She did feel that it was something she could have pursued, but after the accident and the craziness of her life the past few months, she'd stopped returning phone calls to her agent. She didn't need the money and somehow it just didn't seem to matter any more.

Arianna walked into the little French bistro and noticed Douglas seated at a table across the restaurant. He really was a handsome man. Ari guessed that he was roughly the same age as her father had been, putting him in his mid to late fifties.

He got up from his chair to come around the table and give Arianna a kiss on the cheek, pulling out her chair for her. "How are you doing, my dear? You're looking lovely as usual," Douglas said with a broad grin.

"I'm fine, thank you very much. And thanks, as always, for meeting me for lunch. I do look forward to this, you know." Arianna smiled.

"It's my pleasure. Our lunch dates are a great distraction from work these days," Douglas said.

"I do think you work too much, you know. Do you ever take a vacation—and what the heck do you do during your free time anyways?" Arianna teased.

"Oh, you know. The usual. Watching sports, exercise, seeing the odd movie that looks worth my time." Douglas grinned. "Speaking of sports, do you want to go to the game with me this weekend? It should be a good one."

"I won't be able to. I've finally convinced Blu to come down to the beach house with me, but here's a crazy idea. Why don't you ask Gigi to go? She actually loves football. As in, she's a *huge* Niner fan." Arianna was delighted with her suggestion.

Douglas laughed. "Ari, what are you trying to do here? Play little miss matchmaker for me?"

She nodded slightly. "Well, you know there's nothing wrong with going on a few dates. You deserve someone. Someone great."

Douglas's expression changed just a bit and Arianna noticed that look he got in his eyes when he was about to talk about his late wife.

"You might be right. It's just that Melanie was the love of my life. I couldn't imagine my life with anyone but her the day we married, and I still can't imagine my life with anyone else."

"I know, but it's been so many years. I don't think she would have wanted you to be alone," Arianna said. She could still remember the day that Melanie had passed away from the cancer that she had been fighting for so long. Douglas had taken a leave from work and been by her side throughout the last month of her life, and it had all been so painful. Arianna had gone with her parents to see Melanie. She'd been at home for a few weeks, comfortable in her own bed and with Douglas by her side. Arianna remembered feeling scared, as if she could feel a sense of death in the room.

It had been a painful time for everyone. Melanie's funeral was the first time she'd ever seen her father cry. And she knew that his heart had been breaking for Douglas.

Arianna turned her thoughts back to Douglas and their conversation. "Anyways, I'm not pressuring you. Honest. Just think about asking Gigi, okay? Or if not for the game, something else maybe. She's really pretty amazing, Douglas. I do think the two of you would get on very well."

"I'll think about it." Douglas smiled. "And I've known Gigi for as many years as you have. Well, I admit that our conversations have not been so involved, but she does seem nice."

"She's actually quite witty and fun. And very pretty, don't you think?" Arianna asked with a big grin.

"Ari, enough." Douglas laughed. "Let's order, shall we?"

After she'd finished eating, Arianna looked at her phone. "Oh, sorry Douglas, I've got to rush. Doc will not cut me any breaks if I'm late. And I need the full ninety minutes today, that's for sure." She laughed. "Thank you very much for lunch. I really enjoyed the food."

"You're welcome. The pleasure is all mine." Douglas got up to give her a hug. "Call me later to tell me how your appointment went, okay?"

"Yes, will do. Have a good day," Arianna said.

Arianna collected her car from the valet and made her way the few blocks to Doc's office. She took a moment once she was parked in the garage to gather her thoughts. She looked at her reflection in the rearview mirror. *Remain open and honest.* She laughed quietly, thinking that this had become a new mantra of sorts at these weekly therapy sessions.

It had been a bit of a journey to get to where she was now with her therapy. She had tried another therapist right after her breakdown, but there had been zero connection with him and it seemed to be making everything worse for her at the time. It was Douglas that had recommended Doc to her. He'd gone himself for months after Melanie had died. He had told Arianna that talking to Doc had been the only thing to pull him out of the intense darkness that he was in. And he'd been insistent that she stick to it until she found someone that she could open up to. She had resisted at the time, but now she was extremely grateful.

Her therapy sessions with Doc had started out well from the beginning. She liked her and didn't feel at all pressured to talk about anything. Over the months, she'd learned that she could let down her walls, and that it felt pretty amazing to talk to someone about her *real* feelings. For a moment Arianna wondered how life might have been different if her own mother had spent some time in therapy. Maybe it would have made her more open to Arianna and their relationship could have been closer. She sighed. She'd never know.

But now she had something else to deal with. She didn't even want to think about having an actual relationship with Lia. With her mother. But could she? It would be interesting so hear Doc's perspective on it all— if she even thought it was a good idea for her to spend any time with Lia right now.

Arianna glanced at the time. God. She was fifteen minutes late. Not good today when she needed all the time she could get. She grabbed her bag and clicked her car alarm on.

She made her way to the fifteenth floor and turned right out of the elevator. The woman from reception glanced up and waved her on. "Go ahead, Arianna. Dr. Jonas is waiting for you in her office."

CHAPTER 9

Dr. Jonas. Arianna barely remembered her name. The months following the accident, after her breakdown, she'd seen several different doctors. She had grown so tired of the hospital and keeping all of the doctors straight, that she'd devised this little game where every doctor became just Doc to her. Somehow it made everything feel less stressful and major, so it had stuck with her. She did ask Dr. Jonas if she minded, to which she had laughed, telling her that she could call her whatever she liked.

Arianna settled into her favorite comfy chair, tucking her legs underneath her, and grabbing one of the throw pillows to hold in her lap. She loved the clean-scented candle that Doc always had lit on the table in the center of the room.

"Well, Doc, have I got a lot to tell you today. You won't believe what's happened since I saw you last week."

"Okay, where would you like to start, Ari?" Doc glanced down at the notebook in her lap. "When we ended last time, you were telling me about your upcoming meeting with Douglas about finalizing the finances of your parents' estate. Would you like to start with that?"

"Yes. Everything happened that day actually. The meeting went well and I now do have access to everything, including all of the bank accounts, so thankfully that has all been sorted out. I can finally plan this trip with that out of the way…which is another thing that I do want to talk about with you. But first, the bigger issue at hand is that shortly after the meeting that day I got a phone call from my birth mother." Arianna looked up at Doc to see if her expression changed at all at this latest news.

"Wow, that must have taken you by surprise."

"To say the least. It was all I could do to even take the phone from Gigi's hand. Honestly, if I'd had more time to think about it, I probably wouldn't have spoken to her at all. At least not right now," Arianna said.

"Do you want to tell me about the conversation?" Doc said.

"Yes. So—it was pretty short, really. She told me that she was sorry to hear about my parents; and I know, after speaking to Douglas about it, that she has been in the area for a while now. Since before the accident. And I agreed to meet her for lunch. God. I'm not at all sure that it's a good idea." Ari started to feel a bit panicked again.

"Ari, take a deep breath. Why don't you close your eyes for a few seconds and focus on your breathing. I can see that you are starting to get anxious. Do you want to lie down?"

God, Doc had really come to know her well in the short months that Ari had been seeing her.

"Yes, maybe that's a good idea." Arianna moved to the sofa and stretched out her legs, beginning some deep breathing as soon as her head rested on the pillow. "Okay, that's better."

Arianna remained on the sofa with her eyes closed, trying the best she knew how to focus on the way she was feeling.

"Okay, so how are you feeling right now?"

"Well, I guess I feel scared. And also excited."

"Tell me about the scared feeling."

"So...you know that I've spent years trying not to think about my birth mother and why she might have given me up. So now that I'm talking about it, there's also anger. I mean, how could she have done that to me?" The tears started to come, and Arianna knew deep inside that it wasn't only about her birth mother.

She was filled with so much anger. It was the anger that scared her the most, threatening to overtake every other emotion and thought. She was angry, not only at Lia, but also her parents. And maybe most of all at herself. She hated herself most of the time, if she was being honest. Would the guilt ever lesson? She had only really touched the surface of it all with Doc and wondered if she would ever be able to fully open up. Blu knew. And Gigi knew too. But they never pressed her to talk about anything. It would be different opening up to Doc. In her heart, she knew it would be good for her.

"Ari?" Doc's voice brought her out of her own thoughts. "Can you tell me what you are thinking about? Tell me about the anger."

"It's just a lot, you know? I'm not sure how I'm supposed to feel about it, really."

"It's okay to feel however you feel. So let's continue exploring that," Doc said. "Tell me about the excitement you're feeling about meeting your birth mom. Did she tell you her name?"

"Her name is Lia." Arianna smiled slightly. "Actually I loved hearing her voice. She had the same accent as Gigi. She sounded very Italian, and I can't stop wondering what she looks like. If I look like her." She took another deep breath.

"When are you meeting her?"

"Tomorrow. God, my stomach hurts just thinking about it," Arianna said.

"I can imagine that you would feel nervous. This is a pretty major event for you right now, isn't it?"

"Yes and on top of everything else, it's so unexpected. Then again, I've had nothing but surprises in my life these past four months. Why should I be so shocked?" Arianna laughed but there was a tone of bitterness in her voice.

"Is it possible that unlike the other news you've received lately, meeting Lia could be something positive in your life right now?" Doc said, voicing out loud what Arianna had been daring to hope.

Arianna sat up on the sofa in order to look Doc in the eye. "Do you think it could be a good thing? Do you really? I'm afraid to hope for it, and also I'm wondering if getting to know her would even be a good idea. Given everything that is going on with me, I mean." Arianna reached for a tissue and wiped the tears that were now streaming down her face.

"Ari, I wonder about you letting people in right now. Letting the people who care about you be close to you during a time when I would think that you need that the most. Does it feel to you that you are pushing people away?" Doc asked.

Arianna thought about the question for a few seconds. "I don't mean to. I suppose maybe I do a bit. I know that I don't like talking about the heavy stuff with Blu. She has so much on her plate already. She's really the only one that I'd be likely to confide in. There's also Gigi. She's a rock of sorts for me, I guess. She's been there for me my whole life really." Talking about Gigi made her smile. She did feel close to her.

"And what about Douglas?" Doc asked. "It seems like you've been opening up to him a bit more recently?"

"Yes. That's true. There are things I have to discuss with Douglas. Things that I will need to discuss further. And yes, we've also become friends and I know that he worries about me. In more of a fatherly sort of way. And Douglas has been a huge help to me. Helping me to sort things out that I don't have a clue about. Daddy was wise in his decision to make him the executor of his estate. Well, he's been Daddy's attorney and friend for as long as I can remember, so I'm sure it was an easy decision for him."

"Okay, so you've got some core people in your life that really care about you. People that are concerned and want the best for you. Is it possible that Lia might end up being that for you as well?" Doc said.

"Yes, I suppose it's possible. But I'm not sure that there's time for that, you know?" Arianna was overcome with emotion and more tears started to fall. "I've been planning this trip. I told you about that. I need to get on with it and make some decisions as to when I'm leaving. So that's part of it too, really. Should I even bother meeting Lia now right before I'm about to leave?" She looked at Doc, willing her to give her a definitive answer, knowing that it wasn't going to be the case. She knew that she would need to make these hard decisions for herself.

"Ari, what if you decided to be in the moment with all of this? Maybe it's okay that you don't know exactly what's going to happen or what the result will be of meeting Lia. Maybe you can trust yourself enough to know that you will have a better idea after you meet her face-to-face. It will still be okay for you to make the decisions for if and how you proceed after that. How does that feel to you?" Doc asked.

"It feels alright, I guess. I think I'm just worried that seeing Lia—seeing my mother—will open up a whole bunch of new feelings again. Just when I think I'm getting a handle on everything. I don't know that I can bear it." Arianna looked to Doc for some confirmation that she was going to be okay.

"You've come a long way since I met you a few short months ago. You've done a great job of opening up and getting in touch with your feelings. I'm confident that no matter what comes up for you as a result of this meeting, you can handle it. And I can work through it all with you, so I don't think it will be anything that you can't handle. But it's all up to you. You are fully in charge of this situation. That's the most important thing to remember when you start feeling a little overwhelmed and anxious about it."

"You're right," Arianna said. "I'm already feeling better about everything. I knew talking to you would help." She smiled broadly to show her appreciation.

"You know that I'm here for you if you need me. And on that note, we have about ten more minutes left of this session." Doc glanced down again at her notes. "Was there anything else that you wanted to talk about today? Are you feeling comfortable about this meeting with Lia tomorrow?"

"Yes, I'm going to go through with it."

"Try to relax about tomorrow and just be yourself. Let things unfold as they are supposed to, Ari. You're actually getting very good about that, despite what you may think sometimes. I've seen it on a few occasions in here," Doc said, smiling as she got up from her chair, a cue for Arianna that it was time to do the same.

Arianna walked out of Doc's office with a bounce to her step. She felt that it had been a good session and she also felt ready for tomorrow. Once seated in her car, she reached for her phone to check if she'd had any calls and noticed a missed call from Lia. And there was a message. She took a deep breath as she punched in the code to listen to it. Maybe she was calling to cancel. Arianna's stomach knotted.

Hi, Arianna, it's Lia calling. I want to confirm with you our meeting for tomorrow. I hope that everything is still good because I'm very much looking forward to seeing you. There was a brief pause of silence. *It's all that I've been thinking about since we spoke. Okay then. You can just text me back if you like and I'll plan to see you tomorrow. Ciao.*

Arianna sat in the car with her heart racing after she played the message for a second and then a third time without erasing it from her phone. It was strange hearing the voice of her mother on the other end. A voice that soon she would be able to put with a face. She liked Lia's voice. There was something about it that intrigued her, and just hearing it made her feel more excited than scared to meet this woman who said that she was her mother. She was glad that Lia had given her an out from phoning by asking her to confirm via text message, because she didn't think she had it in her to return the call tonight.

She wasn't yet ready to speak with her again.

Arianna bit her lip lightly as she pulled up the number on her phone to send a text.

Got your message. Thank you. I will see you tomorrow at eleven o'clock. Looking forward to it too.

She paused for a moment and then deleted the last line. She wasn't quite ready to open herself up to Lia. She'd have to meet her first and see her face-to-face. She clicked the send button before she could second-guess herself again. She was going to this meeting tomorrow. She was sure of that now.

PAULA KAY

CHAPTER 10

Arianna woke up the next morning to the sound of the alarm on her phone going off. For a moment she forgot why she had bothered to set it and then remembered what day it was. Today was the day that she was going to meet Lia for the first time. Meet her mother for the first time. God, the thought of it was so weird. She still didn't quite know what to feel about it, but had vowed to keep reminding herself about the conversation she'd had with Doc yesterday. *Just go with it Ari. Let it be what it will be.*

She popped out of bed and stopped to buzz Gigi on the intercom. "Gi? Are you there?"

"*Si*, good morning. Would you like some coffee, bella?"

"Yes, please. Can you bring it up here for me with a slice of toast? Thank you," Arianna said, heading into her bathroom.

She stared at her reflection in the mirror, wondering what it would be like to look her mother in the eyes. *I wonder if I look like her.* Arianna had wondered about her birth mom throughout her life, but she never let herself dwell on all of the questions that were in her head. Now, here she was about to meet her and she couldn't think at all of what they might talk about. Well, at least subjects that wouldn't cause too much pain or friction. Not for a first meeting anyways. But she had learned a lot in therapy about being honest when it came to her feelings. Somehow she knew that she'd get through this, and the feeling of fear was mostly being replaced by that of curiosity.

Arianna didn't have time to dwell on these thoughts, as Gigi was knocking on her door with the coffee. "Come in, Gi. You can set it over on the table by the window please."

Gigi placed the tray down on the table and turned to Arianna as she seated herself. "How are you doing, bella? Are you feeling okay?" Gigi had the normal look of concern on her face that she had these days when it came to asking how Arianna was feeling.

"Yes, I'm feeling fine. Just a bit nervous about this meeting, but I suppose that's to be expected, right?"

"I really hope it goes well. It would be pretty amazing to have your mother in your life, especially right now with—"

"Gi, I'm not planning to tell her everything. It's too soon for that." Arianna looked out the window and paused before finishing her thought. "I'll just see how it goes. I want to learn about her, and of course I have so many questions. I certainly don't need to be dumping all of my stuff on a woman I barely know." She could guess what Gigi was about to say and stopped her before she had a chance. "Yes, I know technically she is my mother, but I doubt it will feel like that. Maybe not ever. Right now she's a stranger to me and that's just the way it is." She looked to Gigi now for some assurance of understanding.

"You know what you're doing. Yes, I suppose you're right. Get through today and see how it goes. You can have more time to spend with her if it goes well, yes?"

"Well, I haven't gotten the ticket yet for my trip, and I will want to do that soon. Probably next week." Arianna noticed the worried expression on Gigi's face that always seemed to show itself whenever she mentioned going away on this trip. "I'm still going, Gi," she said gently. "Regardless of what happens with Lia."

"I know," Gigi said. "But you can't blame me for being worried about you. You're like a daughter to me." She paused for a moment. "And I love you as if you were my own. I can't help but worry about you."

"I know, Gi. And I adore you too." Arianna smiled and gave Gigi a big hug. "Now, let me spend a little time with my coffee and my journal, and then I need to start making myself presentable." Arianna winked.

"Call me if you need anything at all. I'll be downstairs in the kitchen."

Gigi left the bedroom and Arianna opened the journal, poised to start writing with her favorite pen. How was is that she'd never written like this before this year? Writing her thoughts over the past months had been so cathartic for her. It was really incredible how much better it made her feel. As if finally she had someone who would listen to her cry and scream without any judgment or interjection. She'd never had that with her parents. She always felt so judged by them.

She couldn't help her thoughts from turning to Lia once again. Would Lia judge her if she knew everything about her past? Arianna thought that it would be crazy if she did, but it was hard to say really. She had heaped enough judgment on herself, anyways. It was something she was constantly working on with Doc. Working through the guilt which Doc said served her no purpose at all.

Before she knew it, an hour had passed. Arianna put her journal away and walked over to her closet. She loved her closet full of designer clothes. Her father had always given her a big allowance to do with as she liked, and her favorite things to purchase were the latest fashion items. She had a closet that any woman would die for. All the latest styles, including matching shoes, handbags, and accessories.

She had a gift for fashion, and before she got into modeling she had thought that maybe she'd go to fashion school. But her father had laughed when she suggested it. Oh, he would have given her the money, but he said that he didn't know why she should bother when she could just continue on with her modeling if she wanted to work at all. Arianna sighed. She realized now that her parents' attitude towards her in regards to work hadn't done her any favors at all when it came to her own sense of self-esteem.

Back on the task at hand, she thought hard about how she wanted to present herself to Lia. She didn't want to make her uncomfortable by being overdressed. After several thoughtful minutes, she chose her favorite designer jeans, a simple white blouse, and some short black boots. She'd add her favorite simple necklace and some stud diamond earrings and she'd be all set. She couldn't help but smile as she made her way to the shower. *I'm gonna meet my mother today.*

An hour later, Arianna was headed into the city. She was nervous, but also excited. She glanced at the time, hoping that she wouldn't be late, and made her way over the bridge, headed towards one of her favorite parts of town, Little Italy. Really it was mostly a small collection of restaurants and shops, but she loved to sip a drink there and imagine what it would be like to finally be in Italy herself. She'd wanted to go there ever since she was a small girl and found out that she was full-blooded Italian.

Gigi had been helping her with a school project on ancestry and she remembered the day that she asked her what that meant. Her parents had told her from an early age that she was adopted, that she had been *chosen* by them to be their daughter. Gigi had known this too, and on that day when an innocent Arianna had looked up at her and asked what it meant to be full-blooded Italian, Gigi had whispered down into her ear so that her mother wouldn't hear from the other room.

"Bella, it means you are like me. You come from Italia. Your mother and your father by birth were from Italy. I think that's true. It is where you get your beauty." She had laughed when she'd said it, but then quickly turned serious. "Quiet now, Ari. Don't let your mother hear you talking about it. It will make her sad."

And Arianna remembered always feeling so guarded with her feelings about being adopted. Gigi's words could not have been more truthful that day. Arianna's mother and father hated when she brought up anything to do with being adopted. So she'd not ever pressed the matter.

Her thoughts turned back to her morning meeting with Lia and the issue at hand of finding a parking spot in the busy area. Tourists and locals alike seemed to be out enjoying the rare day of sunshine. She sighed with relief after noticing the time and the single available parking spot all in the same moment.

She parked her car, swiped some lip gloss across her lips, and looked at herself in the rearview mirror. *Today is the day.* She took a nice deep breath to calm her racing heart. Arianna didn't know what was about to happen but she did know that nothing would be the same after this meeting.

CHAPTER 11

Arianna walked into the cafe, taking a deep breath as she tried to calm her nerves. On her way to speak with the hostess, her eyes did a quick scan of the tables and landed on Lia. She knew at first glance that it was her. Her mother. Their eyes met and Arianna waved slightly, willing herself to smile and not show how nervous she was feeling. *Now just make your way across the room, Ari. Be normal. You can do this.*

When she reached the table, Lia stood to her feet, looking every bit as nervous as Arianna felt. Arianna reached to shake her hand as she would do with anyone she was just meeting. After a slightly awkward moment they both sat and stared at one another while the waiter brought them a menu.

"Just a latte for me, please," Arianna said to the waiter without opening the menu.

Lia nodded in agreement. "Yes, I'll have the same. Thank you."

After what seemed like several minutes, Lia smiled at Arianna. "You're so beautiful. I can't believe how beautiful you are."

Arianna was no stranger to people remarking about her looks, but she could feel herself blushing instantly. "Thank you. I—I don't know what to say. I'm sorry. This is a bit awkward, and I don't want it to be." She took a deep breath, willing herself to take it all in.

She almost couldn't believe it. She really *did* look like her mother. It was amazing, really. It was like she was looking at herself in a mirror years from now. Lia had the same thick dark wavy hair, cut to her shoulders, big brown eyes, and long lovely eyelashes.

"I'm sorry. I don't mean to stare. It's just remarkable to me. Sitting across the table from you right now. I've imagined this day so many times, Arianna," Lia said. "I can't tell you how happy you made me when you agreed to meet. I wanted to call you for months now, and I'm sorry I waited this long."

Arianna took a sip of the latte that the waiter had placed before her on the table. "I talked to Douglas after we spoke on the phone. He told me everything. Or at least the parts he knew, about you contacting my father before he—before the accident." Arianna's voice caught a bit and Lia was quick to interject.

"I'm so sorry about your parents. I can't imagine what you've been going through. The shock that you must have felt. Are still reeling from. I—I want you to know that I did want to call you sooner, but I knew that it wasn't the right time. That it might be too much for you and I didn't want to put you through anything else." Lia reached across the table for Arianna's hand as if it was the most natural thing for her to do.

Arianna instinctively pulled her hand away. She couldn't help it. She wasn't used to being touched so easily, and she had the same wall up that she would have with any stranger.

"I'm sorry. Arianna. It's okay," Lia said smiling.

Arianna believed her. "God, I didn't meant to do that. That was rude. I'm sorry. I just—you know—I just need a little time, that's all." She stopped talking for a few seconds, staring at the woman across from her. "I really do look like you." The shock of it was incredible to Arianna.

Lia smiled. "I think so too. If I'm being honest, you look just as I've imagined you would, if not even more beautiful. You're certainly much more lovely than I was at your age. That's for sure. And it's remarkable. You have the smile of your father."

Arianna noticed a wistful look cross Lia's face, like she was flashing to a memory that she wanted to share out loud. But there would be time for that later. She didn't think she could handle talking about her father too right now, even though she was more curious than ever.

Arianna laughed, trying to lighten the mood a bit. "I suspect there will be time enough to tell me about such things. Today I want to know about you. I'm confused as to where you are living… It was such a shock when you called the other day that I ended the conversation with a ton of questions unasked."

"Oh, I know. And you're right. There will be time to get to know one another. I hope that we can, Arianna. I mean that," Lia said, and Arianna trusted the sincerity in her voice.

Arianna wanted that too. She was surprised at how much she wanted that, now that she was sitting here with her mother. It was unbelievable, but just being with Lia made her feel comforted. She could already tell that it was just a matter of time before her guard would come down. She hoped they'd have the time to spend together before she left for her trip. She felt a twinge of something stir inside her when she thought briefly about her plans, but she didn't dwell on it now. There would be time for sorting that all out later.

Arianna turned her attention back to Lia. "Sorry, I was a bit lost in thought there." She laughed. "It seems to happen to me quite often these days, I'm afraid. Go on. You were about to tell me how you came to be in the area? I'm so curious to know how you found me."

Arianna had already decided that she wanted to see Lia again, and there would be time enough later for the harder questions. Right now she wanted to learn more about this woman sitting in front of her.

Lia shared that she'd been living in New York, working as a housekeeper, when she'd gotten a phone call from one of her friends in San Francisco about a job opening here. She'd been doing this kind of work ever since she'd arrived in the Bay Area from Italy as a young girl.

Arianna knew that Lia must have been working in San Francisco at the time of Arianna's birth, but she didn't mention it now.

"So I began working for the family here. It was a good job. Some cleaning, but mostly cooking, which is what I prefer." Lia smiled. "Then everything pretty much fell apart when the couple decided to divorce. I lost my job a month or so ago, but I have another starting in six weeks' time."

Arianna wondered about the type of families Lia was working for. How odd to think that Lia, her mother, had a role in someone else's home as Gigi did in her own. Thinking of Gigi made her smile and she couldn't stop herself from thinking that the two women should meet.

"Lia, you'll have to meet Gigi, my house—" Arianna stopped herself mid-sentence. She wondered what Lia would think about her lifestyle, her wealth. But why should Arianna be feeling weird about it? It was Lia who had given her to her parents.

"It's okay, Arianna," Lia said. "I know that you are wealthy. That your parents are—were well off. It's what I wanted for you and it makes me very happy. Please know that." Her voice got quiet. "I knew that I couldn't give you the life that you deserved. I wanted something better for you." Lia dabbed at her eyes with a napkin.

Arianna felt a bit stunned at the emotion she was feeling. She tried hard to hold back her own tears. *Take a deep breath, Ari. Just let it be what it will be.*

"I have so many questions. So many things I've wanted to ask you ever since I can remember. I almost can't believe that we are sitting here together right now. It's all a bit overwhelming, if I'm being honest." Arianna glanced at her watch. "Are you hungry? Shall we order some lunch or do you need to be anywhere?"

"*Sì*, yes. I'd love to eat. I was looking at the menu before you arrived and the food looks lovely. Do you like Italian food?"

"I do, yes. Well, I have my favorite restaurants but I don't cook much myself. Really I don't cook at all." Arianna laughed. "Gigi, she's our—my housekeeper— and she cooks too, but to be honest, that's a bit hit-or-miss." Arianna laughed again. "Don't tell her I said that when you meet her." She blushed a little as she realized the unspoken invitation that was insinuated. "Yes, let's order, shall we?"

They both ordered the Tuscan salad, enjoying the meal as the conversation flowed. Lia asked Arianna about her childhood, and Arianna felt herself opening up a bit. Of course she didn't delve into any of the tougher times, but she did share with Lia where she'd gone to school and what life had been like for her growing up in Marin as a child.

By the end of the meal, Arianna wasn't ready for the

conversation to end, but it was getting late; so it was probably time to make a move soon.

As if reading her mind, Lia chimed in. "Arianna, I've enjoyed this. Meeting you and talking to you. Can I see you again soon? My schedule is pretty open right now. I have my resume in at the temp agencies in town, but so far they've not called with anything."

"Yes, I'd like that very much." And Arianna meant it when she said it. "What is best for you?"

"I don't know how you'd feel about coming to my place? It's just a small apartment in South City, but I'd love to cook you dinner, if you're up for that? Something lovely and Italian. Maybe one night early next week?" Lia looked at Arianna with a hopeful expression on her face.

"Yes, I would like that. A lot, actually. Monday night would work for me. Let me know when and where and I'll show up with a big appetite." Arianna grinned.

"Perfect. Let's say seven o'clock. And I'll text you the address," Lia said.

Lia insisted on paying the bill when it arrived, and Arianna finally relented after making Lia promise to let her treat next time. In her mind, she calculated that this meant at least two more meetings between them. She smiled as she thought about how much she wanted to get to know this woman. Her mother.

They walked out into the sunshine.

"Where are you parked? I'm only right here." Arianna waved towards her convertible. "So I'm happy to give you a lift if you've parked a ways away."

"Oh no, that's okay. I don't have a car, actually. I'm going to catch the bus."

"Don't be silly. I can give you a ride, Lia. Really, it's no problem."

"No, honestly. I'm going to run a few errands and it will take me no time at all on the bus. I do it all the time. If you don't mind though, you could drop me right before you turn to go over the bridge. On 19th," Lia said.

"Oh, I'm heading over to that area to drop by a friend's, so I can drop you there, no problem." Arianna was happy to have a few more moments with Lia. She wasn't at all ready for their time together to end.

She unlocked the car and both she and Lia got in.

"I love your convertible," Lia said.

"Thank you. It was a gift from my parents." *God. Was that a weird thing to say?* Arianna glanced at Lia, who didn't seem bothered by the statement. Arianna didn't mention the fact that it was actually the third car that her father had bought her after she'd wrecked the other two during her crazier high school days. She'd really grown up since then.

"Let me know if it's too much with the top down. I can easily put it up." Arianna said after she'd been driving for about five minutes. She didn't want to talk more right now, though. She was just enjoying that they were sitting beside one another in the car...in the silence. It felt nice. It felt oddly right to her.

"No, bell—Arianna." Lia caught herself at the term of endearment that slipped easily from her mouth. "This is nice. I've never actually ridden in a convertible before."

"You can call me Ari if you like." They were at a stoplight and Arianna looked over at Lia. "All my friends call me Ari." She smiled and then added. "And Gigi calls me bella all the time. I don't mind." She felt suddenly shy, but oddly her world seemed a bit more right all of a sudden. She took a deep breath and glanced at her reflection in the rearview mirror. Everything was going to be okay. Today was a good day. Today was a great day, and now she knew her mother.

PAULA KAY

CHAPTER 12

Arianna let Lia out on 19th Avenue after trying to convince her to let her drive her home. After a slightly awkward moment, Lia quickly kissed Arianna on both cheeks and promised to text her with the address to her place for Monday night. They waved goodbye and then Arianna was left alone with her thoughts as she drove the ten minutes to Blu's apartment.

She was oddly calm and feeling quite elated after the day she'd had with Lia. Not at all what she'd expected. She didn't know if it was everything that was going on in her life, her sessions with Doc, or if she was really just becoming a new person, but she found her walls coming down much faster with Lia than was typical for her. She didn't quite know why. Well, if she was being honest with herself she could guess the reason. But she wanted to let Lia into her life.

Now the question was, how much time would there be before she left on this trip? Arianna sighed. Was it possible that she was meant to stay here? Not do the trip? She'd talk about it with Doc the next time she saw her. Then she really needed to make a decision and buy the ticket.

Arianna pulled up to Blu's, scoring a great parking spot, and realizing that she'd not even texted her to let her know that she was on her way. They'd had loose plans but normally she was more polite about showing up on Blu's doorstep unannounced. Arianna smiled, anxious to tell Blu all about Lia.

She reached for her phone to text her and then decided to just ring the doorbell. Blu wouldn't mind. After the third ring of the doorbell, Arianna heard the fast patter of Jemma's feet on the other side of the door. "Who's there?" said a sweet little voice.

"It's your favorite person in the whole wide world," Arianna shouted through the door. "Next to your amazing mommy, I mean."

Jemma giggled as she opened the door for Arianna.

"Hey, J-bean. Good job asking who it is first." She placed her bag down on the table and scooped Jemma up in her arms. "How's my favorite little jelly bean doing?"

Jemma giggled in delight. "What flavor am I, Ari?"

"What's your favorite flavor this week?" Arianna asked.

"Watermelon."

"Watermelon it is. And you taste delicious."

Jemma giggled even harder as Arianna covered her neck with kisses. "You're squeezing me too tight. Put me down." The little girl laughed and took her by the hand. "I made a picture for you." Jemma pulled her into the living room, where it looked like she'd been coloring right before Arianna had arrived.

Blu looked up from the small table in the corner. "She's been working on that masterpiece all morning, I'll have you know." She rose to give Arianna a quick hug. "How'd it go? I'm dying to know. And by the pleased look on your face, I'm guessing you have lots to tell me."

Arianna nodded as she gave Blu a quick hug before sitting down on the sofa to admire Jemma's artwork. "It went *so* well, Blu. I can't wait to tell you about her."

"Let's give munchkin here a few minutes and then I'll send her to her room so we can talk." Blu whispered over Jemma's head. "I'm just finishing up with some bills here." She sighed and made a face.

"Mommy, I wanna stay with Ari," Jemma whined.

Blu laughed. "Ari's gonna stay for dinner, I think."

Arianna nodded to Blu behind Jemma.

"So maybe color one more picture with her and then you can let the grown-ups talk for a few minutes, okay?" Blu said.

Jemma turned to look Arianna in the eyes, putting her sweet little hands on either side of Arianna's face. "Ari, are you going to stay for dinner?"

Arianna put her hands on Jemma's little face, saying "J-bean, I'd be delighted. On one condition."

"What's a condition?" Jemma said with a perplexed look on her face.

Arianna laughed. "It means that I'll stay for dinner if

you do something."

"Okay, what do you want me to do? Color another picture?" Jemma looked up with a hopeful look on her face.

"Well, yes. I would like another picture. That goes without saying, because you know how much I admire your artwork." The refrigerator at Arianna's house was plastered with drawings that Jemma had given her. She nuzzled Jemma's neck with a quick kiss. "I want to know if you will sit by me during dinner, silly. That's the condition I offer to you."

"Sure, Ari. I'll even sit on your lap if you want me to." Jemma grinned. "Easy peasy." Arianna and Blu laughed simultaneously.

"Her new favorite expression," Blu said.

Arianna and Jemma colored a picture together while Blu finished paying her bills.

"Okay, baby girl, why don't you take your coloring book into your room for a little while so Mommy and Ari can talk about grown-up stuff," Blu said as she held out her hand to Jemma.

"But not for too long, okay, Mommy?"

Arianna watched them head off into Jemma's small bedroom with a lump in her throat. The two of them were so amazing together. She thought Blu was a wonderful mother, if not just a tad overprotective. But she didn't ever question Blu about her parenting. She knew that it had been the two of them ever since Jemma was born. Actually Blu didn't talk about Jemma's father at all. It was one of those topics that were off limits. And Arianna had always respected that. After all, she knew what it was to have secrets. She had only opened up to Blu since the accident and—well, it was really only after her breakdown. It was Doc who had taught her so much about trust and opening up to people. She figured that if she couldn't trust Blu, who she knew cared about her maybe more than anyone in her life right now, then who could she trust?

But it wasn't the same for Blu. Arianna didn't push her. She only knew that Blu had had a difficult childhood. As much as her own childhood had revolved around private schools and fancy vacations, Blu had grown up living in poverty with a mother that was an alcoholic. That much Arianna did know. And she didn't press for more.

"Okay then, she's settled for—oh—a good ten minutes. That's *if* we're lucky." Blu said as she passed Arianna on her way into the small kitchen. "Can I get you a glass of wine? I'm dying for one myself. Paying bills seems to have that effect on me." She laughed.

"Yes, please. That sounds great. Sorry, I should have picked something up on my way. I was so distracted."

"Oh, no worries, it's actually one of the bottles that you brought over last week. Thank you very much for keeping my wine selection full." Blu laughed. "Now, tell me everything. I can't wait to hear all about Lia and how your meeting went." Blu handed Arianna the glass of wine and settled herself into the worn but comfy chair across from where Arianna sat in the living room.

"Oh, Blu. I can't believe how great it went. I mean, I was trying not to have any expectations. Well, I kind of did after our initial phone conversation, but then I just decided to try hard to be in the moment."

Blu raised an eyebrow. "Who is this person in front of me and what have you done with my slightly neurotic, yet lovely best friend?"

Arianna laughed in response to Blu's joke. "Okay, okay. So I know I'm not the most zen person, but honestly, Doc is really helping me with that. I guess I've finally realized that there is so little in my life I can control right now, you know?"

"Yep, I do know that, *and* I think you are amazing." Blu got that funny look on her face that Arianna knew to mean that there was so much more that she wanted to say but she was trying to keep from doing so.

"But?" said Arianna.

"No buts. You're amazing. Period. Now go on, please." Blu smiled.

"Okay. So I walked into the restaurant and recognized her right away. And—by recognized I mean that she looked almost exactly like what I would picture my mother—uh, Lia to look like. Blu, I *really* look like her. I mean, as in a lot." Arianna said this as if she still couldn't quite believe it.

"That's pretty amazing. And what happened when you first spoke? What did she say to you? I can't even imagine how nervous you both must have been."

"It was a little awkward at the beginning. I went up to her and basically stuck out my hand and said hello." Arianna laughed as she recounted this to Blu.

"She kept staring at me and telling me that she thought I was beautiful." Arianna's eyes started to well with tears. *My mother thinks I'm beautiful.* The emotions that came with this thought all at once surprised and overcame Arianna, and before she knew it tears were flowing down her face to the accompaniment of big gulping sobs.

Her mother. The mother who had raised her had never once called her beautiful.

Blu grabbed a box of tissues from the nearby table and moved quickly beside her best friend on the sofa, pulling Arianna to her in a big hug. "Oh, sweetie. You *are* beautiful. And how amazing that you got to hear that from your mother—"

Arianna managed a laugh amidst her sobs. "Oh God. It's not that. Really. You don't need to tell me how gorgeous I am." She knocked Blu playfully on the arm. "I don't know what is making me cry right now exactly. It's just all so overwhelming. Not in a bad way, though. Does that make sense?"

"Yes. And what I was gonna say before you practically knocked me out"—Blu got this exaggerated look of annoyance on her face—"was that soon she'd see how much your inside matches your outside. Okay, that sounds corny now, but you know what I mean. Not everyone knows you as the amazing person that I know you to be. That's all. And I know that's important to you. Now maybe more than ever." Blu's voice got quieter and she seemed to be wrestling with her own emotions as she continued.

"Okay, okay. Let's have a deep breath and a drink of our wine so I can get through telling you the rest of this without busting into tears every five minutes. I don't think my heart can take it." Arianna laughed.

Blu crossed back over to sit in her own chair, lifting her glass towards Arianna. "To you, my friend. And to being open to what life has for you *right now.*"

Arianna lifted her glass in agreement and added, "And to Lia—my mother."

The two women spent the next twenty minutes with Arianna recounting the rest of her visit with Lia to Blu. By the end of it all, Arianna was left with even more of a sense of peace about everything than she'd had when she had begun filling Blu in on the details. Her friend's reaction was affirming. It did seem as if Lia had come into her life because she truly wanted a chance to get to know her daughter. Arianna believed that and Blu, although still a bit skeptical, accepted the fact that she was going into this new relationship with her eyes wide open.

"And I'll want you to meet her, of course. After I've spent a bit more time with her. You will, won't you?"

Arianna said.

"Meet who, Ari?" Jemma had snuck back into the living room, after being quite the team player for giving Blu and Arianna the chunk of time that they'd had to discuss Lia and the day's events.

"Jemma, it's not polite to eavesdrop." Blu looked at Jemma with a stern expression.

"Mommy I don't even know what leaves drop means," Jemma said with an expression of utter cuteness on her face.

Arianna and Blu burst into laughter. Arianna reached out to grab Jemma in a big squeeze. "I just have a new friend that I want your mommy to meet, that's all. And you too, probably. If you'll stop being such a little spy with your *leaves dropping*."

"I don't know what you and Mommy are talking about, but I'm hungry," Jemma said with a giggle and rub of her tummy to signify a dire need for food.

"Okay then. Who's ready to order some pizza?" Blu said.

Arianna spent the rest of the evening with Blu and Jemma, having the privilege of tucking the little girl in with a sweet bedtime story before she said goodnight to Blu, letting her know what time she'd be picking them up the next day for their flight to San Diego.

Arianna needed to phone Douglas. He was going to be pleased to hear about her meeting with Lia. At least she thought that he would be. Arianna thought that she might eventually like for him to meet Lia too. Her little circle of people. Blu and Jemma. Douglas and of course Gigi. Maybe she'd organize something at her house next week.

Stop getting ahead of yourself, Ari. Let's see how Monday night goes first.

Oddly enough, when she thought about seeing Lia again on Monday, she had none of the anxious feelings that she'd had before meeting her. Arianna was surprised that all she felt was excitement about the possibility of getting to know this person better. Of getting to know her mother better. *Just breathe and let it be.* And she did take a deep breath and tried to enjoy her drive back to her home.

It was dark, and as she drove across the bridge she looked out towards the city lights, wondering what her mother was doing in her apartment right then. She wondered if she'd made many friends since arriving in the area or if she preferred to spend quiet nights at home alone with the TV or a good book. Arianna wondered if Lia had a love for writing or if maybe she also kept a journal to record her thoughts. So many questions. There'd be time to ask them all, or at least the ones that mattered.

CHAPTER 13

Arianna had the driver pull up in front of Blu's apartment. She could hear Jemma's excited squeals as she went to ring the doorbell.

"Ariiiiiii."

"Open the door, J-bean." Arianna laughed.

The door opened and her favorite little face peeked out.

"Let me see you. Why are you hiding?" The child was always playful and most often in a good mood, and Arianna loved that about her. It was hard to be sad for long when in the presence of the six-year-old bundle of energy.

"Look what Mommy made me." Jemma threw the door open wide, revealing her ensemble—the new black leotard and tutu that Arianna had seen a few days earlier. Jemma twirled a few times and looked up at her with an expectation of approval.

"Ooh, you look lovely." Arianna said, scooping her up for a big hug as she glimpsed Blu struggling in the small hallway with an oversized suitcase. Arianna put

Jemma down. "Let me help Mommy with her bags, and then we're going to go to the airport. Are you excited about flying?" Arianna knew that this would be Jemma's first flight, and she prayed that the small plane wouldn't have any turbulence to deal with.

She felt slightly shocked as she realized that she'd not thought about the fact that this was the first time she'd be flying since her parents' accident. She was used to taking the small charter planes south to their beach house. They'd been doing it ever since she was a little girl, but she hadn't taken the time to think about how it would feel to be in the small plane, so similar to the one that had gone down with her parents just a few months ago. She looked at the excited face of Jemma and knew that she'd be able to deal with it.

The ride to the airport went smoothly, as there was little traffic at this time of day; and before long they were at the airport, meeting with the pilot that she'd hired. Once everyone was situated in their seats, Arianna looked over to where Jemma had her little face squished to the window, peering out in anticipation.

"When are we going to fly?" she asked Blu.

"Soon. Here, Jemma. Have a piece of gum to chew," Blu said, handing her her favorite bubble-gum flavor, one that she only allowed the child to have for very special occasions.

Jemma took the gum with wide eyes. "I'm allowed to have gum today, Mommy?" she said with a big smile.

"Yes. It's a special-occasion day. Jemma's first time flying in an airplane. And also it's good for your ears when we are going up into the air, so be sure to chew fast, okay?"

"You got it," Jemma said with a happy grin as she began chewing the stick of gum.

The flight attendant stood beside them, introducing herself and explaining the safety procedure to them before they were ready to take off. Once they had leveled off in the air she came back to bring them drinks and a snack, taking special care to give Jemma a treat and a fun airplane pin, which Jemma promptly had Blu pin to the bright blue swatch of color around her tutu. "The blue is the sky, Mommy," she said with a big grin.

"Jemma, how are you doing over there? Can you see the clouds now?" Arianna asked from across the aisle, feeling a little less stressed after she'd closed her eyes and did some of the deep breathing exercises that Doc had taught her to do when she was feeling overwhelmed.

"Yes. I can. We're up so high, Ari. In the clouds. It's pretty."

Arianna was happy to be giving Jemma this experience. She smiled to herself as she thought about the little girl who had come to mean so much to her. She had a whole list of things that she wanted to do for Jemma. But she'd have to go over all that with Blu one of these days. She knew that in the end Blu would finally accept some gifts from her. She'd just have to spend the right amount of time positioning them in the right way. She could think of almost nothing she'd rather do with her money—well, aside from her own upcoming big trip, but even that was hardly touching the vast amount of wealth her parents had left her. Yes, there was plenty of money to be shared. It was one thing Arianna had come to know for sure as the last few months passed.

Arianna put her seat back so that she could close her eyes for a quick rest, noticing that Blu had done the same, taking advantage of the fact that Jemma was quiet for the moment, seemingly mesmerized by what she was seeing out her window.

It seemed only moments later that the flight attendant was beside Arianna, gently putting her seat back up and letting her know that they were getting ready to land. She looked out her window at the view she'd known since she was a child. You could make out the stretch where the white sandy beaches met the ocean for as far as the eye could see, and then the city buildings of San Diego, which seemed to appear out of nowhere. Arianna was excited to finally be taking Blu and Jemma to the beach house that she'd told them so much about. She knew that they were going to love it as much as she did.

The landing was smooth, and Jemma was chatting away with excitement for having seen all of the sand out her window. The trio was greeted by the driver that Arianna had hired to pick them up, and soon they were headed towards La Jolla, where Arianna's home was located.

Arianna had always referred to it as the "beach house," and now she was feeling slightly embarrassed as she realized that Blu might be expecting some cool bohemian-themed flat on the beach. It was really anything but that, and one of her father's many extravagances, to provide a certain type of lifestyle for her and her mother. She did have fond memories of playing on the beach with Gigi when she was younger. Her parents referred to those times away as family weekends, but Arianna remembered it being like any other weekend at home in Sausalito. Her parents were always playing golf or tennis, or attending local parties. But she'd had Gigi, and Gigi *was* family to her. She had been the one steady comfort in Arianna's life, and she was so thankful that she had her support, even now—especially now. She had invited Gigi to come down for the weekend as well, but she'd declined due to a previous social commitment.

"So, about the beach house," Arianna said, knowing that she sounded a little funny.

"Yes? I can't wait to see it," Blu said, and Arianna could hear the anticipation in her voice.

"Well, I realized that I may have downplayed it a little, and I'm not sure what you're expecting." Arianna laughed.

"We're expecting just to have a fun time, right, Jemma?" Blu nodded to her daughter, who nodded back in silent agreement, her eyes glued to the window and everything that was happening at the beach next to the coastal road the driver had taken. Blu looked at Arianna's face. She laughed. "I'm sure it will be amazing and, knowing your parents, quite spectacular."

"Okay, yes, I guess you could say that." Arianna laughed.

They continued the drive up the coast towards the home located at the top of a small hill at the southern part of La Jolla. The beach house was a six-thousand-square-foot custom home that her father had had built from the ground up and as they pulled into the driveway, Blu could not hold back her surprise.

"Wow. Ari, you were not kidding. This place looks amazing."

"Just wait till you see inside. And the view in the back." Arianna winked, knowing that they would make full use of the pool, outdoor barbecue, and outside sitting area. She'd called the local service that she used when she was here, and they were to have sent over her favorite housekeeper and a new chef that came highly recommended, to prepare for their arrival and see to it that there would be a nice dinner for their first evening.

As they walked to the door, followed by the driver with their bags, the housekeeper stepped outside to greet them.

"Hello Maria." Arianna kissed her cheek in a warm greeting. "This is my friend Blu and her daughter Jemma," she said, making the introductions.

"It's good to see you, Miss Ari." Maria reached out to shake Blu's hand. "And a pleasure to meet you, Miss Blu." She bent down to shake Jemma's hand. "And you, Miss Jemma."

Jemma giggled and threw her little arms around Maria for a big hug. Maria laughed, seeming delighted. Arianna was pleased, because she hoped that maybe Blu would feel relaxed enough to let Maria stay with Jemma one evening while the two of them had an adult night out. She knew that they were few and far between for Blu, and Arianna was hoping that she could get her friend to let loose and relax a little bit.

They followed Maria into the enormous foyer, greeted with a huge bouquet of fresh-cut flowers sitting on the center table and accented by the low lights of the beautiful chandelier hanging above. Arianna could already smell something wonderful, so she motioned her guests to follow her as she made her way to the gourmet kitchen to introduce herself and Blu to the chef.

They stepped inside and she heard Blu gasp at the ocean view that greeted them from every window of the room. Jemma ran across the space to the window screaming that she wanted to go to the ocean. Arianna laughed as she stuck her hand out towards the chef, who she did notice was quite handsome. "Hi. You must be Chef Parker."

"At your service, and please call me Chase. It's lovely to meet you, Miss Sinclair." He grinned widely, displaying perfect teeth as he reached out to shake Arianna's hand.

"And you can please call me Arianna—or Ari." She motioned towards Blu, who seemed a little tongue-tied. "And this is Blu."

Chase reached his hand out to shake the one Blu offered him, and Arianna thought it lingered a bit as he did so. "It's lovely to meet you, Blu. I hope that I can treat you all to some delicious food while you're here." He flashed a big grin, and Arianna didn't think she'd seen Blu smile so broadly herself in quite some time.

Chase made his way over to Jemma at the window and crouched down beside her. "And who might you be, princess of the dark night in your lovely tutu?"

Jemma giggled and did one complete spin for her new friend. "My mommy made this for me. Do you really think I look like a princess?" she asked with wide eyes.

"I would never suspect otherwise," Chase teased with obvious delight.

Blu made her way to Jemma, smiling at what Arianna thought was the cutest exchange ever. "This is Jemma." She tapped Jemma lightly on the back. "Jemma, shake Chase's hand and say hello."

Jemma stuck out her little hand towards Chase, saying, "I'm six. Can you give me a piggy-back ride now?"

They all burst into laughter as Chase looked towards Blu for approval before scooping Jemma up and placing her on his shoulders.

Arianna and Blu followed Chase with Jemma on his

back out onto the expansive terrace which surrounded a big infinity pool and hot tub. A big stone fireplace sat in the center of a beautiful eating area that had a table set for a dinner and an outdoor sofa placed near the fireplace. The ocean view went on for as far as one could see; it was what Arianna loved the most about the house. Virtually every room had the same incredible view from any of the house's many windows.

At Jemma's insistence, Chase put her down so that she could explore more easily. "Mommy, I want to go to that sand," Jemma said, pointing towards the ocean.

"J-bean, let's get settled and I'll take you for a walk in a little while, okay?" Arianna said to the little girl, who could hardly contain her excitement. "And I have a surprise for you that will happen after dinner. When it's dark," she added with big eyes. She knew that there would be a weekend fireworks display that they'd be able to see perfectly from the terrace.

"Ari." Jemma looked at her. "Is it scary?"

"No, bean. Not scary at all. You're going to love it." Arianna reached out her hand toward Jemma. "Now come on, let me show you where your room is."

PAULA KAY

CHAPTER 14

Arianna looked towards Chase and Blu, who seemed deep in conversation across the terrace, and decided to leave them alone for a few minutes. The wheels were going in her brain, because she was always trying to set Blu up with someone and so far she'd shown zero interest at all in meeting a man. In fact, more often than not, she seemed very anti-men, something that Arianna had given up pressing her about lately. She figured that Blu had her reasons; and Arianna knew, maybe more than anyone, what it felt like to have someone prying or trying to pressure her to talk about something when she wasn't ready. The fact that, at least for now, Chase and Blu seemed to have taken a liking towards one another, made Arianna feel insanely happy.

She led Jemma up the spiral staircase towards the second floor. There were five bedrooms in total, one on the first floor, three on the second, and the master bedroom that she'd taken over on the third floor.

She was feeling so pleased at the moment that, for whatever reason, her mother had not redecorated her childhood room, instead moving her into one of the other rooms when she outgrew the youthful decor. Arianna guessed that maybe she thought she'd have a grandchild to put in that room one day. She felt a quick pang of intense sadness, but it was quickly replaced by the excitement over the delight that she knew Jemma would be expressing shortly.

Arianna opened the door to what would be Jemma's room, feeling pleased as the child squealed in surprise when she saw what was beyond the door.

"This was my room when I was a little girl."

Jemma dropped Arianna's hand, running across the carpet to the hardwood floor and the ballet bar that she'd spotted as soon as they entered the room.

"Ari, were you a ballerina too when you were a little girl?" Jemma said, lifting her little foot up to the bar, like she'd been taught in class.

"No, not really. Mostly just for fun. I wasn't serious about it or nearly as talented as you are, my little ballerina bean." Jemma giggled as Arianna reached down to give her a little tickle as she spoke.

She remembered when her mother had had the room decorated. She didn't think she'd had much say in the room, and looking back she thought her mother just filled it with everything typical of a little girl. There was the ballet bar with a full-length mirror that ran the whole length of that wall. A canopy bed with big fluffy pink pillows and huge stuffed animals took up one other side of the room. There was a big wooden dollhouse complete with every small doll and piece of furniture that could possibly belong in the little replica mansion.

Seeing the dollhouse brought back a memory of Arianna playing here one rainy day after being sent to her room for mouthing back to her mother. All she had wanted was for her mother to play dolls with her, and instead she got in trouble because she wasn't listening the first time when her mother had said that she didn't have time to play that day. Arianna had run up the stairs, and shortly after Gigi came to her, kicking off her shoes and sitting down to play house with her. All of her best childhood memories in this house included Gigi, not her parents, and Arianna thought that it was very sad.

She watched Jemma as she started pulling things out of the playhouse now, obvious wonder and excitement on her face. *You'll never have to worry about not feeling loved, J-bean,* she thought to herself as she helped Jemma to pull out everything so that she could get a look at all of her options for filling the interior of the house. She'd never known a mother who was more loving and attentive than Blu. She envied them their relationship, and she couldn't help the tear that silently fell down her cheek as she thought about it and everything she had lost.

"Why are you crying?" Jemma looked up with a worried look on her little face.

Arianna brushed her hand across her face quickly. "I'm not crying. I'm just so happy that you like your room. Do you like it, bean?"

"I love it." Jemma stood up quickly and took off towards the door. "Mommy. Look at Ari's old room she's giving me."

Blu laughed as she entered the room. "Honey, she's not giving it to you." She winked at Arianna as she scooped Jemma up into her arms. "But is this where you are sleeping? What a lovely room. I can't believe that there's a ballet bar for you, kiddo."

Jemma nodded as she put her head against Blu's chest and yawned.

"Are you tired, honey? I think you should have a little nap before we walk down to the beach."

Arianna laughed, because Jemma's eyelids had already closed. It would actually be a good opportunity for her to have a little chat with Blu about Chase. Arianna was curious to know if her impression about the two was correct and that there had been a little spark she'd seen flying between them.

Arianna went to the bed, pulling down the covers so that Blu could tuck Jemma underneath. On their way out, Arianna reached up to switch the button on the intercom system. "We can hear her from any room when she wakes up. I don't want her to feel scared not knowing where she is," Arianna said to Blu. "Come on, I'll show you your room and then we can have a nice chat about Mr. Gorgeous, downstairs." Arianna winked.

"Oh, stop," Blu said, following her down the hall to the room next to Jemma's.

"This was officially my room, once I outgrew the other. Honestly, Blu it's so nice having Jemma in there. I think that room was created for her and not me." Arianna laughed.

Blu looked around the room with obvious pleasure. "I can see your taste. I love it, Ari. Everything is *so* beautiful." She went to sit on the king-size bed with the big white comforter and plush pillows in a variety of pretty pastel colors. Arianna sat on the bed next to her. "So?"

"So, what?" Blu responded.

"So, spill. What's up with you and Chef Cutie-pie?" Arianna teased. "Is he adorable, or what? God, I had no idea they would send over such a handsome guy. The last chef they sent me was in his sixties, I think."

"He's twenty-eight and recently out of culinary school. Which he did in San Francisco, by the way."

Arianna noticed a blush creeping up Blu's face.

"You're blushing. You like him," Arianna teased.

"Ari. Stop. Seriously." Arianna could tell that Blue was trying to keep herself from grinning. "Is he handsome? Yes. Very." She laughed. "Am I in the market for meeting anyone right now? No."

Arianna looked at her with a raised eyebrow. "But, Blu—"

"Please. I'm just not."

Arianna sighed. She really didn't get it. Blu was obviously attracted to the guy. She'd drop it for now and let things unfold at their own pace.

"Okay. Okay. If you say so. But some day I'm going to get to the bottom of this huge aversion you have towards men or anyone that remotely shows any interest in you."

"Thanks for the warning." Blu winked. "Now how about if you show me the rest of this *palace*." She laughed, slugging Arianna playfully on the arm.

Arianna took Blu upstairs to see the master bedroom, which was pretty spectacular. It had its own sitting area with a fireplace and a huge balcony where she loved to sit and listen to the ocean while writing in her journal. Each of the five bedrooms had big attached bathrooms and walk-in closets, but the closet in this room was as big as any normal-size bedroom. Arianna seemed slightly embarrassed as she opened the door to show it to Blu, revealing the wall-to-wall carpeted space that every girl would dream of. There were rows of jackets, blouses, and formals, and stack upon stack of shoes, each in its own individually labeled container. There were two chaise lounges in the middle of the room, a large vanity table and a full-length mirror in one corner.

"I still haven't cleared out my mother's things." Arianna said, aware of the worry lines that were probably appearing across her forehead. It had been on her mind to do so for a while, but so far she hadn't felt that she had the energy for the task.

Blu came up beside her and put her arm around her shoulder. "I can help you with this, ya know."

"Thanks. It's okay. I don't want to think about it this week. I'll ask Gigi to come down here with me again to help, or maybe she'll want to come down for a week on her own. I really do just want it boxed up and donated somewhere." Arianna sighed. "Anyways, I've just been using the dresser in the bedroom. Even *I* don't have enough clothes to fill that huge closet." She laughed and shut the door behind them.

"Are your sewing things upstairs here or still down in the foyer?" Arianna asked Blu as they walked back down the hall.

"Oh, I asked Maria to leave them downstairs, because I wasn't sure where you wanted me to set up the machine. But now that I see how huge and lovely my bedroom is, I'll grab everything and put it in there."

"Nope. We'll get them now when we go downstairs. I have a great idea for where you should set up shop." Arianna smiled. She couldn't wait to show Blu the sunny room off the breakfast area downstairs. She knew it would be the perfect place for her friend to work.

PAULA KAY

CHAPTER 15

Arianna grabbed the bag of sewing supplies and materials and Blu carried the sewing machine, following her through the kitchen where Chase seemed hard at work doing his prep for the evening meal. He quickly came to help them. "Let me help you with that, ladies," he said and Arianna turned and gave Blu a look, mouthing the words "so nice" as she led them through the breakfast room just off the kitchen to another room nestled on the other side. The windows faced the ocean as well, and the view was equally as grand as the view from the kitchen. A large desk faced the window and two comfortable chairs created a little sitting area in the corner.

"I thought you could set your sewing machine up here on the desk and be able to enjoy the view while you work on your masterpieces," Arianna said with a huge grin on her face.

"Wow." The look on Blu's face was priceless to Arianna. She could always tell when her friend was feeling overcome by emotion, and it made her happy to know that she'd been spot on about Blu needing this time away just as much as Arianna did.

Chase's expression as he made ready to leave the room didn't go unnoticed by Arianna. She caught him staring at Blu, and it definitely seemed to Arianna that he'd wanted to say something. But she knew that the people she hired through the domestic service were very professional. It had taken a few times of Arianna's coming to the house alone after her parents had passed for Maria to really warm up to her and to feel okay with dropping a bit of the professional, less personable way that Arianna was used to, but didn't appreciate that much. Especially now. Arianna was all about dropping pretenses and bridging the gap that sometimes existed between people with money and those with not as much money. She knew money had its privileges for sure, and she was very aware of what it was doing for her now.

So she quietly thanked Chase, who excused himself to go back to the meal preparation while Arianna turned her attention back to Blu; she was staring out the window after setting up her sewing machine and various items on the desk. Arianna went over next to her. "Penny for your thoughts." It was a common expression for the two to use with one another, and one that seemed to get said often these days.

"Oh, Ari." Blu turned and Arianna could see that there were tears in her eyes. "Thank you so much for this. It's perfect. I feel so inspired, and after spending just a few hours here." She turned to give Arianna a big hug.

"It's absolutely my pleasure." And Arianna meant it more than she'd meant a lot of things during her lifetime. Blu had been a great friend to her, and there was so much she wanted to be able to do for her and Jemma. So much that she could do. *If only Blu would let her.*

"And..." Arianna slid one of the wall panels across to reveal a whole media setup lining a good portion of the wall. "Here you have a stereo system and the flat screen complete with surround sound—in case that helps with your inspiration." She knew that Blu loved to crank her rock music while she worked, so she thought she'd find the system especially appealing.

"I love it. I can't wait to get started." Blu grinned.

"I can't wait to see what you create. But how about right now we see about taking some wine out onto the terrace for a bit while the rug rat is still resting? I can ask Chase and Maria to listen for her on the intercom."

"That sounds great."

Arianna thought that Blu looked more relaxed than she'd seen her in ages. She had thought about taking a little nap herself, because she could feel a slight headache coming on, but she didn't want to waste this time that they had alone together; she excused herself for a minute to pop up to her room to take a couple pills, leaving Blu and Chase chatting in the kitchen as Chase prepared a snack tray of cheeses and meats for them. *So, maybe I'm being just a little sneaky,* Arianna thought, laughing to herself. *But she deserves someone amazing, and I have a good feeling about that guy.*

When Arianna came back downstairs she found Chase and Blu still chatting in the kitchen, Chase with a lovely plate of food and Blu getting ready to pour two glasses of wine. "Would you like to join us outside for a drink?" Arianna said to Chase, ignoring the quick look that Blu sent her.

"Oh no, I couldn't. I never drink while I'm on the job, and I have yet to prepare what I hope will be a lovely dinner for you ladies."

Arianna smiled at him, appreciating how professional he was, while at the same time hoping he'd loosen up a bit over the course of the weekend. "Maybe after dinner then."

He nodded and then seemed to remember an additional question that he had for Blu. "About the little one—Jemma, is it?"

Blu nodded.

"I assume that she won't appreciate the grown-up food, so I'll make her something more kid-friendly, but how picky is she?"

"That's nice of you to ask. She's actually not a picky eater, and in general will try anything I put in front of her. What is the menu for tonight?"

"Salmon with grilled asparagus."

Arianna and Blu laughed at the same time. "Well, you're in luck because, believe it or not, that little girl loves salmon," Arianna said. "She's really pretty amazing. I've seen her eat with us at sushi, French, and Mexican restaurants with absolutely no complaints."

"And if she's not into something, I can just make her a grilled cheese, so please don't worry," Blu said.

"I'll be anxious to hear the little lady's review of my menu," Chase said.

"Oh, she'll let you know," Blu said, and Arianna nodded her head in agreement.

Chase went back into the kitchen to finish his prep work, leaving Arianna and Blu sitting on the terrace in the shade of a big table umbrella, sipping their wine and nibbling on the nice array of gourmet cheeses and meats that Chase had served them. Arianna hadn't felt so relaxed in ages; and by the look on Blu's face, she guessed that she was right in thinking that Blu was also feeling pretty good. It was going to be a great weekend.

Arianna and Blu sat outside for a good thirty minutes enjoying the view, their wine, and conversation. Arianna had always found Blu easy to talk to. She seemed to get Arianna, without judgment or any of the other things that she had often felt from girls that claimed to be her good friends during her younger days. She suspected that her relationship with Blu was easy because both of them knew when to press something and when to back off, respecting boundaries, although Arianna could feel them both pressing more often lately; she suspected that it was a good thing, signifying the deepening of their friendship. Doc had said as much to her when she brought it up during a session.

Soon Maria came outside hand-in-hand with a smiling Jemma, who looked well rested and happy. "Miss Blu, I hope you don't mind. I heard her while I was upstairs cleaning and she seemed happy to come downstairs with me."

"Oh, not at all, Maria. Thank you," Blu said, motioning for Jemma to come over and sit by her and Arianna.

"Did you have a good rest, bean?" Arianna asked.

"Can we go to the beach now?"

"Jemma, answer Ari." Blu said with a stern look on her face.

Arianna laughed. "It's okay." She got up from her chair and stretched. "How 'bout if we all go for a short walk before dinner? Let me check with Chase to see what time he is planning to serve."

Jemma smiled. "Okay—and yes, Ari. I had a lovely rest." She turned to look at Blu with the silly devilish grin she put on at times, seemingly to get a reaction from her.

Arianna and Blu both burst into laugher. "You're lucky you are so cute," Blu said, playfully swatting at her bottom. "Let's go up and get your shoes and a light jacket while Ari talks to Chase."

"Can Chase come too? Please, Mommy," Jemma said as her face lit up. "I loved his piggy-back ride. It was one of the best I ever had."

Arianna slowed her walk towards the kitchen so that she could hear Blu's response.

"No, sweetie. Chase has to cook us dinner, but you can see him when we come back."

Arianna smiled as she walked back into the house, Blu and Jemma right behind her as they went upstairs to Jemma's room.

Minutes later the three of them were making their way down the wooden steps that went down the hill from Arianna's house to the private beach below. Just beyond that was the public beach, where one could easily walk for miles along the water's edge. The weather was perfect, as the sun was starting to set and the sky was colored with beautiful reds and oranges.

"Can we put our feet in the water?" Jemma asked, practically kicking her sandals off as she spoke.

"Sure, let's see how warm it is," Blu said as she kicked her flip-flops off in the sand. "Ari, are you coming?"

"You two go. I want to sit for a few minutes." Arianna sat down on a big piece of nearby driftwood and took off her own shoes so that she could dig her feet into the sand; she was responding to a text message that she'd gotten from Lia. She smiled as she realized how much she was looking forward to spending more time with her once she returned home.

CHAPTER 16

After a great weekend away in San Diego, Arianna was feeling better than she'd felt for a very long time. Things seemed a bit brighter than they had a few weeks ago, even if she did find herself in circumstances that threatened to burst this new bubble of contentment she was feeling. Nothing had changed, yet everything had changed. She didn't know yet the part that Lia would play in her life, but she knew that a shift had occurred. She felt just the slightest bit less alone than she had a few months ago.

Arianna joined Gigi in the kitchen for some breakfast and to fill her in on the details of the weekend away. When she began talking about Lia, Gigi seemed optimistic and pressed her again about her trip, expressing concern that maybe this was another reason that she shouldn't be heading so far away right now. Arianna knew that she had to make some decisions about her travel plans, and vowed to put this at the top of her to-do list for next week. *After I've spent some more time with Lia*, she thought. Maybe a small part of her did wonder if she should stay. Get to know Lia better. She brushed the thought aside for now, as it was time to get ready to head into the city for her appointment with Doc.

Driving downtown, she was reminded of how anxious she had felt that last time she'd spoken to Doc about seeing Lia. She felt so different right now than she'd thought she might. There was no stress or anxiety at all. Well, except for the fact that she really did need to start making some decisions about her plans. But in terms of how she was feeling about Lia, she felt she'd done a good job of being open and letting herself be in the moment, of letting things unfold between them.

She smiled as she thought about the quick phone conversation that she'd had with Lia earlier that morning. Lia had phoned and said that she'd wanted to hear Arianna's voice, so she decided to call instead of texting her the address for that night's dinner. Arianna had laughed and told her that it was nice to hear her voice too. That she was looking forward to dinner and couldn't imagine the lovely Italian meal that Lia was preparing. She had told Lia not to go out of her way, that actually she'd also be fine taking her out to dinner somewhere. But Lia had insisted on cooking, telling Arianna that it was one of her favorite things to do in the world. She could hear the happiness in Lia's voice when she spoke about cooking for her.

This will be fun, Arianna thought and reminded herself to bring two bottles of wine from her favorite vineyard in nearby Napa Valley. Her parents had loved wine and had an extensive wine collection in the cellar at their home, so she had grown up around fine wines and learned at an early age which ones she loved the most. It would be a nice gift and something they could enjoy together tonight over dinner.

Arianna pulled into the parking garage at Doc's office hardly even realizing how quickly she'd gotten there. She rushed up and the receptionist sent her straight in.

"Hi, Doc, how are you?" Arianna entered the room with a huge grin on her face.

"I'm doing well, but the real question is how are you doing? From the look on your face, I'm guessing that you have some good news to tell me," Doc said.

"In fact, I have nothing *but* good news. And I can't wait to fill you in."

Arianna proceeded to tell her all about the visit with Lia the previous week. Doc listened attentively, waiting for Arianna to finish telling her about the dinner planned for that evening.

"So, let me ask you a question," Doc said.

Arianna sat up on the sofa, pulling the pillow in closer to her chest. "Yes?"

"Now that you've met Lia, and let's assume that everything goes great tonight, where are you at with thinking about this trip you've been talking about? Is it possible that you might change your mind?"

Arianna took her time as she thought about her answer to the question. "You know, I've been thinking about this a lot. Since yesterday, really. I know it's early stages but something about meeting my mother—Lia— just feels right."

"You just called her your mother. How does that feel?

Arianna shifted her body in slight discomfort at the question.

"It's okay, you know, Ari," Doc said.

"I know. I keep catching myself calling her that. I need to remind myself that she's still a stranger to me right now. It's odd though. I mean, you and I have talked about how fleeting time can be—and what I've learned about that ever since after the accident. How important it is to live in the moment, to not wait for things and people in your life. I guess I'm trying to practice that with her, you know?" Arianna looked at Doc, and she realized that she was feeling a sense of hope that she'd not felt for a long time.

"Yes, I do know, Ari. And you are doing an excellent job of it. You know that I'm not here to tell you either way what you should do. Only you can make those decisions and decide what's important to you right now. I think you'll know what to do. And if you decide to stay here to get to know your mother better, it won't be a wrong decision," Doc said.

Arianna felt so supported here in this office with Doc. God, she'd come so far from that scared girl who could hardly formulate a sentence without breaking into sobs just a few short months ago. She'd learned some hard lessons in a short time. That was for sure. But oddly, after all the bad news that she'd gotten over the past months, she felt more sure of herself than she'd ever imagined that she could. She was a lot stronger than she'd ever thought she was. It was sad that it had taken her parents' deaths and the subsequent tragedies in her life for her to realize this. But she was here now.

Arianna left Doc's office with an assignment to make the decision about her trip before her regular visit next week. She felt good pulling out of the parking garage into the downtown traffic of the city. On a whim, she decided to do a bit of shopping, parking at Union Square to visit a few of her favorite designer shops nearby. It had been ages since she'd done any real damage to her credit cards, and she was dying to do some shoe shopping.

She'd not been going out all that much lately, though, which was probably why she'd not gotten tired of her current wardrobe. *How much clothes does one girl really need?* She laughed as the foreign thought crossed her mind. Maybe she really was changing for the better, because suddenly fashion seemed like the last thing for her to be thinking about.

Well, except I do want to have a great selection of clothes for my trip. Then again, *if* she ended up going, she could always shop in Europe, something that she'd always wanted to do. *God. There's that big if again*, she thought. *Am I actually considering not going on this trip that I've wanted for so long?* Even as she had the thought, the picture of having lunch with Lia entered her mind, and she knew that staying was a consideration now. And that it would be okay.

She finished shopping with hardly any new purchases. She did end up finding a new pair of little black boots that she adored and a lovely new pair of earrings that would go perfectly with a new dress she'd bought last month.

She retrieved her car and started making the drive back to Sausalito, realizing how tired she felt. She'd been on the go a lot the last few days, which was exactly the opposite of what she should be doing. Emotionally, she was feeling great, and that was amazing. But if she was honest with herself, physically she did feel more than a little drained; and if she was going to do any traveling or anything at all over the next few months, she needed to slow down and get some good rest.

She'd call Gigi and see if she could make her some of that lovely chicken soup that was one of her specialties, for lunch. That sounded perfect. And maybe a good movie and a nice nap before she headed over to Lia's for dinner.

Gigi had her lunch ready for her when she arrived home, and the rest of the afternoon was relaxing. Arianna did watch a good movie, curled up in the special cinema room that her father had had built. It was *the* thing to do, and all of her friends at school had had one too. She remembered having a few lame birthday parties at her house that involved private screenings of the latest movies coming out over the summer. So a lot of it seemed to be for show, but now she rarely had anyone over to share the room with her. She'd have to invite Jemma over soon to watch something as the little girl did love it, along with the old-fashioned popcorn maker and corner counter full of all kinds of typical movie-theater sweets.

Arianna could barely stay awake for the entire movie, so when it was over she quickly made her way to her room and comfy bed. She'd get a nice cup of tea and spend some time writing in her journal after her nap.

Arianna woke two hours later feeling completely refreshed and excited about the evening ahead. She buzzed Gigi downstairs over the intercom, asking for a cup of tea. She took her journal out from the bedside table and grabbed her favorite pen. It struck her suddenly as funny that she was even keeping a journal right now. But she had come to enjoy writing down her thoughts and it had helped her to sort out so much about the way she was feeling.

She soon busied herself getting ready for the evening. Again she dressed simply, with a favorite pair of jeans and a simple white t-shirt. She put on the same stud earrings she had worn the other day for lunch. Understated, yet elegant. She put on just a bit of make-up, remembering that it had looked like Lia hardly wore any—which Arianna found rather remarkable, because she had looked so lovely. She smiled again, thinking that she had the same long black eyelashes and dark eyes as her mother. It was a shocking thought after having grown up with two parents whom she looked nothing like, being adopted. She dabbed on a bit of her favorite perfume and headed downstairs to say goodbye to Gigi.

"Have a lovely time," Gigi called out as she heard Arianna making her way down the stairs.

"I will. Thank you, Gi. I was thinking maybe if things go well tonight, I might invite Lia over here. You know, to meet everyone. A small party. You, Blu and Jemma, and maybe Douglas. What do you think? Will it work next week?" Arianna saw the look on Gigi's face and laughed, because she guessed at her discomfort before Gigi could even speak. "Don't worry, Gi, you won't have to cook. I'll hire someone to come in to do the meal. It will be fun. I promise."

Gigi laughed. "*Si*, yes, that's sounds great, bella. I would love to meet her."

CHAPTER 17

It was a beautiful evening for driving with the top down, and Arianna had her opera music playing loud in her speakers as she made the drive over the bridge. As she continued the drive to Lia's apartment just south of the city, she was surprised at how calm she felt. She still didn't know what to expect from their visits but she was looking forward to getting to know her mother better. And if she had to guess, she thought that Lia was going to cook her a delicious meal tonight. She loved Italian food, and being with Lia just reminded her of all things Italian.

She pulled up to the apartment complex, following the instructions Lia had given her as to where to park. She took a quick glance at her face in the car mirror, grabbed her handbag and the wine from the back seat, and headed for Lia's apartment.

Lia answered the door after the first ring of the doorbell, greeting Arianna with a big hug and a kiss on each cheek.

"Oh my God. It smells amazing in here," Arianna said as she made her way into the small dining area off the entry. "What are you cooking?"

"Tagliatelle bolognese. It's my favorite thing to make." Lia smiled and reached for Arianna's hand to pull her behind her into the small kitchen. "Come talk to me while I finish the pasta."

Arianna handed Lia the two bottles of wine. "I hope you like red."

Lia examined the labels. "Ah, very nice. Thank you so much. We'll open a bottle now, yes?"

"Sounds good to me."

Arianna sat on a stool by the kitchen counter while she watched Lia pour two glasses of wine and assemble a plate of bruschetta for them to have before the main dish was ready.

Arianna reached for one of the perfectly done pieces. "Mmmm. This is my favorite. I love bread so much." She laughed.

"You are Italian after all." Lia laughed too.

Lia moved around to finish preparing the pasta, and Arianna noticed that she was using a pasta maker.

"Homemade pasta. Yum."

"Of course. It is the first appliance that I bought when I arrived here. An Italian woman needs her pasta maker." They both laughed.

Arianna watched her put the dough through the machine until it was perfectly flat.

"I wish I knew how to cook," Arianna said, watching Lia. "Who taught you how?"

"My mother. And my grandmother." Lia smiled. "In

Italy the kitchen is always filled with all of the women of the house. Well, the men also know how to cook pasta, but for the women it is part of life growing up. You never cooked with your—your mom?" Lia asked.

"No. Not at all, in fact. I can't even ever remember seeing my mom cook anything other than breakfast, and even that wasn't often. We had Gigi, and for special dinners she would always hire a chef to come in."

"Gigi is Italian, yes?"

Arianna nodded and laughed. "She is, yes. And she would be the first to admit to not being the world's greatest cook. We order out a lot."

"I'll be happy to teach you to cook." Lia looked up and smiled. "If you like."

Arianna's response caught in her throat as instant and surprising tears came to her eyes. "Yes, I'd like that."

"For tonight, I'll show you a few things about the meal that we're having. Let me get this pasta going on the stove." Lia finished preparing the dough and dropped the delicate pasta into the pot of already boiling water. She opened the lid to the other pot and scooped out a small spoonful with the ladle, blowing on it gently as she brought it over to where Arianna sat. "Here, bella. Taste this."

Arianna smiled, taking the spoon from her and bringing it to her mouth. "This is the best bolognese I've ever had. What's in there?"

Lia showed her the herb that was lying on the

counter. "Timo."

"Timo?"

"Ah—in English, thyme. One of my favorite herbs in Italian cuisine. The trick is in the timing of the sauce. You must put the thyme in early. It will get the full flavor that way, and then when the dish is prepared, you can also add a few sprigs on top."

"I cannot wait to eat that. My mouth is watering."

Lia laughed. "The pasta should be done in about ten minutes or so. Enjoy your wine and I will finish with everything in here. Shall I turn on some music? Do you mind?"

Arianna shook her head. "No, not at all."

"I love to listen to old rock music when I cook."

Arianna laughed. "I love to listen to opera when I drive."

"Really?" Lia laughed, unable to contain a look of surprise. "I wouldn't have expected that."

"Yes, all my friends make fun of me and think it's kind of weird, but I guess I grew up with it—it's actually something very nice I think I got from my mother. My parents took me to the opera a few times when I was younger and I was mesmerized by it. I find it relaxing." Arianna felt herself blushing a little.

"I don't know much about opera," Lia said with a wide smile. "Maybe it's something you can teach me a little about?"

"Yes. I actually have season tickets for the opera here.

Two seats, so we'll go for sure. I'd like that." Arianna felt a bit shy all of a sudden, in disbelief that she was making all of these future plans with her mother, of all people.

She went to sit on the small sofa in the living room, with the dining area between her and Lia working in the kitchen. She could see Lia humming along to the music, strands of long curly hair escaping the loose bun at the nape of her neck. Arianna thought she looked perfectly happy and content with her apron on, working in the kitchen, and a lump caught in her throat. How different would her life have been, growing up with this woman as a mother? Would she have learned to cook? Learned Italian? Avoided some of the negative influences that had come into her life…some of the mistakes she'd made? She sighed. No use dwelling on the past or what could have been. All she had was right now. This moment. And this time with Lia was better than she ever could have imagined it.

Lia looked up and smiled when she saw Arianna looking at her. "How are you doing in there?"

"I'm great. How are you doing in *there*? Can I help with anything at all?"

"No, no. I am just about ready to serve, actually. If you want to come have a seat."

Arianna got up and made her way to the table as Lia placed a steaming plate of pasta down in front of her. "This looks and smells delicious. I can't wait to try it."

"Dig in." Lia smiled.

Arianna took her first bite and was immediately transported in her mind to what she imagined a perfect Italian restaurant experience must be. "This is seriously the best pasta I've ever tasted."

"Thank you. That means a lot to me."

"Do you cook often?"

"As often as I can. But I love cooking for others especially."

"Is that why you do the work that you do? And do you enjoy it?"

"Well, if I'm being honest, I don't like the housekeeping part of the job as much, and it's unusual without formal education to get a job strictly as a private cook. So mainly the types of people that hire me want everything. The housekeeper that can also cook as a big bonus." Lia laughed.

Like when my parents hired Gigi, Arianna thought. They had wanted the housekeeper and nanny all rolled into one position.

"But I don't mind so much, really. I love cooking for the families because they do seem to appreciate it. I mainly love to cook Italian, but I'm quite happy to experiment with any recipe."

"It's good that they appreciate it," Arianna said.

"Time will tell with this next job. It's always a little nerve-racking at the beginning, getting to know one another. I have high hopes for this one, anyways. The people seemed nice when I met them and there aren't any kids, so it will be strictly housekeeping and cooking for just them. I think they do entertain a fair bit, so I'll do small dinner parties as well."

"Speaking of small dinner parties..." Arianna chimed in. "I was thinking that I'd love to have you over to meet Gigi and my best friend. She'll bring her daughter Jemma, who is six and adorable, and then I'll also ask Douglas, who I know that you've spoken with before. Maybe later this week. Say, Friday if that works for you?"

"Oh, that sounds wonderful. I'd love to come. See where you live. Oh, and I'm happy to cook—"

"Oh no, not at all. I wouldn't dream of asking you to cook. I'll hire someone to come in and do it. It's no problem, and I'd rather have you enjoy yourself."

"Actually I would love to do the cooking. Honestly. To help you do a little dinner for the people that you're closest to—that sounds like pure joy to me."

Arianna laughed. "Are you sure?"

Lia nodded. "Completely sure. I'll come up with a menu this week and we can go over it together beforehand. Does that sound good?"

"Yes, I'm good with anything you want to do; and you can send me the shopping list to give to Gigi. She's happy whenever the cooking doesn't fall on her." Arianna laughed.

"Great, then Friday it is."

They finished their pasta and then Lia excused herself to clear the plates and get the dessert out of the refrigerator. She came back to the table with what Arianna thought was the most amazing-looking panna cotta that she'd ever seen. She dipped her spoon into the fresh berries on top, scooping up the delicious creamy dessert. "This is decadent."

"I'm glad you like it. You are very easy to please." Lia smiled.

"And you are an incredible cook." Arianna smiled too. "I'm impressed. With the smells, the wine, and this delicious meal, I feel like I've been transported to Italy tonight. And it's been so lovely. Really."

"It's been my pleasure Ari."

They chatted a few more minutes before Arianna realized how tired she was feeling. It had been an exciting couple of days, and the busyness was catching up to her. She stood up to collect her bag and say goodbye.

Lia said, "So I'll call you about the menu and if you'd like, I would love to see you before then too. Anytime— but I don't want to be pushy or anything. I just want you to know that I'll take as much time as you'll give me." She smiled, and Arianna realized how much she was appreciating Lia's honesty.

"Yes, I'd like that too. I come into the city quite often, so we can meet for lunch or coffee—or I'm happy to come back down this way too."

"That sounds great. I'll call you in the next few days then." Lia went to give Arianna a big hug. "Drive carefully, okay? You are okay—to drive, I mean?"

"Oh yes, it was good that we just had the two glasses of wine." She laughed thinking of all the times she'd had to get a cab after too many drinks in the city. But she suddenly felt much older than that young carefree girl that partied too much and didn't care about anything important. "I'm fine to drive. Honest." She hugged Lia back and headed out to her car, feeling completely happy and hopeful for the days ahead.

PAULA KAY

CHAPTER 18

Arianna couldn't remember a time in her life when she'd felt so content. Since Lia's dinner at her apartment, she'd gotten together with her several times throughout the week, and the two had spent hours on the phone together. During their many conversations, Arianna had finally brought up her travel plans and although Lia did seem disappointed that she was planning to leave so soon, she'd said that she understood and was excited for her to be able to travel and see the world.

Arianna wasn't sure exactly why she had felt so nervous about introducing Lia to the others, but the small dinner party was going along without a hitch, and she was positive that everyone felt as good about Lia as she did. The wine was flowing and the conversation was easy. She felt that Lia had gotten a good glimpse of her life here…with the people she loved so much. Lia excused herself to go to the kitchen to get the dessert she'd prepared. Arianna followed her, offering to help.

As she watched Lia by the counter, carefully laying out the dessert, Arianna was overcome with emotion in a sudden and unexpected way. She loved spending time with Lia, and cooking tonight with her had been the most fun she'd had in a long time. Arianna hadn't expected to feel this way, and she didn't allow herself to edit how impulsive she was feeling at this moment.

"Come with me, Lia."

Lia turned around at the sound of Arianna's voice. "What, bella?"

"Come with me. On this trip. We'll go to Italy. To Tuscany together." Arianna shocked herself as the words came pouring out. This was how she wanted to spend her time the next few months. With her mother. Not partying her way across Europe…like the young girl she once was. None of that mattered to her anymore. All she wanted was to get to know this woman standing in her kitchen.

"Lia, please say yes. You won't have to worry about any of the expenses. It will be my treat. And my pleasure," Arianna said, unable to keep the excitement from her voice.

Lia was quiet for a moment, and Arianna could guess the questions in her mind. It was sudden, she knew.

"I don't know, Ari. The idea of it—to be back in Italia, in Tuscany—it's been so many years, so much has probably changed. To be there with you—I never even allowed myself to think of that—"

"Say yes. Please, Lia." Arianna felt like a young child begging her mother for the doll that she'd spotted in the shop window, and she giggled at the irony of it.

"What about my new job—the apartment—" said

Lia. "I don't know if it's smart for me to take off right now when I'm just getting on my feet here. But the thought of spending all that time with you—"

"Don't worry about any of that. I'll help you until you get on your feet. And if that job doesn't work out, you'll find another one. Please don't worry about the money. That's the easiest thing in the world for me to take care of."

"Ari, are you sure?" Lia grinned and crossed the kitchen to where Arianna stood.

"Yes, I'm sure. Say yes and we'll plan everything next week. It will be incredible."

Lia reached for Arianna and pulled her in for a big hug that Arianna did not resist. She was scrapping her round-the-world trip of a lifetime to be with her mother in Italy, and she couldn't feel more pleased. It was a better idea. It was the best idea. She hugged Lia back and noticed her quickly wiping at the tears in her eyes before bringing her attention back to the dessert.

"Are you ready to serve these?" Arianna asked. "I'll help you. And I want to tell the others about our plans."

Arianna noticed a concerned look on Lia's face.

"Lia, they'll be happy. No one has been overly excited about my travel plans and they'll be delighted to know that I'm not going alone any more. Or traipsing around the whole globe with partying on my brain." Arianna laughed. Partying was the last thing on her mind these days.

Lia nodded and gave Arianna a quick kiss on the cheek. "Alright then. Let's serve this to our guests, shall we?"

Arianna smiled broadly. "I think this calls for a little celebratory drink of champagne." She grabbed the chilled bottle out of the fridge, anxious to tell her friends the news.

After dessert and with the champagne poured, Arianna lifted her glass in a toast. "Everyone, thank you for coming tonight. It's been so wonderful having you here in my home and I want to thank Lia for the Italian feast that she's prepared for us."

Arianna waited while everyone nodded in enthusiastic agreement, thanking Lia for what had been a spectacular meal. Arianna continued. "And I have an announcement to make about something that you've all been patiently listening to me talk about nonstop for this past month or so. My around-the-world solo trip has hereby changed to that of a trip to Italy—to Tuscany, to be more precise— and I've got a willing partner in crime. I've asked Lia to come with me and she's agreed." Arianna grinned.

Lia looked slightly embarrassed but had a big smile on her face as everyone clapped their approval.

"Oh, that's fantastic," Blu called out. "Tuscany is going to be unbelievable. Especially for you two, going together."

"Blu, my invitation to you still stands, of course. I want you and Jemma to come for as long as you're able."

Arianna turned towards Gigi. "And Gi, you'll come too? I'll find a nice villa with plenty of room and we'll cook and drink wine and enjoy the views—and Douglas, you too? Say you'll come. It will be fantastic." Arianna looked around the table at the people that she loved. They had been there by her side through so much already. And she wanted them with her in Italy.

They all raised their glasses and in near unison toasted to Arianna and her invitation.

Douglas spoke first. "That does sound lovely, Arianna. Thank you for the invitation, and I will do my best to see if I can clear my schedule to meet you all for a few days."

Arianna noticed the slight blush that seemed to be creeping to Gigi's face as Douglas looked at her while speaking.

"Bella, what a wonderful idea. And to go home after all this time."

Gigi's family was from southern Italy, but Arianna had already thought about either having them come up or helping Gigi to organize the additional time that she should take to visit her sisters and the rest of her family.

Arianna felt completely at peace as they finished their champagne and enjoyed the easy conversation that wound up the perfect evening.

CHAPTER 19

Arianna woke up the next morning feeling great. It was wonderful to have finally made a decision about this trip that she needed to plan. Before Lia had left last night, they'd agreed that she was perfectly fine with Arianna's planning the logistics with the travel agent that morning, so that was the first thing on her mind as she headed downstairs for some coffee.

Gigi was in the kitchen humming to herself and seeming particularly cheerful for that time of the morning.

"What are you so happy about?" Arianna said, giving her a quick peck on the cheek.

"Oh, nothing, bella. Just that last night was so much fun, and I love seeing you so happy these days. Lia seems wonderful and her cooking—my God. It was as if I'd been transported back to Italy. I could eat like that every day. Although it's probably a good thing I don't." Gigi laughed, patting her stomach.

"I know. It really was delicious. Lia loves to cook and she's so good at it." Arianna was quiet for a moment, remembering the look in her eyes when Lia had confessed to her that she'd always wanted to own her own little

Italian restaurant. Arianna couldn't wait to share many meals with her in Italy with the delicious wine, cheese, olive oil, and fresh pasta that they were sure to find there.

"Gigi, forgive me for asking, but are you sure that's the only thing making you smile so much this morning? I saw that little look that Douglas gave you last night at the dinner table." Arianna teased her.

"Oh, stop." Gigi blushed and looked slightly uncomfortable. "You know that I've known Douglas for years. And his wife too—before she passed. God rest her soul. He's practically been a member of this family. If your father were still alive, he'd think that was a crazy idea, you know. He'd never allow it."

"Well, Daddy's not here, God rest his soul. And *I*, for one, think you and Douglas together is one of the best ideas I've ever heard. It makes perfectly good sense and you have my blessing." Arianna gave Gigi a squeeze as she teased her playfully, then went to get her coffee.

"He is very handsome, that's for sure." Gigi giggled lightly. "Never mind, then. We'll not talk about that right now. So, about your trip?"

"You mean, our trip?" Arianna turned around to face Gigi. "I'm going to go to see my travel agent this morning to buy the tickets. I've got a call in to Blu and as soon as I know her dates, I can book yours too. I think Blu and Jemma will come for a week. Shall I book you on that same flight? I know that you'd like to visit your family, and of course I want to meet your sisters, so you can stay on after for as long as you like. You tell me what will work for you. Maybe a month in Italy would be a nice vacation for you?" Arianna asked, guessing that Gigi would be delighted with the suggestion.

"That sounds so wonderful. It's been ages since I've been back. Are you sure, Ari? And when will you come back here? You are planning to come back, aren't you?" Arianna heard the unmistakable question of concern in Gigi's voice.

"Yes, I will come back here. I'm not quite sure how long I'll go for, to be honest. If things are going well and I feel up to it, I'd like to stay for a few months at least. I guess I'll play that part by ear, and you can too if you like. We can always change the date of your ticket—and yes, I would like you to be here when I return. The house would seem way too quiet without you here with me then. And I'm not sure that I could bear it."

Gigi was quiet for a moment. "Ari, have you told Lia? Does she know about—"

Arianna cut Gigi off before she could finish. "No, I've not told her anything yet. I will, but it's not time. I just need to have some more time with her first, you know?" Arianna knew that Gigi respected her wishes, but she did hate keeping this big secret from Lia. She sighed. She would trust herself and believe that she would know when the time was right. And hopefully Lia would understand.

Arianna busied herself with a quick bowl of cereal and

a second cup of coffee as she sat out in the garden enjoying the cool morning air. *God, I love it here so much.* The garden was the perfect setting for everything hopeful and right in her life. She felt such peace when she sat here enjoying the flowers that her mother had spent so many hours poring over with her landscaper all those years ago.

The gardeners that they'd had for as long Arianna could remember had continued to faithfully come by to tend to the space, making it one of the most magnificent in the neighborhood. Arianna was sure of that, because she remembered that her mother's garden used to be on the local tour once a year. God, she'd hated that actually. Her mother had made her dress up every day that week and play the part of the perfect child out playing near the garden, close enough for strangers to see but not close enough to be a bother.

Arianna bristled at the memory, willing herself to focus on more positive thoughts.

CHAPTER 20

As Arianna and Lia entered the first class section of the plane, Arianna felt very tired. The past week had been a whirlwind, between getting ready for the trip and organizing everyone's tickets. But everything was in place now and she could look forward to the two weeks that she'd have with Lia before everyone else would join them in Tuscany at the lovely villa she'd rented for a month. She hoped that the next two weeks would go well anyways. She glanced over at Lia beside her, settling in and seeming rather pleased with the ample amount of room she had and the little extras that first class offered.

"Can I get you ladies some champagne?" the flight attendant asked as she came by with some warm towels.

Arianna and Lia smiled, both replying at the same time with a heartfelt "yes."

"This is the first time I've flown first class," Lia said. "I definitely see what all the fuss is about. How lovely." She laughed. "Have you traveled a lot, Ari?"

"In the states, yes. But not so much overseas. My parents—they mostly preferred to spend our holidays in

Nantucket or the beach house in La Jolla. Once when I was young—maybe about five or so—we did take a trip to London. Mother had been invited to see an opera there." Arianna had a flash of a memory of being with her mother. She'd begged her to let her go, and her mother had finally relented and managed to get another ticket for the young girl. They'd had to shop for a new fancy dress for Ari as well. When the day came she could hardly believe that she was inside the theater.

She remembered sitting in the box seating and feeling mesmerized by the beautiful music and the scene playing out before her. She had grasped her mother's hand tightly midway through the first act, as her mother tried unsuccessfully to stifle the young girl's sobs. "Shh. Ari, honey. It's not real," her mother had said. And just when Arianna thought she might be in trouble for making so much noise, her mother bent down to kiss her on the cheek and wipe her tears away with her gloved hand. It was one of the fondest memories she had of her mother, and she wiped a tear away now as she remembered the moment.

"Are you okay?" Lia reached over, lightly touching Arianna's hand. "Do you feel okay flying? I'm sure it can't be easy for you." Lia had a slightly worried look on her face.

Arianna had never had less fear of flying than she did in this moment, actually. She knew what the odds were and she also knew that when it was her time to go—she'd be ready.

"I'm okay, thanks." Arianna gave Lia's hand a quick squeeze before reaching for her bag under the seat in front of her. "I have a bit of a headache. I'll just take something, and I'm sure I'll be fine in a little while."

The flight attendant returned with their champagne, two bowls of plump red strawberries, and bottles of water. Arianna raised her glass of champagne towards Lia.

"To Italy."

"To Italia…and spending time with my lovely daughter," Lia said, her eyes sparkling.

Arianna smiled and got comfortable in her seat as they got ready for take-off, taking her smartphone and earbuds out of the seat pocket in front of her to listen to her favorite opera.

Lia looked over at her. "What are you listening to?"

"'La Traviata.' Would you like to listen? I have a splitter, so you can plug your headphones in also if you like."

Lia nodded and the two fell asleep enjoying the opera music together.

Arianna woke up to find Lia reading beside her. "How long have I been sleeping?"

"A good two hours. Do you feel better, bella? Has your headache gone?" Lia sounded concerned, and Arianna didn't want to ruin the flight with worry over how she was feeling, even though her head was still hurting her a bit.

"Yes, much better, thank you. What are you reading?" Arianna leaned over to glance at the cover of Lia's book.

"Oh just some cheesy romance novel about a woman who meets her hot Italian lover." Lia laughed.

"Hey, stranger things have happened, you know." Arianna smiled and entertained the thought before she spoke it out loud. "Lia, you're quite beautiful, you know." Arianna felt her face grow slightly warmer.

"Thank you." Lia looked at her with genuine delight at the praise. "Most of the time, I don't feel so lovely. Just older. I think I've given up on the idea of meeting my Prince Charming. But what about you—you're so young. Maybe there is a handsome Italian in your near future," Lia said in a teasing tone.

"Nah, you know, honestly—before I met you—when I was planning my trip—that's all I wanted to do. Party and maybe hook up with some handsome men along the way. But now—I don't really care about that anymore. Not for this trip."

"Maybe you say that now—but never say never. You're young and beautiful. Don't you want to be married one day—have kids?" Lia asked and Arianna thought she looked worried, as if maybe the conversation was too personal.

But that's what this trip was about, right? To get personal. To get to know her mother. But the question stung, and Arianna tried to hold back the tears that she was fighting. It was too soon and not the right place to talk about everything with Lia. There would be time for that later, after they'd enjoyed a bit of this vacation that she'd organized for them. She smiled as it occurred to her to wonder what her father would think if he knew that she was basically buying time with her mother—whom he'd tried to keep from her—with some of the money he'd left for her. And Arianna had spared no expense on this trip. It really was going to be amazing, and for some reason the thought of doing that for Lia, of giving her the trip of a lifetime, delighted her greatly.

Arianna was jolted out of her own thoughts and back to Lia, who was awaiting her reply. "Oh, I don't know. I guess there will be time enough for that later, right? For this trip, all I want to do is see the beautiful Tuscan countryside, eat delicious Italian food, and sip some amazing wines from the vineyards near our villa."

"It does sound lovely, Ari. Thank you." Lia's eyes filled with tears. "I can't thank you enough."

"It's my pleasure. Really." Arianna could see what it meant to Lia and it made her feel wonderful.

"But Ari—not only for the trip. I don't mean that. I mean—for letting me into your life. For allowing me the time to get to know you. I never would have imagined—"

"I know." Arianna placed her hand over Lia's. "It's like that for me too."

Lia looked like she was holding back tears now, and Arianna didn't know if she should encourage her to say what was on her mind or try to change the subject. It seemed she needed to be so careful lately about her emotions—that is, if she didn't want to collapse into a puddle of tears. But she glanced at Lia beside her looking so small and honest, knowing that she did want to know this woman. Knowing that she could handle anything now. She took a deep breath. She believed that now.

"Lia, why did you give me up?" Arianna was almost shocked to hear the words coming out of her mouth but she was ready to have the conversation now. It needed to be talked about.

Lia looked at Arianna and took a deep breath. "I never wanted to give you up, bella. When I found out I was pregnant with you, I was at first incredibly scared; but I always knew that I would have you. I want you to know that. I never once thought about not having you and it—it was only after you were born that I realized I couldn't keep you myself—I couldn't raise you." Lia was crying softly now. "I knew that you deserved so much more than what I could give you. I was basically alone. In America for the first time. I didn't know what to do." More sobs—and Arianna also was fighting back the tears.

"And my father?" Arianna asked in a whisper.

"Antonio. He was the love of my life." Lia smiled as she continued. "We were high school sweethearts, but it was one summer that we started seeing each other. He'd been working at one of the vineyards near my family's house. I knew who he was from school, but we seemed to instantly click that summer. One thing led to another and we started spending a lot of time together. We were in love—well, as much as you can be at a young age. God, my father would have had a fit if he'd known what was really going on all of those times I'd said I was out riding my bike in the countryside."

"Did your parents—my grandparents—ever know about me?" It was a question that had been on Arianna's mind for a while now. Somehow it seemed to matter to her if Lia had been alone with her pregnancy or if her parents had known. Arianna took a breath as she waited for the answer.

"No, bella, not at the time. I didn't tell them I was pregnant. I couldn't bear to do that to them. But at last— it was only a few years ago—my father was dying and my mother called, begging me to come home to be with them. I managed to scrape enough money together and get a week away from my job in New York to make the trip." Lia got a faraway look in her eyes. "I couldn't bear for my father to pass without telling him the truth. So I told them—both my parents. And he forgave me. They both did. And it was just a month later that my mother had a heart attack and passed also, so they are both gone now. I'm sorry for that, Ari—that you won't ever know them. But I'm mostly sorry that they won't ever know you."

Arianna had never been close with her grandparents. There had always seemed to be a certain distance there, probably due to the lack of closeness between her parents and them. She thought about what it would have been like to be taken into a loving Italian household, and she wished it were different now. But it wasn't.

Lia interrupted her thoughts with another admission. "I never told him at all—your father."

Arianna raised her head at the words. "He doesn't know anything?" She couldn't contain her surprise, and hoped that her question didn't sound too judgmental.

"No, I just—I just lost my courage. When I first found out that I was pregnant it was two months or so after arriving at my cousin's in San Francisco. I didn't know what to do and Antonio—at first we wrote each other every week and it seemed our love for one another was only getting stronger. But then his letters stopped coming. By then I'd found out that I was pregnant and I didn't know how to tell him. I was so confused. After he'd not responded to a few of my letters, I assumed that he'd met someone else, and tried to put him out of my mind. I never heard from him after that." Lia looked like it was all a bit much to retell and remember.

"And didn't you ever go back—before the death of your father, I mean?"

"No, I never did. I don't know. I suppose I felt too much shame. Like I'd done something really wrong. My parents never would have allowed me to give their grandchild up for adoption. They would have been devastated about the pregnancy. They would have insisted that we be married back then. I thought about it. Going

158

home and telling them everything, but then Antonio stopped writing and I just couldn't bear it." Lia turned to Arianna with tears streaming freely down her face now. "It's the biggest regret of my life, Arianna. That I didn't fight to make a way to keep you."

Lia broke down in sobs and Arianna, caught off guard and crying now herself, reached over to pull her in for a big hug. "We're here together now." She let a few minutes of silence go by. "We have today and these next weeks together. For what it's worth, I forgive you, and I think I'm starting to understand more than you could ever imagine." She wiped a stray tear from her own eye as she thought about the things that she had yet to share with Lia—things that would wait for another day.

PAULA KAY

CHAPTER 21

Lia pulled away slightly and wiped her tears. "Ari, there's something that I want to show you." She reached under the front collar of her shirt to pull out a small locket at the end of the silver chain that hung around her neck. Arianna had noticed that she'd worn the necklace each time that they'd been together.

Lia carefully opened the locket to reveal two small pictures inside. On the left was the picture of a handsome boy with dark curly hair and a smile that stretched across his whole face. On the right was a small picture of an infant with a headful of dark hair. It looked as if the picture had been snapped during a moment of surprise, as the small baby had a lopsided grin and big dark eyes that were opened wide to the camera.

"Is it—this is my father?"

"It is—Antonio. And that's you, bella. You're about a week old there." Lia wiped away more tears.

"You—you had me for a week?" Arianna asked carefully, trying to contain what she didn't know yet to be anger or confusion.

"I had you for two weeks.. I brought you home to my

cousin's house from the hospital."

"I—I don't understand." Arianna was genuinely confused. Nothing was making sense now.

"I tried, Ari. I thought I could do it. But then my cousin had to move out of her apartment, which meant I needed to find a place to live too. I had already been struggling to provide anything for you. Formula, diapers, clothes. I just started having such doubts that I could really give you a good life." Lia looked at her with eyes that seemed to be willing her to understand. "You were so small and you needed so much. The only thing I was sure of was that I wanted you to have everything. And I—I could barely take care of myself."

Arianna nodded at Lia to encourage her to continue, wiping away her own tears at Lia's obvious discomfort in reliving those days after her birth.

"My cousin had been working as a housekeeper in the city and she knew of another family that needed help. The room and board was provided and they said that they would give it a try. We moved in and I tried to make it work for those first weeks. It wasn't just about me, I promise you, Ari. Please believe that."

Arinna nodded.

"I wanted so much more for you. And the family I was working for knew a couple—the Sinclairs—your—your parents. When they told me about them and how much they wanted a child of their own—the kind of life that they could provide for you. At the time they—your parents—lived in the city, and I went there. To see the house. I think they knew then that they were moving—building the house in Sausalito. I couldn't believe everything that they had, and they seemed so desperate to be parents. I—I just had to consider it. And in the end I made the decision to do what I thought was best for you. And I do regret it. I do, Ari."

Arianna didn't know exactly how to feel. It was hard to process everything that she was learning but as she looked at Lia, at the locket around her neck, she knew that she could finally truly forgive her. That Lia had wanted her and loved her when she was born. Even for a few weeks more than Arianna had realized.

"I mean, I know that you had a good life with the Sinclairs—" Lia stopped herself. "At least I hope that you did—that you feel that your life with them was good. Was it? I mean—before the accident?"

Arianna was quiet for a moment. "Yes, it was good," she said quietly. It would be too much for both of them if Arianna said more right now. And she didn't want to hurt Lia more than she seemed to be hurting. "I just—I always felt like something was missing." She was trying very hard to balance being honest about her own feelings with being careful of Lia's. "And what did you do after that—after my adoption?"

"It wasn't long after that I moved away to New York. I couldn't bear living so close to you. I thought I might run into you or start stalking the Sinclairs, and I'd—I'd signed the contract and they were so wealthy and powerful. No. There was no changing things once I'd realized my mistake." Lia seemed to gather her strength with one last deep breath before continuing. "But I always knew that I'd find you one day, Ari. And from the moment I bought this necklace with that first paycheck at my new job, I've never gone a day without this picture of you around my neck." Lia fingered the locket and seemed pensive for a minute before she unlatched the clasp and put it in Arianna's hand. "I want you to have this now. It's the one thing I can give you now and maybe…" Her voice trailed off. "Maybe one day you can know your father too.

Arianna thought that Lia looked frightened at the thought of it, and she had no clue if it was a good idea or not, but the thought of actually meeting her birth father was incredible to her. Time would tell. She didn't know if there would be time for everything, and she had to be okay with that.

Arianna took the necklace from Lia. She could see that it was important to her, as if she was finally being absolved of just a bit of her guilt. It was something that Arianna could do for her. And she wanted to spend some more time alone with the picture of herself and of her father. Studying the face of the man whose genes she carried. Her Italian father. Arianna smiled.

"Thank you." Arianna closed her hand around the necklace. "This means a lot to me. And you—you opening up—telling me about the past. It means a lot to me too. It does. These are questions that I've had for as long as I can remember. Questions that my parents—the Sinclairs—always seemed unwilling or unable to answer for me. Thank you for that." She took a deep breath and they both laughed, noticing that they seemed to be deep-breathing in sync after the intense conversation.

"Now, shall we lighten up the mood a bit with a glass of Italian wine and a peek at which movies we have to choose from?" Arianna said, motioning for the flight attendant as she turned on the screen in front of her to check the estimated remaining flying time. "It looks like we have about four more hours before landing in Paris—and I, for one, could use something light-hearted and maybe another nap before we land."

Lia smiled at her. "I second that idea. Especially the wine. I could use a drink." She laughed. "I have the feeling that we'll be having our share of lovely bottles of your favorite over the next few weeks."

"I can't wait." Arianna laughed, happy that she and Lia shared a love for nice Italian wine and food. This was going to be a great holiday. Arianna would make sure of it."

She relaxed into her seat for the remaining hours of the flight, enjoying a movie and the silence between them that was perfectly comfortable after the deep conversation that had taken place.

PAULA KAY

CHAPTER 22

After a short layover in Paris, the flight to Florence was a quick two hours. Arianna and Lia arrived feeling fairly rested after another little nap on the short flight to Italy. Once through passport control and a fairly quick baggage retrieval, Arianna spotted the driver that she'd arranged with the Four Seasons Hotel. Within minutes they were out in the bright Italian afternoon sun ready to take in the view during the twenty-minute ride to the hotel.

"I'm *so* excited." Lia grabbed Arianna's knee and gave it a little squeeze in the back of the sedan they were in.

"Me too." Arianna grinned as she looked out the window. "I've been dreaming of this trip forever."

"Is your first time to Firenze, no?" the driver said, smiling in the rearview mirror at them.

"My first time to Italia." Arianna replied with a big smile. "And she was born in Tuscany," she said, nodding towards Lia.

"Ah, lovely. And mother, daughter, *sì?*"

Arianna and Lia looked at one another and grinned.

"*Sì*, we are." Lia replied.

"*Si sono entrambi belli*. Understand, no?" The driver said with a wide smile. "You are both very beautiful."

"*Grazie*," Lia said, blushing a bit.

"Thank you very much. *Grazie*." Arianna laughed and whispered to Lia, "I think I'm going to like it here if all the men are so charming."

They continued the drive in silence, the two women peering out the windows to try to catch a glimpse of the famous Italian city they were entering. When they pulled up to the hotel, Lia gasped at the sight of it.

"Wow, Ari. This looks incredible. I can't believe I'm actually staying at the Four Seasons."

Arianna smiled, happy that she had held nothing back when it came to booking this trip for them. She had grown up staying at various Four Seasons in the U.S. and knew that it was one of her parents' favorites for good reason. She did trust their taste when it came to such things.

"Lia, wait until you see the suite I arranged for you. The description and pictures of it struck me as something that really suited you." Arianna was so pleased that she could do this for Lia; she knew how wonderful everything would be for her.

The driver delivered their bags to the bellhop while Arianna checked in without hassle, collecting the keys to their two different suites. Their plan was to spend a few days in Florence seeing some of the sights and enjoying the city before heading to the villa where they'd spend the remaining weeks of their time in Tuscany. Arianna was feeling pretty good and was anxious to get a glimpse of the city.

"Shall we each go to our rooms to freshen up a bit and then I can meet you at your suite? I'd love to see your garden view." Arianna smiled, wanting to take in all of Florence, including the luxurious hotel they were staying in together. "We can decide then what we want to do for dinner. The receptionist told me that they'd have a light snack and beverage in our rooms ready for us just now, so that should tide us over for a bit."

"Yes, that sounds perfect." Lia reached over to give Arianna a quick hug before following the bellhop to her room. "See you in a few minutes."

Arianna followed the other bellhop to her suite, tipped him generously, and walked into her own private little Italian dream. She had chosen the Duomo Suite for herself; it consisted of two levels with two different living-room areas and two full bathrooms, and was known for having an amazing view of the city. She had thought that it might be nice to have more space in one of the suites in case she and Lia wanted to spend some time together lounging around.

When she walked into the luxurious living-room area, she was not disappointed. Everything was very plush. There were beautiful paintings, exquisite rugs, and thick curtains that were tied back to reveal a peek of the spectacular view off the terrace.

Arianna resisted stepping outside onto the terrace for a moment, as she wanted to unpack upstairs in her bedroom. She walked up the stairs and was pleasantly surprised to find that the other sitting area was as big as, if not bigger than, the one on the main floor. She continued walking into the adjacent room where she would be sleeping. Several big pillows and a beautifully designed thick comforter topped her bed, which was looking quite inviting at the moment.

She slipped off her shoes and lay back on the bed, closing her eyes as she thought about the great travel day that she'd had with Lia. It seemed that they'd crossed a bridge with Lia opening up to her, and Arianna could feel herself doing the same. And soon enough she'd be sharing some secrets and feelings of her own with Lia. She sighed. She'd wait as long as she could so that they could enjoy their first few days here in this beautiful city. She stretched her lean body across the bed, which felt good after being on the plane for so many hours.

I must make a move to freshen up before I fall asleep.

Arianna collected her toiletry bag and headed into the full marble bathroom, immediately taken with the size and grandeur of it. Several candles lined the huge tub and there were luxurious soaps and bath salts as well. *Ooh, I can't wait to have a nice bath later tonight.* The idea of it sounded absolutely divine, but for now she mustn't keep Lia waiting long.

She quickly washed her face and brushed her teeth,

examining herself in the well-lit mirror. She did look tired, but not too bad. Nothing a little blush and lipstick couldn't fix. She finished her quick make-up application, changed into a pair of black pants and bright top, and grabbed one of her favorite fitted jackets to head down to Lia's suite.

She had booked the Garden Suite for Lia, and she was anxious to see how everything was. It was separate from the main part of the hotel and overlooked the hotel garden, which she walked through to arrive at Lia's door.

She had only knocked once lightly when Lia threw the door open and then threw her arms around Arianna before she even had a moment to say hello.

"Arianna, I love everything about this room—this suite. God, I can't believe I'm staying in a suite and it's so gorgeous. Come in, let me show you." She grabbed Arianna's hand, pulling her into the beautiful sitting area.

Arianna was impressed, as it was equally as beautiful as her suite although each had its own unique decor and design. The room was quite lovely, and she enjoyed seeing Lia so happy as she showed her the bathroom and then her huge king-size bed. "And I can't wait to take a bath in the amazing-looking tub."

Arianna nodded her agreement. "We had the exact same thought. There's a lovely collection of soaps and bath salts. A lot of my favorite European brands, I noticed. Did you get a bite to eat? They had a lovely cheese and bread platter waiting for me in my room. I assume they had the same for you?"

"Oh yes. I've already sampled the Italian cheeses, and everything is wonderful. There's a bottle of champagne in the fridge. Shall we have a glass out on the terrace here before we go?" Lia said.

"Now that might just be the best idea of the night. I'd love that."

Lia poured them each a glass and they carried them out to her private outside terrace overlooking the well-maintained lawn, lush and green.

Arianna raised her glass. "To Firenze."

"And may our time in Italy be the beginning of many wonderful memories together," Lia added and clinked her glass with Arianna's.

Arianna looked down and hoped that the quick pang of sadness hadn't shown on her face during Lia's words. It always took her by surprise, and it was getting harder and harder to hold it all in. *Soon*, she thought. *For now, I'll just enjoy this garden and Lia's company.*

They finished their champagne and determined that they'd head into the reception area to talk to the concierge about finding an evening activity that would lead them to their first beautiful Italian meal.

They found out that the Piazzale Michelangelo was the place they needed to be to enjoy what looked to be a spectacular sunset shaping up. The air was perfect and lovely; just the hint of an evening chill coming on. Arianna had arranged a car and driver for their time in

Florence, and he arrived to pick them up shortly after the hotel contacted him for her. Lia seemed giddy with excitement and Arianna noticed a lovely flush to her face. They sat back to enjoy the ride and admire the city bustling around them.

This is going to be quite the adventure. Arianna wasn't ready for a lot of things, but she'd been dreaming about Italy all her life, it felt. She was going to enjoy every minute of it.

The driver took them to the Oltrarno district of the city and straight up to the observation point where so many famous photos of Florence had been taken. The sun was just setting, and as they got out of the car the view took Arianna's breath away. From here she felt that she was glimpsing the whole city; it was a wonderful welcome to the place where they'd spend the next few days.

The bridges that crossed the Arno River seemed to go on and on. There was the beautiful Duomo in the distance and beyond the city, the hills that they'd be driving through on the way to their villa in a few days.

"Oh my God, it's beautiful," Arianna said to Lia as they both stared in silence.

Lia nodded in agreement and held her smartphone up. "Okay, not to be total cheesy tourist or anything, but I'd love to get some shots of us while we're on this trip together. Okay?"

Arianna laughed. "I'd love that actually. Shoot away."

They both turned so that the view was behind them.

Lia put the phone at arm's length as Arianna put her arm around her, and they both grinned for the camera.

"Perfect," Lia said as she showed the picture to Arianna.

"I'll want a copy of that one for sure." Arianna grinned.

They found a bench and enjoyed several minutes of admiring the view and sitting in silence. Arianna could feel that it was already so comfortable to be around Lia. She felt as if she'd known her all her life. It was wild to think that they had only met a few short weeks ago. She smiled and linked her arm with Lia's.

"How do you feel about going down to one of the busier parts of town to find a restaurant that looks good? I didn't make any reservations tonight because I wasn't sure how we'd be feeling after the flight, but I'd love to find a nice local spot to people-watch and taste some great Florentine cuisine."

Lia nodded her head in agreement. "That sounds perfect to me."

When they got back to the car, Arianna asked the driver if he could take them to a great restaurant where locals liked to eat. He smiled, telling them he knew just the place.

Within minutes, they were at a bustling square with several trattorias, one of which the driver pointed out to her. "Eat here. The bistecca al fiorentina is the best around."

Arianna looked at Lia. "Are you in the mood for steak?"

"Yes, I think I can be." Lia laughed, and they got out of the car with Arianna making arrangements to text the driver when they were ready to be picked up.

Inside the small restaurant, the tables were packed but the hostess managed to find a table near the kitchen for them. "It smells fantastic in here," Arianna said.

"You have no idea how much I want to peek my head in that kitchen." Lia laughed.

"Correction. I bet you'd be in there with an apron on in two seconds if you could get away with it." Arianna giggled.

The waiter came to take their orders, and they chatted easily over a glass of wine while waiting for their steak to arrive. Arianna loved the feel of being surrounded by what looked like mostly locals in the restaurant. She could hear the sounds of the language being spoken and thought to herself that she wished she would have pushed Gigi to teach her more before she left for the trip. *I should speak Italian*, she thought.

Lia looked right at home; Arianna guessed that her Italian was perfect, even though she'd only heard her speak a few phrases. Their meal arrived and they ate as much as they could before pushing their plates away. "Wow. I don't want to overdo it or I won't be able to move tomorrow, let alone walk around the city." Arianna laughed.

"I agree," Lia said. "Let's quit while we're ahead. I think *that* was the best steak I've ever had."

"Shall we walk a bit before I text for the car?"

"Yes, let's. That sounds great."

They walked around the piazza and then decided that they would go for a little stroll towards the river to admire the pretty bridges that they'd seen from a distance earlier in the day. Arianna was enjoying their time together even with the easy silence.

"How does it feel to be back here?"

Lia shrugged and then stopped, looking thoughtful. "You know, it feels pretty wonderful actually. Especially with you. I never in my wildest dreams would have imagined that I'd have the opportunity to come here with you. It means everything to me."

Arianna nodded. "I feel very fortunate too. I'm glad I asked you to come with me. So, does it feel like this is your home? Do you miss it when you are in the states?"

"Yes. It does feel like home to me. There's nothing like it really. I feel different when I'm here. More of myself, I suppose. Before everything bad happened. If that makes sense?"

"It's funny. I almost think that's part of what I'm feeling here, now that you mention it. Like more of myself. I haven't particularly embraced my Italian heritage even though it has intrigued me so much; and having Gigi around has helped, I suppose. But I was never really sure of who I was. To find out now that both my mother and my father are full Italian. Well, that's kind of amazing to me."

"Bella, are you so surprised, what with your love for Italian food, wine, and opera?" Lia laughed. "And you are one of the most gorgeous Italian beauties I've ever seen. And I'm not being biased."

Arianna felt herself blushing. "Thank you. And I think you *are* biased. Well, you can't say that to me without also acknowledging your own beauty, now can you?" She winked.

They came upon one of the prettier of the many bridges that crossed the Arno River throughout the city. "Look, bella. It's so lovely, isn't it?"

"It looks like something from a postcard. Magical."

They found a bench near the water and chatted for several minutes before they were both yawning and decided to call it a night. Arianna texted their driver, who was there to retrieve them within minutes; they were back at the hotel, saying goodnight, thirty minutes later.

"Now for that hot bath," Lia said with a yawn and a big grin.

"That sounds like the perfect way to end a great day." Arianna reached over to give her a hug. "So tomorrow should we get an early start? I'm thinking we can head towards the museum with the statue of David and find a nice little cafe to have some coffee and a bite to eat first. I'm dying to see it. It has been so high on my must-see list for years."

"Sounds great. Enjoy your bath and sleep well."

CHAPTER 23

Arianna woke the next morning feeling so restful and happy. She waited until what she hoped was the reasonable time of eight o'clock before ringing Lia's room to make a plan for the day.

"Good morning."

"Someone sounds wide awake and cheerful this morning," Arianna said.

"I've been up since five o'clock and am well into a first cup of coffee already. Sorry, I couldn't wait once I smelled the strong coffee brewing near the garden cafe."

Arianna laughed. "If you're ready, you're welcome to come up here while I do the same. It won't take me long, and I'll have two coffees delivered right now."

"I was hoping you'd invite me to your suite. I'm dying to see it. I'll be over in ten minutes?"

"Sounds perfect." Arianna clicked off the phone and then called room service. She was really looking forward to the day. Another chance to spend time with her mother. The thought still seemed rather foreign to her but she was getting used to it, and she definitely was enjoying her time.

She let Lia in a few minutes later and gave her a quick tour of the suite before carrying their coffees out onto the expansive terrace.

"Wow. This is so pretty. I love it."

"I know it's bigger than the one you're in. But I thought you would enjoy it more—"

"Ari, I love my suite. There is nothing to explain." She leaned over to hug her. "You've been so wonderful to me. Really. I'm still pinching myself for being on this trip with you."

"Me too. As a matter of fact, I was just thinking a similar thought about having you here with me. I guess it was meant to be. Now, let me go put some clothes on and freshen up these tired-looking eyes. I won't be long. Make yourself at home."

Arianna went to get dressed, opting for a simple but elegant summer dress, with her favorite sandals. She grabbed one of the knit shawls that she'd brought with her, stuffing it into her oversized bag with her sunglasses, phone, and keys. She was back downstairs within ten minutes, ready to go.

"You really are pretty low-maintenance in terms of how much time it takes you to get ready," Lia said.

"Good genes. And little patience." Arianna laughed. "Alright then, let's head out. I've called the driver and he should be waiting for us outside."

Their car was waiting; Arianna instructed the driver to take them near the Accademia. It looked to be another gorgeous day, with not a cloud in sight. According to the weather forecast, their time in Florence was shaping up to be full of sunshine and reasonable temperatures.

They thanked the driver and had him let them out near a small cafe that they spotted near the museum. They went inside and ordered one more coffee, and did not resist the beautiful-looking pastries that were being showcased near the register. "Oh, this is a fine start to the day." Arianna laughed.

"You can say that again," Lia said, wiping a bit of raspberry filling from her lip.

"Have you been to the Accademia before? To see David?" Arianna asked.

"I have, but it was a long time ago." Lia had a wistful expression on her face. "It was when I was little and with my father. For some reason, and totally out of the ordinary, he'd taken a day off from work and brought me into the city to see David. I remember him saying it was important. That he wanted me to know art and culture. Funny, because I haven't thought about that for a very long time."

"Do you remember the day with him? Was it nice?" Arianna was curious to know more about this man that Lia was talking about. This man that had been her grandfather.

"Yes, it was very nice actually. I remember going to the museum and not being totally taken with everything, but the statue of David was mesmerizing to me. As I was pretty young it might have had something to do with the fact of the anatomy I was seeing, even though my father had explained to me that it was true art and not for making jokes about being naked. And I remember we went for huge gelatos afterwards. Way bigger than anything my mother had ever let me eat." Lia laughed. "Yes, it was a good day. Just like today will be." She wiped her mouth again and finished her coffee. 'Shall we go?"

"After you," Arianna said as she grabbed her bag to leave.

They headed over to the Accademia Gallery, where they were able to bypass the long lines of people because Arianna had had the hotel concierge get them advance entry tickets. They walked around the museum, enjoying the art and sculptures, before they came to the famous statue of David.

"Wow. Seeing the sculpture in my art history books really does not even compare to the real deal at all, does it?" Arianna asked Lia.

"No, nothing compares to seeing Michelangelo's work in person. It is all so beautiful. I never tire of looking at it."

The two stood near David for several minutes, taking it all in, before swarms of tourists flooded the room. "Okay, I'm ready to move on. You?" Arianna said.

"Yes."

They walked around the whole gallery for a few hours

before deciding it was time to head to another famous part of the city. "Arianna, are you ready for some shopping?" Lia said with a teasing nudge.

"I'm always up for some shopping," Arianna said. Although not as much these days, she supposed. It didn't seem to be all that big a deal to her anymore, although of course she did want to check out the leather in Florence—it was supposed to be some of the best in the world.

They decided to walk to the San Lorenzo market to check out the popular spot for shopping for Italian specialties. There were stall upon stall of souvenirs, clothing, and leather. Lia was looking at a beautiful leather wallet and talking to the shop owner in Italian. "Is it a good deal?" Arianna asked.

"No, it's too much," Lia said as she grabbed Arianna's hand to walk away, winking at her as she did so.

"Miss, miss, come back. Okay, okay," the shop owner said. He came down in price closer to what Lia had been asking.

"You should have it. I'll get it for you," Arianna, said taking out her own wallet to pay.

"No, no, Ari. I won't have it. You've done enough for me as it is. I love it and I'll buy it. It's okay. The price is good, and surely I can splurge on at least one souvenir." She laughed, paying the man and tucking the wallet into her purse.

They continued walking along the stalls, and Arianna

became very taken with a little leather box that she'd found. It was rectangular and looked like a cigar box, only deeper. It was lined with deep red velvet, and Arianna couldn't stop touching it. She knew that she had to have it, and with the realization came the seed of an idea that she'd have to accomplish once she got back home to Sausalito. "I'll take it," she said to the woman running the shop, without even bothering to ask the price first.

Lia shook her head, laughing. "Ari, you're a terrible bargainer."

Arianna laughed. "Oops. I totally forgot. I guess I don't bargain that much where I shop in San Francisco."

"I guess not."

Arianna was pleased with her purchase and suddenly very hungry. "What do you think about finding a cafe for some lunch?"

"I know just the place, and it's right here. How adventurous are you feeling?"

"Go on," Arianna said with a narrowing of her eyes.

"There's a Florentine dish that you must try. There's a great spot that serves it here at the Central Market, and it's very popular among the locals. Follow me, I'll show you." Lia took Arianna by the hand to lead her through the stalls to the indoor food market, which was bustling during this time of day and a great display of what lunchtime looked like in Florence.

Arianna grinned as she followed behind Lia, letting her weave them both throughout the tourists and locals on the crowded street. "So what's this dish that I need to try?"

"You'll see soon."

As they entered into an eatery, Arianna could see something that she didn't recognize hanging over the counter. It didn't look like meat exactly, but she wasn't sure what she was in for.

"It's called panini di lampredotto, which is fresh bread rolls stuffed with hot lampredotto and topped with salsa verde. It's something you will only find here in Florence and it's delicious. I promise."

"Lia, what *exactly* is lampredotto?" Arianna tried not to wrinkle her nose as she asked the question, but she had the feeling it was going to be unlike anything she'd ever eaten before.

"Well…maybe you should try it first." Lia laughed, getting closer to the counter to order. "Shall I get us some Chianti also?"

"Yes, most definitely, to the wine; and I promise you that I will try whatever it is you're ordering, but I think I would like to know what I am eating." Arianna laughed.

"Lampredotto is the fourth stomach of a cow." Lia looked at Arianna to see her reaction.

Arianna laughed. "How many stomachs does a cow even have? Okay, honestly it sounds a bit disgusting to me, but I promised. You only live once, right?" Arianna laughed. Wow, she really was taking risks these days and being quite the adventure girl.

Lia ordered everything, and within minutes they had found a little table in the crowded seating area and Arianna was biting into her first lampredotto sandwich. Lia watched her curiously as she devoured her own. "Well? What's the verdict?" she asked, noticing that Arianna was going in for a second, bigger bite.

"I kind of can't believe that I'm saying this, but it's actually pretty tasty. Go me, being Miss Adventurous with my cow stomach tasting and all." They both laughed and lifted their glasses for a toast.

"To Ari's adventurous tastebuds."

"Cheers to adventure," Arianna said.

They had finished the rest of their meal and polished off another half liter of wine, when they looked at each other and both yawned at the same time.

"Are you thinking what I'm thinking?" Arianna turned to Lia.

"That a nap sounds really good about now?" Lia laughed.

"We have reservations tonight at the hotel restaurant, which is supposed to be one of the best in the city, so I'm thinking it makes sense to go back and have a rest and kind of chill out there for the afternoon. After we both have a little nap, you're welcome to come join me in my suite if you like."

"That sounds perfect, and I'm anxious to try the restaurant too."

They called for their driver, who was waiting nearby,

and made their way back to the Four Seasons, where they could relax a little bit before dinner. Arianna felt like the two days that they'd had in Florence had already been so incredible, and there was yet so much more to do. And the villa. She couldn't wait until they'd arrive at the gorgeous villa she'd rented for them just outside of Siena.

PAULA KAY

CHAPTER 24

Back in her suite, Arianna pulled out the journal that she'd brought along to get caught up with all of her thoughts and reactions to Florence. And her time with Lia. She wasn't exactly sure why she continued to write, but it made her feel better and she was starting to get an idea of something she could do with the journals that she'd been keeping. She smiled even as a lone tear snuck its way down her cheek. There was no time for crying now. She'd shed more than enough tears these past few months and now it was time to let go. She'd been doing a great job of that lately. Largely thanks to Doc, who had given her some great tools for dealing with all of the crazy emotions since the accident.

She finished writing in her journal and decided to take a hot bath before she crawled into her luxurious sheets for a nap.

She awoke to a blinking light on the room phone alerting her that she had a message. It was Lia, letting her know that she was up and ready whenever Arianna was. She phoned her back to let her know that she'd get dressed for dinner and that Lia should come up to have some wine with her. The hotel staff had left her a bottle of her favorite Chianti, and she couldn't wait to try it. She reminded herself that she wanted to be sure to check into the winery tours once they got settled in the villa. This was something that she thought they'd all enjoy, and she was really looking forward to it.

Dinner that night would be a more formal occasion, and Arianna was looking forward to dining in the hotel's Michelin-starred restaurant. The classic Florentine menu was supposed to be amazing, and they had a wine list that compared to nothing she'd ever had before. She stepped into the sleek fitted black dress that she'd brought and then eyed her jewelry carefully. She chose some small elegant diamond-drop earrings and a matching diamond necklace that hugged her neck. She laid out her favorite black heels and Chanel handbag, placing her lipstick and other essentials inside the bag.

Her doorbell rang and when she greeted Lia, she was taken aback by how lovely she looked. "Wow, you look gorgeous."

"Thank you very much, as do you," Lia said, twirling as she walked in the door. "I've only had one occasion to wear this splurge of a dress, so it feels pretty wonderful." Lia had on a dress equally as body-hugging as Arianna's, in a beautiful deep red that perfectly accentuated the curves of her body and the olive color of her Italian skin.

Arianna stepped back to admire her and called over her shoulder as she left the room, "I'll be right back, don't move." She returned with a perfect strand of pearls in her hand. "May I?" she asked Lia as she moved to put them around her neck.

"Oh, they're beautiful. Yes, I'll borrow your jewelry any time," she said with a big grin.

The two women moved into the living room and Arianna went to retrieve the bottle of wine and two glasses. They sat and chatted for a good hour or so before it was time to make their way downstairs for their dinner reservation. "I'm famished, and so ready for what I think is going to be a gorgeous meal," Arianna said.

"Me too."

They entered the restaurant, and Arianna was immediately taken with the elegance and decor of the place. There was a beautiful chandelier that hung in the center of the room from the vaulted ceiling. Paintings lined the walls and the tables were set with the finest white tablecloths. At each table was a centerpiece of bright-burning candles in the prettiest shade of pink.

They sat down and Arianna examined the wine list that the waiter handed her. After asking his recommendation, with anxious anticipation she ordered the finest bottle of Chianti that they had. Sipping her wine, Arianna looked around the restaurant, taking in her surroundings. The clientele was a mix of international, which she assumed were mainly hotel guests, and also many Italians. There was a reason that this restaurant had won so many awards, so she'd assumed it would be pretty busy and it was. She loved hearing the Italian chattering around her and the life that seemed to fill up this room.

The two woman opened their menus and listened to the waiter explain the specials of the day and his recommendation. For their appetizers, Lia ordered the seared scallops and Ariannna the foie gras, which she only ever ordered on special occasions. They each chose a first-course pasta dish, and Arianna chose the sea bass fillet, while Lia went with roasted pigeon. Arianna read out loud, "with Vin Santo and Caramelized Fruit with Thyme—ah, I know why you chose that dish," she said.

"Well, you know, that thyme with caramelized fruit sounds like something I have to try. It sounds amazing, doesn't it?" Lia said, her eyes shining in anticipation.

Arianna nodded. She loved how excited Lia got about Italian food. She'd mostly witnessed it in relation to the rustic and authentic dishes that Lia loved preparing herself. But now, sitting with her in one of the finest Italian restaurants, as the two of them tasted first their appetizers and then the delicious dishes of home-made pasta, Arianna could see that she was the best dining partner that she could ever hope for, appreciating every mouthful of the food.

Arianna had grown up frequenting expensive restaurants and was used to the highest quality when it came to dining out. Now she realized that this was something that Lia and her adoptive mother did have in common. They both thoroughly enjoyed a good dining experience. But she doubted that Lia had many opportunities when it came to expensive restaurants such as this. Arianna could not be happier to be able to give that to her now.

Over the course of the next hour, they enjoyed their main entrees, delighted with both of their choices. Lia shared a taste of the caramelized fruit with Arianna, and they both agreed that it was something that Lia needed to experiment with right away.

They capped the meal off with dessert, Arianna ordering an almond tartlet with white peach and Lia choosing the dark chocolate cremoso with Amarelli liquorice meringue. And this they coupled with a recommended dessert wine that left them feeling completely satisfied and just a bit tipsy as they ended the night.

"That was absolutely, hands down, the best meal I've ever had in my life," Lia said as they were leaving the restaurant. "And you? I'm sure that you've enjoyed many dinners of that quality over the years—which is incredible. Really." Lia smiled, and Arianna knew that Lia was only appreciating the privilege that Arianna had grown up with.

"The best meal I ever had"—Arianna was thoughtful and her voice grew quieter—"was the meal you prepared for me that first time at your apartment." Her voice caught and she had to hold back a sudden burst of emotion. "Being with you that night—watching you cook in your kitchen—and knowing that *that* was my mother. It was magical to me. I remember feeling as though I'd been sitting in the kitchen watching you cook for a lifetime."

Lia stopped walking and Arianna could see the tears streaming down her face. "Ari, you'll never know what meeting you has done for me. It's a completion that I never thought was coming, that I never thought I deserved—"

"Me too." Arianna tried to hold back her own tears as she reached over to give Lia a big hug. She waited a minute while they both collected their emotions. "So, are we still thinking that we're going to go to the Duomo tomorrow morning?" Arianna really wanted to attempt to make the climb to the top of the cupola, famed for the extraordinary view of Florence, as well as the full interior of the dome. But she could feel another headache coming on, and she hoped that she'd feel up to what was known as a decent hike up the four hundred-plus steps.

"I'm up for it, if you are," Lia said, wiping her eyes and smiling broadly. "Say around nine o'clock, my suite, for a coffee and bite?"

"Perfect. Sleep well."

Lia reached over to kiss each of Arianna's cheeks. "You too, bella."

CHAPTER 25

Arianna woke up the next morning with a slight headache which felt more than a little annoying to her. *I really need to try to get through these last two days in Florence without ending up in bed. Then I can relax a bit once we settle into the villa. But I want to get as much out of the time here with Lia as I can.* She poured a full glass of water and took a couple of her pills, determined to think happy thoughts and be rid of the ache in her temples before they left that morning.

She washed her face and dusted it with a little powder, putting on a dash of blush and her favorite lip gloss. This morning she dressed in her favorite pair of designer jeans, some short boots that wouldn't be difficult to walk in, and a light long-sleeved blouse that was just right for a warm day. She grabbed her sweater, her bag, and her keys and was off to meet Lia for some much-needed coffee.

Lia had coffee and a breakfast of scones and pastry waiting for her outside on the terrace when she arrived.

"Oh, this looks so perfect," Arianna said as she scooped up a scone and took a gulp of the strong Italian coffee. "Exactly what I need right now."

"Good, good. I'm excited about this morning. I've never actually walked the steps to the top of the Duomo, so it will be a fun experience. I'm doing so many new things here with you. It's really fun for me." Lia had the look of an excited child.

"Me too. I can't believe we've only been here a few days. It feels like so much longer."

"And we have the villa to look forward to. I'm excited about being back in Siena. Especially to be able to show you around," Lia said.

"Me too. The villa sounds heavenly. And being so near my favorite wineries. I can't wait to experience all of that." Arianna got up from the table. "Let's go meet the driver. He should be there waiting for us."

They made their way through the city towards the dome that they'd been admiring from afar from different vantage points within the city. It did look so beautiful, a true work of art. They began their tour visiting the cathedral at the base, which in itself was quite spectacular. It was getting crowded with tourists but Arianna had a feeling that it would only get busier as the day progressed.

As they made their way towards the staircase that led up through the interior of the dome, Arianna stopped for a minute to catch her breath, rubbing her temples slightly as she did so.

"Arianna, are you okay, bella?"

"Yes. I have the slightest bit of a headache."

Lia had a worried frown on her face. "Do you want to

come back tomorrow? I think we'd have time in the morning if you're not feeling well. Or we can skip it altogether. Whatever you want."

"No, no. I think I can manage. I might want to take it a bit slow." Arianna laughed. "Man, since when did I start acting so old?"

"Well, you don't want to get sick. We have too many fun things planned. You tell me if at any time you want to turn back, okay?"

"I will."

The two women followed several others as they began the climb up the steps. Arianna tried not to think about the fact that she'd just read at the bottom that the exact number of steps totaled four hundred sixty-three. Soon her worry was replaced by a sense of awe as they entered the interior of the dome and admired the frescoes of Giorgio Vasari's *Last Judgment*.

"This is incredible, isn't it?" Arianna said.

"It's so beautiful." Lia had a sense of awe in her voice too as she spoke.

They continued upward after stopping for several minutes to admire the artwork. The stairs now led them through the outer part of the cupola onto the lantern structure. It was here where they could step out into the sunny day and get a magnificent view of the city stretching out in front of them.

"Wow. This place really is beautiful. It seems that everywhere we go, we catch another glimpse of Florence that leaves me breathless and in awe of its beauty."

"Can you imagine ever living here?" Lia asked.

Arianna considered how to answer the question being posed to her so innocently. *In a heartbeat,* she said, but only to herself. "I don't know. It might be one of those cases where to live here would be to lose some of that magical feeling. Does that make sense? Although I suppose people might say the same thing about visiting San Francisco or where I live in Sausalito. It's hard to imagine living somewhere else. But I do wish I had traveled more. A lot more. I wanted to see the world—" She caught herself, but not in time.

"Ari, you're so young and you've plenty of money. You *can* see the world if that's what you want to do." Lia said it with so much conviction, as if she wanted that for her daughter more than anything.

Arianna looked out over the view and waited a beat before she replied. "I'm here with you now and that's what matters to me. In all my years of dreaming about travel, Italy was the place that I most wanted to visit one day and the fact that I'm here with you—with my mother… It's more than I could have imagined really."

Lia gave her a big hug. "Well, I think that it's pretty great too, and I think that you have lots of fun adventures ahead of you, young lady." Lia laughed, and Arianna turned so that she wouldn't see the tears that were welling up in her eyes.

Arianna quickly rubbed her sleeve across her face.

"Shall we head down and go find some lunch?"

"Sounds like a good plan to me," Lia said.

They made their way carefully back down the stairs and into the late morning sunshine once again. "I think I spotted a few nice-looking restaurants just down from the square here. Maybe some pizza?" Lia said.

"Pizza sounds great. I'm anxious to compare the authentic experience with that back home," Arianna replied.

They found a great little cafe that wasn't yet too crowded for an early lunch. They each ordered pizza and a glass of wine, and spent the remaining time taking in the view and watching the people pass by.

After lunch, even though Arianna was still feeling a bit unsettled, she decided to get in a little more sightseeing, and by mid-afternoon they were both pretty wiped out. They agreed that they would go back to the hotel to rest and take it easy for the remainder of the night, maybe even ordering in room service to share in one of their suites.

CHAPTER 26

Arianna dragged herself out of bed the next morning, feeling rough. *God, what was she going to do about this headache?* She reached for the pills that she'd been carrying with her in her purse. She thought about phoning Lia's room to cancel their breakfast meeting, but then decided against it. She really needed a nice cup of strong coffee; maybe it would help her head. She'd wait to see how she felt after breakfast before she made any decisions about the day.

She made her way down to the hotel restaurant promptly at nine o'clock to find Lia already there looking lovely and ready for her day. "Good morning," Arianna said as she sat down opposite Lia in the plush-looking dining room.

"Morning." Lia grinned. "How'd you sleep?"

"The bed is like a little piece of heaven, isn't it? I slept great, thanks. And you? How's your room?"

"I love it. Really. Everything is so beautiful and perfect. I feel so lucky to be here with you. I can't thank you—"

"Stop." Arianna smiled. "You've thanked me enough,

and besides, it's my pleasure. I'm so happy that you came with me."

Their waiter came over to take their order and bring them coffees. Arianna sipped hers and tried to forget about the pounding in her head. "Yesterday was wonderful, wasn't it?"

"Oh, it was *so* wonderful. It was like a little gift of discovery around every corner. I can't wait to see what today holds." Lia was peering thoughtfully at Arianna. "Are you okay, Ari?"

Arianna realized that she had her fingers pressed up against her forehead, either trying to pressure the pain away or willing herself to stop thinking about the dull ache. "Yes—well, no, actually. I do have a bit of a headache." She sighed. "I just took something for it and I'm hoping that some food and coffee will help."

Lia looked worried. "Maybe you should go back to your room after breakfast. I hate for you to miss anything, but we should stay in today if you're not feeling well.

"Yeah, maybe I will have to lie down for awhile, I guess. I definitely don't want you to stay in, though. You should go out exploring. Enjoy the morning."

They ate their breakfast and enjoyed some easy conversation before parting ways for the morning. Arianna back to her room, and after some convincing, Lia headed out into the Tuscan morning to check out her surroundings.

Arianna slept, but as the morning progressed, she felt increasingly worse instead of better. Lia checked in with her around noon, and then was back to her room an hour later with some lunch that she'd picked up at one of the nearby restaurants for both of them. They sat at the table in Arianna's room and chatted about Lia's morning.

"I'm sorry you're not feeling well. I'm bummed out for you."

"It's okay. I think I should rest for what's left of the day, and then I'm sure I'll be well for tomorrow." Arianna hoped that she could knock this headache and get back on her feet. "You should go. Explore some more and then report back to me." Arianna grinned. "I love hearing your description of everything."

"I feel like I'm living a dream," Lia said with a strange look in her eyes. "It feels different, yet everything is the same. I've missed it, I suppose." She looked down for a second. "No, that's not true. I missed it a lot. I probably never should have left. If I hadn't—everything would be different. We would have been together."

Arianna noticed the tears in Lia's eyes. "You know, I've been doing a lot of thinking lately about regrets. The ones I have and the ones I don't have. And it's something I've been working on a lot with Doc in therapy. Can I be direct with you?"

Lia nodded her agreement.

"Don't do it Lia. Don't spend your time worrying about the past. That's one thing I've learned since I—

since my parents' accident. Life is way too short and we just never know, do we?"

Lia nodded and wiped her tears away with her hand. "You are wise, my child." She laughed. "I'm not sure where you get that from."

"Well, I just think—we're here now. Together. And I hope we're making some incredible memories together. I know that for me, I never would have imagined this. And I'm okay with the past." She really believed it as she spoke the words out loud. She had come to some important conclusions about her life lately, and Arianna felt strong voicing them out loud now.

"You are right. Absolutely right. And I'm going to make an effort to start focusing on the future. A future that has you in it. And *that* makes me insanely happy." Lia reached over to grab Arianna's hand across the table.

"Alright then," Arianna said as she got up from the table. "You go. Enjoy the rest of the day, and come back and tell me all about it."

Lia checked back with Arianna later that afternoon and they discussed plans for the next morning. They'd decided to leave for the villa in the late morning, and Arianna had already arranged the car and driver to take them there. The drive would be about ninety minutes, and she was looking forward to seeing some of the Tuscan countryside along the way.

The two women ordered pasta delivered to Arianna's

suite and enjoyed a relaxing evening in, with Arianna still nursing her headache. She didn't have a huge appetite but the delicious food was hard to resist; and it did seem to help her to get something in her stomach.

"Oh, I hope I feel better tomorrow."

"Me too." Lia frowned. "I'm so sorry you're not feeling well and haven't been able to enjoy this last day in Florence. I predict that you'll be back here another day in the near future."

Arianna smiled but inside she doubted that she'd be back.

CHAPTER 27

Arianna slept soundly during the night and woke up feeling better, although she still noticed a dull ache in her head that she hoped would lessen as the morning went on. She thought that being in the villa and spending some good time in the fresh air of the countryside would do her a world of good, and she couldn't wait to get settled there to explore Siena.

Whenever she had thought about traveling to Italy, it was mostly the picture of the rolling hills of Tuscany that came to mind. She was anxious to finally explore it a bit, along with the wine tours and bike rides that she was hoping for.

And it would be fun when the others arrived. She still wanted more time with just Lia, but she was also missing them, especially Blu. And she and Lia would have a few more weeks together after they left. It would be a great time, and one that she hoped would create some good memories for everyone.

Arianna spent a few minutes packing up her things before breakfast so that they could take their time, enjoying the food and coffee before they left. They both agreed that it was bittersweet to leave but they were looking forward to a new adventure at the villa.

They met the driver outside at the designated time; and with one last glance towards the hotel, they were off for part two of their trip.

When the driver asked if they wanted the faster route or the slower scenic one, they opted for the more direct because Arianna still wasn't feeling very well.

The drive was very beautiful, though, and did go through a good portion of Chianti, which was so lovely to Arianna. The vineyards and rolling hills were just as she'd pictured them, and she couldn't keep her mouth from hanging open as she saw a new view around every turn. She glanced at Lia, who was looking out her window and seemed to be enjoying the view too, lost in her own thoughts—which Arianna guessed had to do with her childhood and being back here.

"Are you okay?" Arianna asked.

Lia turned towards her. "Oh, yes. I was thinking about how I might feel being back home now. It seems like such a journey that I've been on, all of a sudden. And it wasn't always good. Being back here the last time wasn't good, really. It was sad and tragic saying goodbye to my father. And I can't help but think how much I would have liked for my parents to have met you. They would have adored you, and I wish that I could have given that to them. And to you too," she said softly.

Arianna reached out to touch Lia's arm. "I'm sure

that I would have loved them. It's funny, but I think being here with you will give me a good idea of who they were. And if we can go to where you lived—where you were raised—if you're comfortable with that, I think it would be lovely." Arianna hoped that it was something Lia would enjoy doing and not feel pressured into in any way.

"Yes, I've been thinking of that too, actually. I think it's a good idea, and of course we should do it. I'm so happy to show you my Tuscany, even though it's been so long since I've really felt that way about it."

"Well, I look forward to seeing it all."

They sat back and enjoyed the remainder of the ride in comfortable silence, each lost in their own thoughts and marveling at the changing landscape outside their window.

Soon they came upon road signs for Siena, and the driver said that he would continue to the villa, bypassing the city unless they wanted to drive in. They opted for going straight to the villa, knowing that there would be plenty of time for driving into town. Arianna had booked them into the best villa that she could find in the area, sparing no expense. It included a driver, housekeeper, and cook, although Arianna had a suspicion that Lia would happily be doing most of the cooking that would be enjoyed at the villa. And Arianna didn't want Gigi to lift a finger while she was here. This was to be a vacation for her; she was a guest and friend, to be treated accordingly.

Within a few more minutes, Arianna could spot the villa in the distance. It looked regal atop a small hill in the middle of the countryside. There was a gorgeous landscaped garden, a tennis court, and a large swimming pool. Beyond the immediate grounds was an olive grove. The villa had nine bedrooms and ten bathrooms, so there was more than enough room for everyone. Arianna smiled to herself as she thought about the fun that Jemma would have outside in the garden and playing in the pool. She was definitely ready to see the little girl that she was really starting to miss.

They pulled up to the front walkway, and immediately the staff was there to greet them and collect their bags. They stepped out of the car, taking in the incredible view of the olives groves and Siena beyond. "Wow," Lia said.

"You can say that again." Arianna felt quite pleased so far and was anxious to check out the inside. "Let's go in and check out the house. We'll have a wander around outside here in a bit. Sound good?"

Lia nodded her agreement and they followed the housekeeper inside.

The foyer immediately inside the front door was simple but charming. There was a huge bouquet of flowers which gave off a lovely scent that was perfection. The foyer opened up into a huge living room with a big fireplace and comfortable-looking sofas and chairs. Beyond the living room was a formal dining room, and beyond that a sitting room that opened to the outside into a courtyard with big tables. There was also a wood-burning stove and everything one would need for some great evening dinners outside.

Arianna and Lia peeked their head into the kitchen, which had been converted to a full-size chef's kitchen, while still retaining its original charm. Arianna heard Lia catch her breath.

"About that cook we just met…" she laughed.

"I was wondering about that. I don't want you to lift a finger if you don't want to; if, on the other hand, you'd like to cook while you are here, the kitchen is yours." Arianna winked.

"I can't wait to get in there." Lia laughed.

"I figured as much and will look forward to it."

There were three bedrooms on the first floor, four bedrooms on the second, and another two bedrooms in the unattached pool house, all with their own en suite bathrooms, so there was going to be more than enough room for everyone. Lia chose one of the bedrooms downstairs that overlooked the garden flowers and gave a magnificent view of the rolling hills beyond.

The housekeeper showed Arianna to the master suite upstairs, which she admired with a smile. It was so gorgeous. There was a small terrace and a huge bathroom with a big old-fashioned bathtub. Arianna immediately noticed the high-quality towels and the lovely assortment of soaps and powders. She'd be enjoying a soak in the tub soon enough. She opened the door out to the small terrace and caught her breath at the view. For as far as she could see were rolling hills and olive groves. It looked so magical, and she smiled to herself as she thought about the exploring that they'd do once they were settled.

After Arianna had thoroughly examined her sleeping quarters, she wandered through the rest of the house to check out the remaining bedrooms. There was a set of two bedrooms with an adjoining door that would be perfect for Blu and Jemma. Blu's room was extravagant and exactly what Arianna wanted to give her, and the other room was done up for a child, including a sweet little playhouse villa with little dolls and furniture that she knew Jemma would love.

Arianna felt very happy for her choice with the villa. The travel agent had done a great job choosing the property. She wandered down to the kitchen to get a drink and see what Lia was doing. Lia was already in the kitchen examining all the gadgets and the fully-stocked refrigerator and pantry. "They've thought of everything," she said with obvious delight. She pointed towards a bottle of wine on the counter. "The cook showed me a cheese platter prepared in the fridge for us. Shall we take it and this bottle out to the front terrace for a little snack?"

"That sounds amazing," Arianna said, taking two wine glasses from the shelf near her. "You grab the cheese and I've got the wine."

They took their food outside and got everything

organized on the large table that overlooked the garden, pool, and olive grove beyond. "I feel like I'm dreaming. This is so exactly how I pictured it would be that I can't believe it. I mean, look at the view."

Lia nodded her head in agreement. "Being back reminds me of how truly beautiful it is. And it is magical, isn't it?"

"That's exactly what it is." Arianna was thoughtful for a moment. She wished that the magic she was feeling would rub off a little on her now. If only. But she had to just keep living in reality and enjoying the moments with Lia for what they were—and they had been special so far. She felt such a bond to her that it was surprising, even though she knew how much she'd wanted that deep down from the moment they first met a few short weeks ago. It was surprising how much had happened in such a short time. And there was still a bit more time. They'd enjoy the remaining days of their vacation together before, as Arianna knew, she'd have to have a serious talk with Lia. She dreaded it, but at the same time she felt that the time was coming.

"Penny for your thoughts," Lia teased.

Arianna laughed, getting out of her own head and back to her conversation with Lia. "Oh, sorry."

"Where were you just now?" Lia pressed. "Anything you'd like to talk about?"

Arianna could sense that Lia was feeling more comfortable now about her and about their relationship.

She probably felt that they were past the point of not being able to ask more serious questions or talk about things that really mattered.

"Oh, nowhere. Just thinking about how wonderful this is. How great the trip has been so far, and what I think remains to be another adventure. I'm excited to check out Siena and also to see where you grew up."

"Yes, I'm excited to show you, bella." Lia smiled.

"We have some time before the others arrive, so I say we start with a little tour tomorrow. Does that sound good?"

"That sounds perfect."

Arianna poured them each another glass of wine while they discussed what they'd do the next day and for the remainder of their trip.

Lia agreed, at Arianna's insistence, to let the cook prepare their dinner for their first night. Arianna felt that Lia should relax and enjoy a home-cooked meal to get the full experience of their first night at the villa. They'd noticed that the pasta maker was out in the kitchen, and good smells started wafting through the house by late afternoon.

Arianna could hardly believe how great their stay at the villa had already been after only their first day. She couldn't wait to explore a bit the next day and decided to retire early, taking some time to have a nice bath in her deep tub and write in her journal, which had been a little bit neglected lately.

CHAPTER 28

The next day Arianna was up early and feeling good. She made her way across her room to pull back the curtains and let in some early morning sun and fresh air. The weather looked lovely and the rolling hills of the olive groves out her window were breathtaking, with the morning sun causing the most incredible colors.

Arianna made her way downstairs to find some coffee already brewed and fresh scones laid out on the table. She didn't see or hear Lia up yet, so she assumed that it was the cook that had been up early preparing the little feast. She made a mental note to be sure to commend her on the impeccable service.

She had brought her journal downstairs with her and decided to have a seat out by the pool for a bit. It was so relaxing. She could already feel any tension and anxiety that she'd had melting away with each glimmer of sun shining down on her. Why hadn't she learned how to rest and relax earlier? She thought of a time not so long ago when all she cared about was shopping and partying. All of the wasted days she'd spent being hung over, with not a thought to her future or what would truly make her happy. But there was no use worrying about it now. The important thing was that she was making the most of her time here in the place that she had dreamed of for years, and with her mother—the mother that she had given up hope of ever knowing. So there were a lot of blessings to count. That was for sure.

She spent the next thirty minutes or so writing in her journal. She was trying hard to capture her initial impressions and feelings about the place, and more importantly the insights she was learning about the progression of her relationship with Lia, which seemed to peel back a new layer every day. She smiled as she thought of Lia now. She really did seem as though she belonged here. Not back in San Francisco at all. Just as Arianna was contemplating that thought, she heard the door opening from the house.

"Morning. Mind if I join you out here?"

Arianna closed her journal, looked up, and smiled at Lia.

"Oh, sorry. I didn't realize that you were writing. I can leave you if you'd like some time to yourself," Lia said.

"Oh, no. Not at all. I'm finished and I'd love some company. You've found the scones, I see. Word of warning. They're delicious." Arianna laughed.

Lia laughed too. "I've already nibbled one and definitely agree with you." Lia pulled up a chair next to

Arianna by the pool and got situated with her coffee.

"So, I was thinking…"

Lia looked up. "Yes."

"What if instead of doing Siena today, we visited Castellina in Chianti? I'm dying to see where you grew up, and I figured that we could go to Siena another day this week. I guess I'm kind of craving a quiet pace today, and from what I've read, I think we'd find less crowds there, don't you think?"

Lia was thoughtful for a minute. "Yes, I suppose we can do that today."

Arianna thought that she detected some hesitation from Lia. "Or if you'd rather wait. We can do that too."

"No, I guess I have to get a bit of courage up—or not courage, really. Just that it might be strange being back. I want to show you, though. And I do love it there, so yes, we'll do it." She smiled broadly to show her approval of the change in plans.

"Great. If you're sure?"

Lia nodded her head in agreement again. "Yes, I'm sure."

"Super. I'll let the driver know that we'll aim for going around ten o'clock. Does that sound good to you?" Arianna said.

"Yes, perfect. The place is not so big at all. We'll have him drop us in my old neighborhood and then I can give you the basic tour. That should take us right up to lunch, and I'm sure there are some new places that would be fun to try. God, when I lived there, the food was magnificent. I used to dream of opening up a restaurant there. To have my own business, just like my father's bakery."

"That must have been pretty fun growing up with a father as a baker. I can't imagine having access to all of those delicious breads and pastries." Arianna laughed.

"Oh, it was very nice, really. I worked in the bakery when I was young, and even before that I spent almost all of my free time there. I knew all the regular customers and my father would have me take deliveries out on my bicycle during the week. It was a fun time."

Arianna noticed the change in Lia's face as she talked. She seemed to light up, and it was beautiful to see. She'd noticed that a lot on their trip so far. It was part of what had her thinking about Lia and San Francisco and what her own reasons were for being there. Arianna would maybe make a different decision later. After they'd been back from their trip. Time would tell. She reminded herself not to worry about the future or anything right now. Just be in the moment. In Tuscany. With her mother.

They finished their coffee and scones and went inside to get dressed for the day. Lia told Arianna to dress casually, so she was going to wear her designer jeans and a plain white blouse, simple earrings and her normal light dusting of make-up. Lia had a simple skirt and short-sleeved top on with super-cute red sandals that made Arianna smile when she saw them.

"Love your shoes."

"Thanks. They are actually quite comfortable, and I figure we might be doing a little bit of walking today," Lia said.

They collected their handbags and let the cook know that they would not be home for lunch but planned to be back for dinner. Lia had enjoyed the meal so much the night before that she'd agree to forgo cooking herself for one more night, which made Arianna very happy for some reason. Nevertheless, she loved to see Lia bustling about in the kitchen and very much looked forward to the meals that she'd be preparing in the villa soon.

Arianna's first impressions of Castellina in Chianti were that it was just how she'd pictured a quaint little Tuscan village. The homes had the old Italian charm, and she loved the feel of the hustle and bustle of the locals going about their daily lives.

"I can't believe that this is where you grew up," Arianna said. "It's *so* charming. And so unlike where we live."

"You can say that again," Lia said. "Being back here makes me realize how different my life has become in the U.S. Not bad really, just different."

"Would you ever want to come back here?" Arianna was curious about this after seeing Lia in Italy. To her, it seemed that Lia belonged here.

"I don't know. I mean, I guess I've never really let

myself think about coming back. With my parents gone and—well, finances have been tight for me. I'm not complaining—" She glanced at Arianna, who got the feeling that Lia really wanted her to believe this, that she was careful when it came to talking about her financial situation with Arianna. "—And I make good money in the states, doing what I love, for the most part." She laughed.

Arianna knew this was in reference to the cooking part of her job and not the cleaning, which had to be hard work as far as Arianna was concerned.

"So, would I come back some day?" Lia said, as much to herself as to Arianna. "Not as long as you are still in San Francisco. *That* I know for sure."

Arianna looked away for a brief moment so that Lia couldn't see what was in her eyes. "And if I weren't in San Francisco?"

"Then I would beg you to let me move near you." Lia laughed. "I've waited so many years to meet you, to know you, Ari. I would never give that up. Not for Italy, not for anything. So unless you'd be coming back here with me, I guess my answer is an emphatic no." Lia laughed.

They'd been walking along the old stone-paved road through town as they talked, and Lia stopped in front of a bakery. The smells wafting out into the morning air were undeniably tempting.

"Is this it?" Arianna asked. "Your father's bakery?"

"This is it." Lia smiled. "God, I have so many

memories of this place, this street." She peered through the window. "My mother sold it right after Papa died. I know the owner. He's an old family friend. Shall we go in?"

Arianna grinned. "Do you even need to ask?"

The little bell above the wooden door clanked to announce the arrival of customers.

"*Buongiorno.*" The man looked up from behind the counter to greet them. He squinted his eyes as if trying to remember something. "Lia?" His face broke into a wide grin of recognition. "*Sei tornato. Buono a vederti.*"

They continued for a few seconds in Italian and then Lia gestured towards Arianna. "*Questo è Arianna...lei è mia figlia.*"

The man looked genuinely surprised, but delighted, as he kissed Arianna on each cheek. She knew enough Italian to know that Lia had introduced her as her daughter. Arianna grinned as she told him in Italian that it was lovely to meet him. They ordered one of the delicious-looking pastries and took it to go so that they could continue walking in Lia's old neighborhood. Arianna was anxious to see more and was enjoying her time in the sweet village so far. She knew from their earlier conversation that the bakery was not far from the home where Lia grew up.

PAULA KAY

CHAPTER 29

They meandered their way through a few more roads, then came upon the sweetest little square. There were a fountain and benches along each side, forming another little interior square. Arianna walked over to one of the benches and Lia followed, but Arianna noticed the strange faraway look on her face. "Penny for your thoughts," Arianna said.

"Oh, sorry. I guess I was a little lost for a moment there."

"Memories?" Arianna asked, suspecting as much.

Lia nodded, looking slightly sad.

"I take it they aren't good memories?" Arianna asked, not feeling that she should pry but knowing that she could now with Lia, at least just a bit. If she was fully invested in their relationship, she had to press at times. And she supposed that she should allow Lia the same privilege. Her attention turned back to Lia, who seemed a little better.

"They aren't bad memories, no." Lia smiled slightly. "This was the place where I last saw Antonio. Before I left for America. We'd had such a great day together.

We'd gotten gelatos and brought them here to enjoy and say our goodbyes."

Arianna leaned over and gave her a slight hug. "I hope you're okay. Being here, I mean?"

"Yes, I am. I really am. I want to be here with you. I guess it just hit me all of a sudden, but I'm okay." She looked up as if to convince Arianna with the grin plastered on her face as she reached for Arianna's hand. "Now, let me show you my house. It's right over there." She pointed to one of the small lanes jutting out from the square.

Arianna followed and they walked around Lia's old neighborhood, carefully peering into the windows at the house where she grew up and giggling at the prospect of getting caught by the new owners, whom Lia said she didn't know. Lia pointed out Antonio's old house, saying that it too had been sold when his mother passed away long before the death of Lia's own parents.

Lia showed Arianna where she'd gone to school in the small elementary school that was still home to small children learning to read and write. She showed her where she used to ride her bike and deliver the baked goods to all her father's best customers. It had been a good morning, and when they came upon the most perfect-looking little restaurant, they both raised their eyebrows and said at the same time, "Let's have lunch."

Arianna laughed as they both noticed the sign with the name of the restaurant. Thyme. "And it's named after your favorite herb. That has to be a good sign, right?"

Lia nodded her head as she took in the interior of the little restaurant, a big grin spread on her face. "It reminds me so much of my childhood." She grabbed Arianna's hand, giving it a squeeze. "And it feels amazing to be here now with you."

Arianna nodded her head in agreement. They'd eaten at fancier spots in Florence, but this was the kind of rustic environment that she imagined suited Lia. She only hoped that the food matched the decor.

They found a little table near the window and a smiling waitress came over to greet them. "*Buongiorno*," she said as she handed them the menus.

Arianna smiled wide and said in English, "This place is so sweet."

"*Si, grazie*. My uncle—he owns the restaurant," the waitress said, pleased with her halting English. "Where do you come from?" She turned to Lia. "You are Italian, *si*?"

"I was raised here—in Castillina—and my daughter"—Lia gestured towards Arianna—"she grew up in America. In San Francisco."

"Ah. San Francisco. I want to go there one day." The waitress smiled broadly and continued to tell them the specials of the day, leaving them to make their selection while she got their wine.

"This menu is really good. I want everything," Lia said. "Ari, I'm dying to get in the kitchen at the villa. I think tomorrow night I should cook dinner, yes?"

"If you'd like to. I'm all for it."

They both ordered pasta dishes with bruschetta to start, and chatted easily, each with a glass of wine, as they waited for their food.

Arianna could see Lia's eyes darting around the small seating area, taking it all in. She'd noticed that a lot when they'd been dining out and wondered what it was that she was thinking. Now she felt brave enough to ask.

"If you'd have stayed here—in this town, or another in Italy—do you think you would have been cooking in a restaurant like this? Would you prefer it to the kind of work you are doing now?"

Lia seemed thoughtful, as if she was hesitant to say what was on her mind. "If I'm being honest, my dream was to open my own restaurant. It's all I ever thought about as a child, while cooking with my grandmother. She used to tell me *'il cibo è un dono di Dio.'* " She smiled as she recounted the memory to Arianna.

Arianna grinned. "I agree wholeheartedly with your wise grandmother. Your food *is* a gift from God." *And my great-grandmother.* She wanted to hear much more about the family that she'd never known, but before she could ask another question, the waitress was delivering hot plates of delicious-looking food to their table.

"Oh my goodness. It this not the most delicious pasta you've ever eaten?" Lia said as she wiped her mouth with her napkin and went in for another bite.

"Well, it's certainly great, but I'd say second to yours."

Arianna winked. "But it is good." She laughed, twirling her spaghetti around her fork. "If I'm not careful, I'm not going to be able to fit into any of the clothes I brought."

Lia laughed too, with her hand on her stomach. "You can say that again. We'll have to get on the bicycles or be sure we start taking some nice long walks near the villa."

"That sounds lovely, actually. I want to soak up every bit of this gorgeous Tuscan sunshine."

"And really, Arianna, I don't think you have much to worry about. I think you could stand to gain a few pounds, if I'm being honest." She looked worried, like she may have said something she wished she could take back. "I'm sorry. You're perfect. Just the way you are."

"What, are you worried you're sounding too much like a mother?" Arianna teased with a wink. "It's okay, Lia. Really." And she meant it. Growing up, her mother had been quite critical of her weight, always monitoring what she was eating, and Arianna learned how to battle the curviness of her Italian genes. Her mother had been very thin, so Arianna suspected that her curves, as she grew older, were just another reminder to her mother of their differences. It was a wonder she hadn't ended up with an eating disorder, but she'd loved food too much for that. She smiled thinking about it. She'd learned how to manage so that she could maintain the figure that would still land her the modeling jobs, while not becoming obsessed with dieting like so many others that she knew in the industry.

And these days, she didn't usually have so much of an appetite; so the fact that she was hungry and eating so much while in Italy, she counted as a good thing.

Lia seemed to relax after Arianna had reassured her that she could, in fact, speak to her as if she were her mother. They finished their meal and when the waitress came to check on them, Lia told her how fantastic they thought it was and asked her to please tell the chef.

"*Sì*, my uncle is the cook." She grinned. "Would you like to come back to the kitchen? Say hello?"

"*Sì*." Lia's face lit up as she turned to Arianna. "I never pass up the chance to see a chef's kitchen." She laughed.

Arianna stood up too and they followed the waitress back behind the swinging doors into the kitchen. She spoke to her uncle in Italian and the middle-aged Italian man made his way towards them, wiping his hands on the apron tied around his waist.

"*Buongiorno*," he said, kissing first Lia, and then Arianna, on both cheeks. "Welcome to Thyme. I am Carlo and this is my niece, Sofia," he said gesturing to the young waitress. "I hope your lunch it is good, *sì*?" he said in his broken English.

"*Il cibo era delizioso*," said Lia.

"Very delicious," echoed Arianna with a big grin, rubbing her stomach with the palm of her hand. She noticed Lia eyeing the kitchen and smiled inwardly. Arianna loved Lia's dream, and wondered what part having her had played in its not coming to fruition. She didn't dwell on that. There wasn't time to. The cook was showing them around the kitchen with pride, and Arianna noticed how delighted he was when, in Italian, Lia shared her thoughts on his good-quality ingredients. By the time they were walking back out of the kitchen, Lia and Arianna had promised that they'd be back with the whole gang for a good old-fashioned family-style dinner in the upcoming weeks.

As they walked out of the restaurant, Arianna couldn't help but notice all of the smiling customers sitting at the tables outside chatting as if they all knew one another. She had a great feeling about this little restaurant, and looking beside her at Lia, Arianna didn't think she'd seen her looking so happy since the day that they'd met. She reached over to give her a quick hug. "That was wonderful. I like it here."

Lia smiled and Arianna thought she looked radiant in the moment, as if years of stress had melted away.

"I'm not quite sure what we could do now to top that. Gelato?" Lia asked with a grin.

"With extra toppings." Arianna laughed and they continued walking down the quiet street towards the gelato place that they'd noticed earlier.

After their dessert, they decided to ring the driver, who was parked nearby, and go home for a little rest and later a walk around the property. Arianna had been eyeing the olive grove and the paths that she'd glimpsed winding their way through the crooked vines.

What a perfect day it had been. Arianna leaned her head back in the car to shut her eyes for a few moments. It felt good, and she realized how tired she was feeling even though the morning outing hadn't been strenuous. She also felt the creeping of a slight headache coming on and sighed. She'd have to take a couple pills when they arrived home, in the hopes of knocking it out before the evening.

Lia turned towards her. "What's wrong, bella? Are you okay?"

"Yes, I'm okay." Arianna smiled in the hopes of reassuring her. "I'm just tired. A nap sounds perfect right about now."

"We'll be home soon. And nothing to do until dinner if you don't feel like it."

"I think I'd like to have a nice walk after my nap. That sounds perfect." Arianna said.

CHAPTER 30

The rest of the week was spent in the most glorious of ways that Arianna could imagine. She would sleep in and wake up to the most delicious smells of fresh scones and strong coffee. After breakfast, she and Lia had gotten into a nice little routine of walking through the olive grove and back via the country road that ran along one of the bigger neighboring vineyards. She still marveled at the breathtaking beauty that she saw around her every day and thought that if she'd die here, she'd have lived a happy life.

Lia actually said that to her one day while they were out walking and Arianna surprised herself, and probably Lia as well, by bursting into tears. It had led to a great talk that was deep and meaningful and all about how happy they both were that Lia had found her and reached out—how happy they were that they were building a new future that included one another.

Arianna tried to be as honest as she was able to be about her feelings, and kept reminding herself to be in the moment. She could almost hear Doc's voice in her head saying as such on several different occasions when the conversation and emotions got rather intense. Every morning, Arianna tried to write her innermost thoughts in her journal. It was a process that had helped her so much so far, and one she suspected that she wouldn't give up until it was no longer necessary. But she had a new idea about that too.

She'd gained a lot of clarity since arriving in Italy. Particularly, since arriving at the villa. The days were easy and full of sunshine. Hope and happiness was all around her and it was hard not to get caught up in that.

They started developing a little ritual of dropping by Thyme every other morning. They'd go in late in the morning for a cup of coffee and then end up staying for lunch and conversation with Carlo and Sofia. One day, while telling Lia of the beautiful ingredients he'd found that morning, he invited her into the kitchen to cook with him. Her face had lit up like that of a kid in a candy shop, so Arianna suspected he really had no choice but to ask her to join him.

Arianna especially enjoyed these days in the restaurant, and she could tell that Lia did too.

They had gone into Siena a few times as well, mostly for dinner and for Lia to show Arianna a few highlights of the city. But Arianna enjoyed Castellina the most. When she told Lia that, she had seemed surprised, saying that it was so different from San Francisco, with many less choices for eating and shopping. But Arianna liked the small-town feel to it.

So they continued on like this, getting into an easy and enjoyable pattern. Often Lia would cook the evening meal and invite all of the staff and their families to join them. These were the evenings that Arianna enjoyed the most. They'd sit at the big tables in the courtyard with her favorite operas playing in the background and plates full of steaming pastas, meats, and sauces. There was always so much laughter and smiles. They got by with their broken Italian and English on both sides, and Arianna found herself picking up on the language much faster than she thought she would.

She couldn't wait to share this little home they'd created with the rest of her friends. Gigi was going to love these nights as well, and Blu and Jemma wouldn't know what to make of it. Arianna was content and counted every minute as a blessing, knowing that these moments were some of the best she'd ever have.

A few days later, like the flip of a switch, Arianna felt something shift inside her. She knew that she was going to have to make the time to talk to Lia sooner rather than later and she dreaded it.

CHAPTER 31

Arianna awoke with another pounding headache and tried not to cry over the frustration of knowing she'd be unable to join Lia on the bike ride that they'd planned. Maybe this trip hadn't been the best idea. But she only let herself think that momentarily. She'd already had more great memories than she'd ever imagined possible. She'd just have to figure out a way to deal with Lia and the questions that were sure to come. Maybe it was time to tell her. Arianna didn't have much time to think about this before she heard a quiet knock on her door.

"Come in."

"Morning, sleepyhead. I brought you some coffee and a scone from this lovely shop I found just down the way." Lia put a tray on the table beside Arianna's bed. "What's wrong? Are you feeling bad again?" Lia had that look of worry on her face that Arianna had come to know.

"Morning—thanks for the coffee, and that does look divine." Arianna struggled to prop herself up a bit in her bed. "Yeah, I'm afraid I have a pretty bad headache again today. I really hate to keep you from anything..."

Lia was quickly beside her with a hand upon her

forehead. "Bella, you're not looking well. Do you think maybe I should find a doctor? That's several days now with this headache, no?"

Arianna shook her head and struggled a bit to disentangle herself from the covers, and sit up at the edge of the bed. "No. No, I don't need a doctor. I'll be alright. I just—I just need—" Arianna pressed hard with one hand on her forehead, stood up, and immediately fell to the floor.

"Ari! Oh God—"

Arianna heard Lia's panicked pleas as she struggled to open her eyes.

"I—I'm okay. Water. Can I have some water?"

Lia got the glass of water on Arianna's bedside table and knelt down beside her, bringing it to her lips. "I'm calling the doctor. This is not normal, and I'm very worried about you now."

Arianna struggled to sit up and get her thoughts together enough to talk to Lia. She knew that if she couldn't convince her soon, Lia would be calling for help in a matter of minutes; there was no mistaking the panicked look on her face. It was time. Arianna needed to get the strength together to have this conversation with Lia—with her mother.

"No, no. Please don't call anyone. Just—can you help me get back into bed, please? I'll be okay. I—I just need to talk to you." She hoped that the pleading in her voice was enough to convince Lia of this.

For the moment Lia was focused on helping her get back into the bed and seemed a little less likely to go running to the phone, so Arianna focused on some deep breathing and thinking about what she was going to say. This was it. She had to tell her. She owed it to Lia now. She hoped that she wouldn't be too angry with her. *If it were reversed I might be furious.* And then, just as quickly, she reminded herself how much she'd changed these past few months. She'd become someone who was much more in the moment and zen-like. She couldn't help but smile as the word came to mind.

Lia helped tuck the covers in around her, and she was sitting up in the bed now, feeling a little less like she was going to pass out again. Arianna reached for the coffee and then took a little bite of the scone.

"Ari, why won't you let me call for a doctor? I think you need to see someone, don't you, bella?"

Arianna felt bad for how worried Lia appeared to be. She'd hoped that they would have much more time here together before she started to feel unwell. Before she would have to tell Lia the truth. And probably ruin her vacation, Arianna thought.

"Lia, there's something I need to tell you. Pull that chair up by me, will you?"

Lia pulled the nearby chair up close to her bed and looked every bit as nervous as Arianna felt.

"What is it? Are you okay? You look so serious— you're making me worried."

Arianna took a deep breath and tried to sit up a little straighter in her bed. "No. I'm not okay. And I'm so sorry for telling you like this. For not telling you sooner." Arianna glanced up to look Lia in the eyes. "I'm sick. Well, that's not true exactly." She took another measured breath and decided to blurt it out. "I'm not just sick. I'm dying—"

"What are you talking about?" Lia reached out to grab Arianna's hand, giving it a squeeze as she did so. "You've probably just gotten something from the air travel. People get sick all the time when they spend time on planes. I'm sure we can go to a doctor here and—"

"Lia. Stop. Listen to me." Arianna thought she looked genuinely confused, and it reminded her of her own initial reaction when the doctor had first given her the diagnosis, and then the rotten prognosis, mere months ago. She'd have to make her understand. To prolong it now wasn't better for her.

"The headaches I've been having…"

"Yes." Lia nodded for her to continue.

"It's because of what's wrong with me. I have a brain tumor, if you can believe it." Arianna was surprised herself at the lack of bitterness in her voice. She'd had time to adjust, and it had been awhile since she'd had to tell anyone the news. At this point, it was almost laughable. Well, not really. But to anyone that knew what she'd been through these past months since the accident, it was way too much to be real. To imagine any one person could go through. Arianna did get that.

Now she could see the tears springing up in Lia's eyes, and she felt that she was prepared for it.

"What? I don't understand. When? How long have you known this, Ari? And why—why didn't you tell me?" Lia wiped her tears with her hand, waiting for Arianna's response.

"It's crazy, really. It's crazy for me now to even think of everything that's happened. They don't know for sure, but it's likely that I've had it for a while now. I've always had to deal with headaches for as long as I could remember, really, and then before—before the accident, they started to get pretty bad. I remember thinking it was weird, but I was also partying a lot—I had a lot of hangovers, so I didn't think too much about it." Arianna squeezed Lia's hand that she was still holding as Lia wept quietly.

"After the accident—my parents' funeral and everything—I just couldn't hold it together anymore. It was too much. I pretty much had a complete mental breakdown, and the headaches were also very bad at that point."

"Oh, Ari, I wish I'd been there for you then—that I could have helped you through all of that."

Arianna thought that Lia looked like she was a bit in shock. She'd already witnessed a similar reaction from her friends, so she understood it. But she knew that she was hearing her now and believing her. Lia nodded, encouraging her to continue.

"I can't imagine how hard all of that must have been for you. And then to find out that you've been dealing with this too." Lia reached over to give Arianna a big hug and Arianna didn't resist. It felt good to have her mother's arms around her. To breathe in her perfume and the clean scent of her hair.

Arianna hugged her back for a long moment before she continued, and now she was wiping at tears also, thinking about the time lost for her and Lia but also knowing that it couldn't have been any other way. *Just trust the timing, Ari.*

"Once they determined that my mental health was okay, that I'd basically suffered from being under too much emotional trauma, the doctors wanted to look into the headaches I'd told them I was having. Then they discovered the tumor right away." Arianna said this matter-of-factly but noticed new tears streaming down Lia's face. It was hard, telling someone you loved this kind of news. *And I do love her.* This new realization about how she felt towards Lia both surprised and pleased her.

"But I don't understand. Why are you here? Why aren't you getting treatments? Chemo, radiation, or something? I can help you. I'll take care of you. We should go back right away and—"

"Stop." Arianna gently grabbed hold of Lia's arm as she continued quietly. "There is no treatment. No cure. Trust me, Douglas helped me when I first found out, and we spoke to the best doctors. The location made it inoperable. The odds were so small—Lia, I decided to make the decision—my decision—of how I wanted to live the remaining months of my life; I didn't want to be in a hospital. I still don't want that and I've been counting on the others—Douglas, Gigi, and Blu—to help me when it comes time for that part. And I hope I can count on you too…" They were both crying now as Lia hugged her close.

"Of course, Ari." Lia sobbed and struggled to get the words out. "I'll help you with anything. Why—Ari, do you want to be home? Why did you—did we come here? I hope that you didn't make this trip for me. I would hate to think—"

"No, no. This trip. This is what I've been wanting. The only thing, really." Lia had a puzzled look on her face as she waited for Arianna to continue.

"Ever since I can remember, I've wanted to do this amazing around-the-world trip. I wanted to backpack, like so many other young kids I'd heard about, but my father wouldn't hear of it. Well, my parents didn't want me to go anyways but finally they relented."

Out of guilt at my increasing unhappiness, I suppose.

"And my father organized everything for me. The tickets were purchased and everything was booked just weeks before the accident, before everything changed. I—well, Douglas helped me to postpone everything that had been booked, and as you know, he, Gigi, and Blu were very resistant to the idea of me going on this trip—which I wanted more than ever once I found out about the tumor."

"But, the around-the-world—Oh, Ari, did you change your trip because of me?"

"I did." Arianna smiled now. "And with no regrets. The place I most wanted to go to was Italy. It had always been my dream and the place I most wanted to visit. When I met you—well, I wasn't sure, of course, until the day I asked you, really." Arianna laughed lightly. "But then it all made perfect sense." She was crying happy tears now, thinking about the past weeks in Italy with Lia. "And Lia." Lia looked at her, smiling, with tears falling down her face too. "I've been having the best time. Honestly. I don't want it to end and I'm hopeful that today is just a minor setback, okay? I hope that you can try not to worry too much and trust me as to how I'm feeling, so that we can continue to enjoy our time here together." She looked at Lia with a smile that she hoped was reassuring to her.

Lia sighed. "I'll try. But I can't make any promises, if I'm being honest. It will be hard not to worry." She looked at Arianna with a somewhat stern expression on her face. "But do you promise to tell me if you're not feeling well? I don't even mind what we do. I'd love to stay here in the villa and cook some meals for you. If you're feeling up to it, we can go for short walks and the others—Ari, do you think you're up for all the company?"

"Oh, yes. It's what I want more than anything. To have all of you here in this beautiful place. It's exactly what I want now."

Lia reached over to give Arianna another big hug. "Okay, then that's what we'll do. I'll do some shopping and get the house all ready. There is nothing that gives me greater pleasure than cooking for you and this crew. It will be wonderful. You rest here today. And I'll stay close by too."

"You don't have to. If you want to stick to our plan to go riding, I mean."

"No, no. I love it here. I'll just have a walk down the road and enjoy the view that we have here. Maybe you'll feel well enough later to come have some lunch with me outside."

"Yes, I'm sure that I will." Arianna smiled and felt a huge weight lifted from her shoulders. In her heart, she knew that Lia was putting on a smile for her—that she probably needed some time alone to process the news that Arianna had just given her.

PAULA KAY

CHAPTER 32

Arianna felt a huge sense of relief. The conversations that she'd been having with Lia the past few days had gone better than she'd imagined, and she was feeling really good about finally having everything out in the open. Lia deserved that. She had made such an effort to not hold back her own feelings since they met, and Arianna felt good to finally be able to be as real with her.

She made her way downstairs, where she found Lia sitting in the kitchen with a cup of coffee.

"Good morning."

"Hi. How'd you sleep?" Lia said.

"I slept great, and actually I feel pretty good this morning. How bout yourself?"

"Well, you know. I'm still kind of in shock, I guess. If I'm being honest." Arianna couldn't help but notice the sadness passing on Lia's face, and she did understand it. "But, I'm determined to enjoy every moment that we have here together, and I want that for you too." She smiled, and Arianna guessed that it was a forced smile.

"Good. I'm glad to be here and I one hundred percent agree. And on that note, what do you want to do today?"

"I have a surprise for you. I think you'll like it. At least I hope that you'll feel up to it."

"Go on." Arianna smiled as she poured herself some coffee. "I do love surprises."

"Have you heard of the Puccini Festival?" Lia asked.

"Yes...opera, I believe?" Arianna smiled.

"And guess what is showing today?"

"*La Boheme*? Really?"

Lia nodded.

Arianna suddenly felt that the day was going to turn out to be pretty special.

"It's about a two-hour drive to Torre del Lago and the performance will be in an outdoor theater, overlooking the lake, that is absolutely fantastic. Well, I've not been myself, but I've heard such good things about it. I figured that if you are up for it, we could leave in a few hours to get there for a nice lunch and a stroll in the gardens by the lake. What do you think? And Arianna, I don't want you to feel pressured at all—if you're not feeling up to, I mean."

"No, are you kidding? It sounds fantastic, and today is a good day." She smiled, hoping to reassure Lia. "Honest. I'm feeling fine. And besides, we'll be sitting a lot—in the car for the drive and then for the opera—so I shouldn't get so tired. I think it sounds terrific. I'll go let the driver know and then pop upstairs to get ready. Shall we aim for ten thirty?"

"Sounds good to me."

They both took a last sip of their coffee and headed to their rooms to get ready for the day ahead.

The drive to the festival was relaxing. Arianna loved to be driven somewhere new, being able to sit back and watch the scenery out the window—especially here in Tuscany where everything was so beautiful. Watching the green hills as they drove towards the coast, once again Arianna felt that she had to pinch herself that she was finally in this place that she had dreamt of for so long. And seeing Lia there beside her was more than she could have imagined.

They had decided to go to Viareggio, the little seaside resort town nearby, for lunch; and then the driver would take them to the lake to have a little walk outside before the opera started in the early evening. They were both feeling rested and ready for a good meal when they started exploring their options for food. They settled on a little place that was busy but not too busy to get a table, ordering some appetizers and a bottle of Chianti, figuring that they could take their time over a nice leisurely lunch.

Arianna enjoyed her food, the view, and all of the people that were out and about, although she'd grown accustomed now to the quieter life they'd been living at the villa and quite liked it, much to her surprise. But it was nice to be somewhere different for a change, and it was sweet of Lia to think of bringing her to the opera here. Arianna loved it that Lia had been so open to experiencing it even though she knew that the music wasn't her favorite.

They finished their food and the bottle of wine and called the driver to come pick them up. It was a quick drive of only a few miles to Torre del Lago and when they arrived, Arianna could understand the draw that it had. The lake was like a little oasis inside the park. She could imagine that the opera they were going to be seeing under the moonlight would be quite unique and magical, and she was very excited.

They decided to take a walk through the sculpture garden and park beside the lake. The weather was perfect, and Arianna loved seeing the families and young couples out enjoying the beautiful outdoor setting. She seemed to be noticing things like that more frequently these days. It wasn't necessarily regret or longing that she was feeling, just a sense of what was important. She knew that there were certain things that she wouldn't have now, and she had made her peace about that. She also knew that she couldn't change the past, but she suspected that there were still things that she could do that would change the lives of those she cared about for the better. She felt pretty determined about this.

She drew her attention back to Lia, who had been speaking to her.

"God. I'm sorry. Kind of zoned out for a minute there. What did you say?"

Lia laughed. "No worries. You look pretty content, so I'm not that worried about you. I was just saying how nice the weather is here."

Arianna nodded her head in agreement, gathering the swirling thoughts in her head. "Lia, can we sit here for a minute? There's something I want to talk to you about." Arianna walked over to one of the nearby park benches.

Lia followed after her, and when they were both seated, Arianna saw a familiar look of concern on her face.

"What is it? Are you feeling okay?" Lia reached over to take Arianna's hand in her own and at the simple touch, Arianna felt the tears streaming down her face.

Arianna willed herself to speak. It was time for Lia to know everything. There was no reason to keep any of it from her, and Arianna needed to talk about it.

"There's something I haven't told you—something that's very important to me." Arianna felt Lia's hand tighten around her own as she leaned over to give Arianna a slight hug.

"Bella, you can tell me anything."

Arianna took a deep breath before she continued, looking Lia in the eyes as she spoke. "When I was sixteen, I had a child—a little girl."

There was no mistaking the shocked look on Lia's face, and Arianna saw the almost instant tears that matched her own.

"I was so young—and stupid. And things between

my parents and me had already gotten pretty bad. When they found out I was pregnant, they nearly went out of their minds trying to fix everything." Arianna could hear the bitterness in her own voice as she remembered her parents' reaction to her news.

Lia was nodding her head, listening intently as Arianna continued.

"I didn't really have a chance to think about anything—to make any decisions. I was already several months along—thank God, or I think my parents would have made me have an abortion." Arianna's voice broke and she sobbed when she'd uttered the words that she'd thought about many times since then.

Lia reached over and pulled Arianna close, and the irony of the gesture made Arianna sob even more. How different would things have been with Lia beside her during that time in her life? She had needed comfort and it wasn't something she'd gotten from her own mother— not ever, really, and the distance between them only seemed to intensify after Arianna's pregnancy.

Finally Lia loosened her embrace as she looked intently at Arianna. "I'm so sorry, bella. I know that must have been an incredibly hard time for you."

The two women stared at one another in silence for a moment. Of course Lia knew. She knew exactly how it felt to have her child—her baby girl—taken from her arms. It was something that Arianna had thought about daily ever since Lia had told her about the time after her own birth. She needed to finish telling Lia everything that she knew. It was important to her that the people who loved her would have as much information as she had at the very least.

Arianna took another deep breath before continuing. "So my parents took me out to Connecticut to live with an aunt that I'd never met. We told everyone that I was going away to be part of a student exchange program—none of my friends knew the truth. No one ever knew—except for Gigi." Arianna smiled despite the seriousness of the conversation. Gigi had been her rock during that time—after she'd returned and been so filled with rage and sadness. She'd always been there for Arianna in a way that her parents had not been.

Arianna felt new tears streaming down her face as she thought about that day—the day that she'd delivered her baby girl. She'd had her in the private wing of a nearby hospital, her mother beside her, not offering much in the way of comfort, while her father waited anxiously with the young couple who would become parents to Arianna's daughter.

It had all happened very quickly once her contractions had started, and before she knew it, her baby girl was being placed on her chest for mere seconds before she'd heard the frantic voice of her mother telling the nurses to take the child away.

Arianna remembered that feeling of intense panic and longing as she cried out to the nurse to bring her baby back.

"I only saw her for a second—" Arianna was crying quietly now and when she looked at Lia she saw tears that matched her own. "—when they took her out of the room away from me. She had the most beautiful thick dark curls." Arianna smiled as she looked up at Lia. "I imagine that she looks like me—that she looks like us."

Lia reached over to grab Arianna's hand in her own as the two wept quietly without speaking.

Finally, Arianna spoke again, her voice quiet. "Blu knows too—and Douglas. When I met Blu, it was hard for me to be around Jemma at first, to see the mother that Blu was to a daughter around the same age as—as my own daughter. But once I shared everything with her, it was as if a weight had been lifted and—well, you know how much Jemma means to me now.

Lia nodded, just listening and, Arianna guessed, trying to process the information that she'd just shared with her. It was a lot to take in—everything that she'd told her mother the past few days.

Arianna stood up, taking a deep breath as she did so. "I feel much better now." She looked at Lia, who had risen to stand beside her. "Now I feel as if you know everything, and it's a huge relief to me for some reason."

Lia reached over to link her arm in Arianna's, flashing her a big smile. "I'm glad, Ari. The last thing I want is for you to feel any kind of burden or added stress right now.

The two women embraced and then walked around

the park until it was time to get seated in the theater. Arianna had seen *La Boheme* performed several times before, but nothing measured up to the performance she saw that night under the stars there in Tuscany with her mother. Never had the voices sounded so lovely, never before had the music meant so much to her. It was an absolutely perfect night.

They rode much of the way home in silence, tired and lost in their own thoughts about the evening. Arianna wondered if it had meant as much to Lia as it had to her, and she guessed by her reaction that it had. There had been a few occasions during the performance when their eyes met, both with tears streaming down their faces.

They returned to the villa late and retired to their rooms. Blu, Jemma, and Gigi would be arriving the next day, towards evening, and there were a few things that Arianna wanted to do yet to prepare for their arrival. She wanted everything to be just right. She couldn't wait to show them this place that she'd grown to love.

CHAPTER 33

Arianna was feeling exceptionally well the morning that her friends were due to arrive. She'd talked to both Blu and Gigi the night before and they seemed very excited; Jemma, too, seemed to be bouncing off the walls with excited pre-travel energy. Arianna had booked them all first class tickets, so she suspected that the flight would be exciting for Jemma, who had only ever flown on the small plane to San Diego.

Lia had bought fresh flowers for all of the bedrooms and the day was particularly crisp and sunny. Perfect weather for their arrival. Arianna smiled to herself as she thought about her dear friends seeing this magical place for the first time. Well, with the exception of Gigi, but for her it was even more exciting. Her two sisters were flying up towards the end of the week, and then the three of them were traveling back down south so that Gigi could spend time with them before returning to San Francisco from Rome.

The house smelled of strong Italian coffee and fresh bread. *God, this house always smells so wonderful. Thanks to Lia.* Arianna still marveled at how amazing her cooking was, and also at the fact that she had so obviously not inherited that skill from her mother's gene pool. Arianna laughed again. Thank goodness she could afford to have people cooking for her, or she'd probably starve.

She found Lia in the big kitchen, music playing in the background. Arianna stood back in the doorway for a moment, quietly watching her. She seemed to glide across the floor, in her full-length apron, skilled fingers working some type of dough that Arianna guessed would become one of her favorite pasta dishes tonight for dinner.

Lia turned and then jerked slightly. "Oh. You startled me." She laughed and came to give her a kiss on the cheek. "How are you feeling this morning? It's a lovely day, isn't it?"

"I'm well, thanks. Really well, actually. And yes, it's the most beautiful day that we've had yet, I think. Although we certainly have lucked out with the weather, haven't we?" Arianna moved to the counter to pour herself a coffee from the coffee press, not able to stand any more of the delicious aroma without taking some in.

She asked, "Can I help you with anything?"

"Do you want to help me?" Lia laughed, knowing that cooking was not Arianna's most favorite thing in the world to do.

"Uh, not really. But I will." Arianna grinned.

"Nope, just sit here and talk to me, will you? That's perfect for me."

Lia continued to knead the dough while Arianna

watched in silence for a few minutes. "I like to watch you cook," Arianna said. "There's something about it that feels so relaxing to me. You know, I've sat in the kitchen with Gigi hundreds of times but it never seemed to have that effect on me. Probably because, like me, she's a bit frantic in the kitchen." Arianna laughed. "Let's not ever tell her I said that."

Lia laughed too as she flattened the dough into careful little squares. "Your secret is safe with me, bella."

"You're just so—so calm and lovely in the kitchen. It's like your love for that dough is vibrating off the walls or something." Arianna surprisingly felt her face getting a bit warm.

"Well, I don't know about my love for the dough, but I do love cooking very much for the people I care for and you,"—she crossed the distance quickly between them, planting a quick kiss on Ari's forehead—"daughter, dear—I adore." Their eyes met and Arianna's filled with tears. She looked down to compose herself and then back up at Lia, who was now filling the little pockets with some type of meat.

"I adore you too." Arianna said quietly and then wiped away the stray tear that had managed to escape.

A few hours later the house was filled with wonderful smells of cooking; Arianna had woken up from a nap feeling rested and anxious to greet everyone who she knew had arrived at the airport by this time. They'd flown to Milan, and she had a car and driver waiting to pick them up at the airport to make the drive to the villa. Soon she heard Jemma's happy squeals outside the door, followed by a knock with the old-fashioned door knocker.

Arianna opened the door wide, just in time for Jemma to jump into her arms, causing her to almost lose her balance. Blu grabbed Jemma, scolding her to be gentle. Arianna laughed.

"It's okay. Hi, J-bean. I've missed you so much," Arianna said, with big smiles directed towards Blu and a tired but happy-looking Gigi.

"Ari, I went on a big airplane." Jemma had her little hands on either side of Arianna's cheeks, forcing her to look right at her, as if Arianna's adoring gaze would be directed anywhere else.

"You did? Could you see the clouds?"

"Yes." Jemma's eyes grew huge. "And I even got my own movie screen with a lot of movies that I never watched before."

"Oh, I'm so happy bean, that sounds wonderful. Let me put you down a minute so I can give Mommy and Gigi big hugs too."

Blu and Gigi looked happy, but tired. "How are you two? How was the flight? Did you get any rest?"

"Not so much, I'm afraid." Blu said.

"But this one"—Gigi gestured towards Jemma—"she should be well-rested. She slept from Paris to Florence and then again in the car on the way here."

Arianna laughed as she noticed Jemma hopping around in the kitchen with Lia, who seemed to be making an effort to keep her occupied for a few minutes, allowing Arianna to greet her guests.

"Jemma's going to help me in the kitchen, if that's okay with Blu? And welcome!" Lia called out, sounding happy.

"That is perfect." Blu said. "Thank you so much."

"Let me show you two to your rooms—and maybe you'd like to have a little rest before dinner? Lia is cooking up something amazing, and I can't wait to share the local wine and the view here with you."

Blu and Gigi both sighed at the same time, then laughed.

"That sounds amazing, bella." Gigi pulled Arianna to her to give her a big hug. "I've missed you *a lot*. How are you doing? Is everything okay? Are you feeling okay?"

"Yes, yes. I'm fine." Arianna smiled. "We've been having such a good time, and now I can't believe that I get to share it all with you. I can't wait to show you around. So, Douglas is arriving tomorrow? Is that right?"

"Yes, he'll get in on this same flight tomorrow," Gigi said.

"Great. I can't wait until we're all together. And have you been seeing him at all since I've been gone?" Arianna winked as she asked the question that had been on her mind.

"Oh, stop." Gigi blushed a little. "Yes, we've been out

a few times, actually. To talk about the trip and logistics, you know."

Arianna laughed. "I'm sure. Well, you know how I feel. He'd be a lucky man if you considered spending any time with him. You'd both be lucky." She smiled.

While Blu and Gigi rested, Lia and Arianna took the energetic Jemma for a walk outside to explore the vineyard and land around the villa.

"I love it here!" Jemma was full of excitement, and to Arianna's delight had changed into one of her favorite pink tutus. Arianna stood back as Jemma did her sweet six-year-old version of pirouettes as they walked the length of the vineyard.

"How's your dance class, bean?" Arianna had given Jemma, with Blu's approval, a year of ballet classes at one of the best schools for little kids in the city. And to her delight, Jemma had seemed to take to it like a fish to water. She seemed way more graceful than Arianna had been at her age when her own mother had enrolled her in ballet. Arianna had been shy as a little girl and hung back, not wanting any attention at all, which wasn't going to fly in the competitive world of dance; so her mother soon seemed to give up on the idea. But Jemma—she was different. Arianna smiled as Jemma ended her little dance with a flourish.

"I looooove it so much. Thank you, thank you, thank you, thank you." She hurled her little tutu-ed body at

Arianna for another one of her big bear hugs.

Arianna squeezed her tight. "And I love you, you little bug."

Jemma laughed and complained that she couldn't breathe. "I like it here, Ari," she said as they walked along the vineyard hand-in-hand.

"I like it here too." And she did. It was beautiful. If only things could be different. She lost herself in her own head for a few minutes while Jemma was unusually quiet beside her.

"What are we going to do today?" Jemma was ready with more questions, always the inquisitive child.

"Are you tired at all, bean? Do you think you should have a little nap before tonight?"

"No, I'm not tired *at all.*"

"Well then, how do you feel about seeing what Lia is making in the kitchen? I bet she has an extra apron if you'd like being a little Italian sous chef today."

Jemma looked thoughtful. "Ari, her name is *not* Sue."

Arianna laughed and reached over to tickle Jemma. "You're funny, bean. A sous chef is a helper chef. So you'd be a helper to Chef Lia."

"Ohhhh. Okay. Sure. Let's see if Lia will let me be a Sue's chef."

Arianna laughed and they headed back to the villa.

Lia was delighted to have Jemma's help in the kitchen and did, in fact, find a lovely little pink apron to match the little girl's tutu. Arianna sat at the small table watching the two of them prepare more pasta together. There was an Italian opera track playing in the background and Arianna felt totally at peace. *This was the right decision. Coming here.* She felt content and was lost in her own thoughts for a moment. Her attention turned back to the two working in the kitchen.

"Do you have any kids, Lia?" Jemma asked innocently as they were kneading out the dough.

"Remember? Ari is my daughter," Lia said carefully.

Jemma wrinkled up her nose. "But did Ari have two moms?" Arianna knew that this was probably confusing for Jemma, who had spent a great deal of time at the Sinclairs' home and had known Arianna's mom.

"That's right, Jemma. Arianna came out of my tummy when she was born, and then Mr. and Mrs. Sinclair adopted her." Arianna could see that Lia seemed slightly uncomfortable about the conversation.

"What's dopted?" Jemma said innocently.

Just then Blu appeared, and Arianna guessed that she had caught the tail end of the conversation. "What's going on in here?" She winked at Lia as she scooped Jemma up in her arms.

"Mommy. I'm a Sue's chef for Lia. Look at our raviolis." Jemma beamed with obvious pride at her little pockets of pasta.

"That's great, lovey. You are such a good cook. Are you having fun?"

"Yes. It's so pretty here. We have to go for a walk in the vines. Ari took me there. Can we, Mommy?" Jemma started dragging Blu by the hand towards the door."

"Okay, okay. And we're off exploring, I guess." Blu laughed and called out a goodbye to the two women in the kitchen.

After they left, Lia came over to sit with Arianna at the table. "That child is full of questions, isn't she?"

Arianna laughed. "Oh yes. If you're ever lonely and need someone to talk to—er—more like listen to, Jemma's your girl." She laughed. "Sorry if that was getting uncomfortable. I thought you were handling it well."

"I really didn't know what I was going to say next." Lia laughed. "She's a delight." Lia seemed pensive about continuing her thought.

"What is it?" Arianna asked. "What are you thinking?"

"I can't help but think about all those days in the kitchen that I've missed with you. As a little girl. It's one of those regrets, I guess. That I need to put out of my mind now."

"And just enjoy me watching from a close distance?" Arianna laughed. "Or if you really want me to help you cook—"

"Say no more. I've heard the stories." Lia laughed. "Seriously, Ari. I just like having you near. It's fun. It's the most fun I've had in a very long time." Lia reached over to give Arianna a hug. "And I have you to thank for that."

Arianna hugged her back and smiled. "I think it's safe to say that I have *you* to thank for this lovely dinner that's being prepared here. Are you sure you want to spend your time cooking this week? I certainly can hire someone local to come and prepare the meals too. If you'd rather enjoy someone else's cooking. I just don't want you to feel like you are working here *at all*."

"Oh no, are you kidding? I love this." Lia swept her arms to the kitchen. "And the fact that I'm cooking all of my favorite meals in Italia—Tuscany at that—it's amazing to me. I feel like it's truly a dream come true," Lia said, and Arianna could tell how much she meant it. This woman was born to cook. That was for sure.

"Well, alright then. I'll leave you to it while I go have a short nap before dinner."

CHAPTER 34

Arianna awoke early to find Gigi bustling about in the kitchen. "What's the matter? Too excited about Douglas coming to sleep?" Arianna teased as she brushed her cheek with a quick kiss.

"You're silly. And yes, for your information, I am looking forward to his arrival." Gigi smiled as she poured Arianna a cup of coffee and offered her one of her homemade scones, a recipe that she was happy to make and had perfected over the years.

"You know I'm just teasing you. And I think it's absolutely the best thing ever that you two have been spending some time together. Nothing makes me happier." Arianna grinned.

Gigi hugged her tight. "I know, bella, I know."

Before long Arianna heard the sound of little footsteps above them and, soon after, a shout from the stairs. "Ariiiiiii."

"J-bean, is that you?" Arianna called from the kitchen.

"Yes, can I come down?"

"Of course you can. Come in the kitchen and we'll

make you a cup of yummy hot chocolate."

The pitter-patter of feet got closer real fast. "Morning." Jemma made her grand entrance with a big smile and then headed straight for Arianna's outstretched arms.

"Good morning, munchkin. How'd you sleep?"

"Very good. I love my big bed here."

"Do you want one of Gigi's delicious scones?"

Jemma's eyes widened as she saw the plate on the table. "Yes," and then added, "please, Ari."

"Oh, what good manners you have," Gigi called out from where she was making Jemma a cup of hot chocolate. "Here you go. Careful now. It might need to cool a little bit before you drink it."

"Thank you."

Arianna kissed the top of the child's head and nuzzled her neck.

Jemma laughed. "Ari, that tickles."

"Oh, sorry, sorry. I just can't help it. You taste so delicious." Arianna laughed as Jemma wiggled out of her arms to sit next to her in a chair of her own.

Arianna asked, "Is Mommy still sleeping?"

Jemma shrugged her shoulders. "Dunno."

"Well then, if you didn't go in to wake her before you made your way down here, I suspect that she is. Good job, J-bean."

"Mommy likes to sleep sometimes," Jemma said.

Arianna and Gigi laughed at the same time. "I bet she

does," Gigi said.

"So, what do you want to do today?" Arianna asked the little girl.

Jemma looked like she was deep in thought for the next ten seconds. "Go on an adventure," she said with a mischievous expression on her face.

"Oh, that sounds great. I'm always up for an adventure. How about you, Gigi?" Arianna winked at Gigi.

"I might leave the adventuring to you all today. I want to pop in to town to visit the market before Douglas gets here."

"Okay, then. Leave the adventuring to us. And we'll ask Mommy if she wants to join," Arianna said to Jemma.

"Of course," Jemma said, causing Arianna to laugh out loud again.

"Munchkin, you sure do make me laugh."

"You make me laugh, too Ari." Jemma looked very serious all of a sudden. "I love you."

Arianna's eyes instantly filled with tears before she could turn away from the little girl. She grabbed her again and pulled her close. "I love you too, J-bean." She pulled away to put her hands on either side of Jemma's face as she looked her in the eyes. "Don't you ever forget that, okay?"

"I won't. And you either, okay, Ari?"

"That's a deal," Arianna said.

Arianna, Blu, and Jemma spent the day close by the villa, playing in the pool and taking some long walks in the nearby olive grove. Gigi and Lia were busy in the kitchen preparing a nice lunch for everyone as well as the evening meal which would welcome Douglas to the villa. Gigi and Lia had become quite close, which made Arianna very happy. She smiled to herself as she thought that she'd never seen Gigi spend so much time in the kitchen. She seemed to have taken an interest in watching and helping Lia cook, which Arianna thought was both funny and endearing. She wondered if the new interest had anything to do with Douglas and his fondness for Italian food.

They enjoyed a nice lunch out on the terrace, and when it was time for Jemma to take a nap, Arianna opted for a rest too. She found herself growing tired faster, and she had a headache nearly every day now. The pills seemed to be helping less and less, and she was growing worried that she'd need to start thinking about going home soon. She knew that that was where she needed to be as the time drew near. At home, in her bed, with the view that she loved so much.

She'd have to start having some conversations, because it would affect the travel of Gigi; Arianna didn't think Gigi would be able to stay until her sisters were due to arrive. She felt bad about that. She wanted Gigi to be able to visit her family down south, but Arianna needed her at home and she knew that it was where Gigi would want to be. *She'll be able to come back soon.*

Arianna woke up feeling a bit better. She glanced at the clock by her bed, noticing that it was time for Douglas to be arriving any minute. She went downstairs, where she found everyone in the kitchen. Gigi and Lia were still bustling about preparing food, while Blu and Jemma seemed engrossed in an art project at the breakfast table.

"Ari, I'm making a sign for Douglas," Jemma said as she held up her picture.

"Oh, that's so nice, bean," Arianna said, smiling as she made out the landscape of the olive grove, the villa, and Jemma's version of the little family that lived inside. "You're quite the artist."

Jemma smiled broadly. "Mommy says I can be whatever I want when I grow up." She looked up at Blu. "Right, Mommy?"

"That's right. Is that what you want to be? An artist?" Blu asked the little girl.

Jemma took on a serious expression, as she did when she was thinking about such serious questions. "No. I will be a ballerina." And at that she climbed out of her chair to display the tutu ensemble she'd chosen to put on after her nap. It was bright pink and perfectly suited her personality as she did a few twirls around the kitchen.

"I think you will make a lovely ballerina," Lia said from across the room.

"You be sure to invite me to your first performance," Gigi said, smiling at the little girl.

"What about you, Ari? Will you come to watch me dance?" Jemma asked as she went over to take Arianna's hand.

Arianna's eyes met Blu's and she tried hard to hold back the instant tears. The room grew quiet and Arianna scooped the little girl up into her arms. "You know what I wish?"

"What?"

"I wish that you would put on your first performance for us tonight. After dinner."

Jemma's eyes grew wide as she seemed to think about it.

"Do you think you could go practice and come up with a dance to a song from my favorite opera?"

Jemma nodded. "Yes, I think I could do it."

"Okay then, it's a deal. You'll have your first official performance tonight and we'll all be there." Arianna squeezed her tight before putting her down and watching her run off to practice.

The three women looked at each other and smiled. Arianna could feel the sadness in the room. It was heavy. It was too much for her. "Okay then, speaking of music, let's get some going around here. Douglas will be here any minute, and we want to have some nice Italian ambiance going." Arianna laughed as she found the music that she wanted on the stereo in the corner. No sooner had she got it going than the doorbell rang. She looked over at Gigi, who was rushing out of the kitchen towards her room. Arianna guessed that she was going to freshen up, and it made her grin.

She crossed the foyer to the door, opening it to a tired-looking but smiling Douglas, who greeted her with a kiss on both cheeks and a huge bouquet of flowers. "Douglas. It's so great to see you. How was your flight?"

"It's good to see you too." He seemed to be looking over Arianna's shoulder. "And you, little ballerina," he said to Jemma as she twirled over to give him a hug. He took a step forward to greet Blu, who had come out of the kitchen to say hello. "What an amazing place, Ari."

Arianna noticed Douglas's eyes scanning the room, and she guessed that he was looking for Gigi.

"My flight was good. Tiring, but now that I'm here, I feel like I'm getting a second wind. And something smells fantastic in here."

Just then Gigi came from her room down the hall. Arianna noticed that she had changed into a simple but lovely dress, and she watched Douglas's reaction to seeing her. Oh, there was something between them. That was for sure. His eyes seemed to light up when he finally saw her, crossing the room to say hello with a quick kiss on both of her cheeks. Gigi seemed different too, and it was making Arianna really happy. Gigi left to get some drinks started while Arianna took Douglas to show him where he'd be sleeping and to give him a quick tour of the villa.

They finished out on the main terrace, where Lia and Gigi were sitting with a glass of wine waiting for them.

Arianna could see Blu and Jemma in the distance walking in the olive grove. Gigi poured two more glasses of wine, which Arianna and Douglas happily accepted as they took a seat at the big table.

"Oh, this is so lovely," Douglas said, raising his glass for a toast. "To Italy and the wonderful days ahead of us."

The three women raised their glasses and smiled.

"Cheers to that," Arianna said.

"And to Arianna," Gigi said, raising her glass for a second toast.

"To Ari," Douglas said, clinking glasses with Gigi and everyone.

Lia leaned over and gave Arianna a quick hug and a kiss on the cheek.

"Oh, I'm so happy to have you all here. It means everything to me." Arianna could feel the tears behind her eyelids but she refused to let them fall. *Not now. There'll be time for tears later, but not now.* She just wanted to enjoy her friends, grateful for the time they had together in this place.

The four sat there for a while catching up with Douglas and telling him about the area, before Lia and Gigi excused themselves to go make the final preparations for the dinner that would be served shortly.

CHAPTER 35

When it was just Arianna and Douglas alone at the table, he reached out to touch her hand. Arianna didn't pull away, and it even registered to her that it was just months ago that withdrawing had been her natural inclination when someone reached out to touch her. She'd come a long way; she knew it was all about trust, and a lot to do with Lia. She grasped Douglas's hand.

"I'm so glad you're here. Really, Douglas."

He looked at her with such kind, caring eyes that for a moment it reminded her of her father. Not so much the kindness that she saw, but the memory of the two of them together, and she could almost hear her father laughing as he often did when Douglas had been around.

"How are you doing, Ari? How are you feeling?"

"I'm doing okay." She smiled, as she knew better than to think that she could be anything but honest with him in this moment. "Well, I'm starting to have some bad days. The headaches are getting worse and they never really go away. I don't say much to Gigi and Lia though. I don't want to ruin this time for them."

Douglas squeezed her hand. "Don't worry about any of us. This is *your* time, you know. All of this should be about you."

Arianna looked him in the eye. "It is. Honestly. Nothing is making me happier than having you all here. It's all I wanted when I invited you." She smiled. She sensed that Douglas believed her, which made her feel better.

"You tell us when you need to do something different, okay? Just say the word and we can go home. I know that's where you said you want to be. Is that still the case? Or I can find the help you need here, too, you know."

"I know. And thank you. It has crossed my mind, because I do love it here. But there are things I need to take care of. To do yet. And I think I need to be at home for—for the end." She took a deep breath. "But I want you all there. The three of you—not Jemma. I think it would be too much for her. But I want you there too."

Douglas got up from his chair, guiding Arianna up as well so that he could give her a big hug. *The kind I never got from my own father*, she thought as the tears flowed freely.

"Whatever you need, Ari. Anything at all." He took a small step back so that he could look her in the eye, and Arianna saw the tears in his own eyes. "I love you, you know. I want you to know that. You've been like a daughter to me."

Arianna closed the space again as she gave him

another hug. "And you've been like a father to me. I could never thank you enough, Douglas—for everything. And I love you too."

The two broke apart, and each wiped the tears off their face with their hands as Jemma came running up to the terrace with Blu right behind her.

"What's up, bean? You having fun?"

"Yes, Mommy and I are having some adventures."

Arianna laughed and looked at Blu, who seemed to be moving kind of slowly. "I bet you are. It looks like Mommy might need a little rest."

"Mommy might need a glass of that wine," Blu said, laughing, eyeing the bottle of wine on the table.

Arianna laughed too, and Douglas was quick to pour a glass.

"Sit." Douglas said, pulling out a chair for Blu. "Jemma, what do you say about you and I going into the kitchen to see if we can find something refreshing for you to drink?"

Jemma looked up at Douglas with a serious expression on her face. "Yes, I don't drink wine yet."

They all laughed.

"I think Gigi has some sparkling cider for you inside," Blu said.

"And if you ask her nicely, I'll bet she'll even put it in a wine glass like ours," Arianna said.

Jemma looked at Blu with wide eyes. Arianna knew, after she'd witnessed a few accidents at Blu's apartment, that Jemma wasn't typically allowed to use glass dishes.

"Be careful," Blu said.

Jemma nodded and skipped away hand-in-hand with Douglas.

"How are you?" Blu said when the two women were alone on the terrace. "Is everything okay?"

"Yes, I'm fine." Arianna said.

"Okay, good. I just saw you with Douglas as we were walking up and it looked kinda intense."

"Well, yeah. I guess you could say it was a bit intense." Arianna looked at her friend with a light smile. "But good intense."

"Okay, good." Blu gave Arianna a small hug. "I love it here, Ari. I'm so glad you talked me into coming."

"Me too."

Hours later they were all sitting around the big table outside. Arianna looked around at all the happy faces and steaming plates of pasta and appetizers. The wine was flowing and Jemma was chattering away happily as she ate her pasta and bread. Arianna could not be happier, and as she looked at all the smiling faces, she felt that everything was perfect. She was with the very people that she wanted to say goodbye to. And she knew her time was coming.

After that first night with everyone at dinner, Arianna grew much weaker very quickly. There were a few outings to Castellina. Lia and Arianna did have an opportunity to take everyone to Thyme, the little restaurant that they'd grown to love. Carlo and Sofia had become like a little family of sorts; and especially those last few visits there, Arianna was able to pull Carlo aside and get to know him a little better. Lia had grown comfortable there in the kitchen, and he was delighted to have her cook with him any time she was able to.

Gigi, Douglas, Blu, and Jemma seemed to love it there as much as Lia and Arianna did. Jemma had become a welcome fixture, and the waitresses delighted in playing with her and getting out the paper and crayons whenever they saw her coming.

It was a good time, and even though Arianna was growing weary and her headaches were getting worse, she wasn't yet willing to give up the magic of the place. She hadn't shared her situation with Carlo and Sofia. She didn't want their pity, or anyone's pity for that matter, and she wanted them to remember her as she was now.

The day came soon after, though, when Arianna was slow to get out of bed one morning. Gigi had come up to check on her, coming over to her bedside when Arianna didn't answer her knock on the door.

"Bella, are you okay."

Arianna opened her eyes to a worried-looking Gigi that morning, thinking for a few moments before she answered. "No. I don't think I am." A single tear rolled down her face. "I'm not ready. I don't think I'm ready." She couldn't stop the sobs as Gigi sat down on the edge of the bed, pulling her near to her chest.

"Shhhh. It's going to be okay. Everything's going to be okay, bella." After a few minutes, Gigi smoothed Arianna's sweaty hair off her forehead and tucked her back under her blankets. "Let me go talk to the others. I think it's time to leave."

Arianna could only nod.

Within the hour, Lia was by her side, letting her know that Douglas had made all of the arrangements. There was a doctor coming to the house to check on Arianna's comfort and give her something stronger than the pills she was taking, so that the flight would be as comfortable as possible for her. Douglas would go ahead, flying that day. He would make all the arrangement so that there would be a nurse at Arianna's house the next day when the rest of them arrived back home.

Arianna smiled with gratitude, finally willing to be taken care of. She was so tired and the pain in her head was growing more intense. She hoped that she still had at least a few decent days left to finish the things she still had to do before it was time.

She looked down at Jemma, who had curled up in bed next to her to take her nap. Blu had resisted when Jemma had asked, but Arianna had insisted, telling her best friend that it was exactly what she needed. The two of them had slept soundly for an hour, and Arianna had never appreciated the warmth of the little body next to her so much as during that time. It was a comfort to her.

And all too soon it was time to leave. They had said their goodbyes to Carlo and Sofia the last time they'd been in for dinner, and even though Arianna had tried to insist that Lia go to the restaurant, she hadn't wanted to leave the villa. They had helped Arianna outside that last day to the terrace overlooking the olive grove. With her dark sunglasses, the sun was bearable and didn't make her head hurt too much more. And she wanted to breathe in the Tuscan air one last time before she left to go home.

Douglas had done his best to make the arrangements as easy on everyone as possible. They had booked the whole section of first class, and the flight crew was aware of the situation. Arianna had been given something that would help her sleep soundly, once she was settled on the plane, and the flight itself went smoothly.

Before long, the small group was arriving in San Francisco with Douglas and a driver there to meet them, taking them back to Arianna's house in Sausalito. Arianna turned to Gigi, Douglas, and Blu, who were all sitting together in the car. "I'm so sorry your time in Italy was cut short."

They all shook their heads.

"Don't you even worry about that," Gigi said. "Italy will be there. We're exactly where we want to be."

Everyone nodded, and Blu gave Arianna's hand a little squeeze. "You just focus on feeling better."

Arianna nodded and rested her head back against the

car seat, closing her eyes for the duration of the trip home.

They arrived home and Arianna met Nurse Sheila. Before her trip, and at Douglas's insistence, they'd had a meeting with Arianna's doctor so that she could get the information she needed to be able to spend her final days the way that she wanted to. She desperately wanted to be at home—to spend her last days there, rather than in a hospital—so they had made arrangements to have everything she needed when the time came.

And Arianna wanted her friends there. She had tried to remain strong, but finally she was honest with herself about not wanting to die alone. It wasn't that she was scared exactly. She'd made her peace about it. It was more that she felt in her heart of hearts that it would be the best thing for those she loved—Gigi, Blu, Lia, and Douglas—to be able to say their goodbyes to her, and for Ari to tell them the final things that were in her heart. She'd been busy making plans, and she needed to be sure that she allowed the time to explain these things.

And Jemma. She'd debated how to handle the little girl. She didn't want to scare her and she didn't want Jemma's last memories of her to be the image of Arianna sick in bed. But Jemma was smart. They had talked about Arianna's being sick and that she was going to go to heaven soon. She would have one last time with Jemma, and she'd do her best to draw together the strength she had left to make it a happy time, with smiles and laughter.

Between the nurse, Gigi, and Lia, they'd gotten Arianna settled into her bed with everything that she needed to be comfortable, including some pretty strong medications which she would have for at least right after the long trip. Blu and Jemma had taken the car and driver into the city to pack some things to stay at the house for a few days, and Douglas had gone to his home to do the same.

Lia hadn't left Arianna's side, and Arianna knew that there'd be no convincing her to take a little time for herself.

CHAPTER 36

Arianna awoke with a start, looking at the lit clock next to her bed. 3:30. Was it morning or afternoon? She had no concept of how long she'd been asleep or even what day it was, but as she pulled the curtain back, she realized that it was dark out and the middle of the night. She suddenly felt panicked, and had a singular focus as she stumbled across the room towards the door.

She rushed into her parents' bedroom, no longer holding back her sobs. She was filled with such intense anger and sadness—for everything that had happened to her and for the pain that she was afraid she'd caused. Why couldn't her parents have listened to her? Let her have a voice?

She began frantically searching through her mother's things; she hadn't bothered to do so before now. Gigi had told her that she would take care of it later—after Arianna was gone was what she meant, most likely. She tore through the dresser drawers, pulling out her mother's expensive undergarments and the t-shirts that Arianna had rarely seen her wear.

She made her way to the closet, pulling each

expensive designer item off the hanger in a rage. She couldn't hold her anger back any more. It was all too much bottled up inside her. Arianna screamed at the top of her lungs as she made her way to her mother's desk in the corner of the spacious master bedroom.

She flashed back to a memory of her mother sitting there looking out the window when Arianna had appeared after playing in her dressing room. Arianna thought she'd been about five at the time, and had gotten into her mother's make-up drawer. She smiled for a single moment now as she seemed to recall that even then she'd drawn a perfectly red smile on, not coloring out of the lines of her already full lips.

Her mother had looked up at her with the strangest look on her face, before she'd rushed up scolding Arianna and wiping everything off her face. She realized now that it was the look that had always divided her and her mother. Arianna wasn't hers. Arianna was beautiful and could never have truly been hers.

Arianna glanced up at the careful vases and china picture frames that lined the pretty shelf near her mother's desk, and in one second she was on her feet screaming to let loose all of the rage she felt inside. Rage towards her parents and the inconsolable anger she felt towards herself for not having stood up for her own daughter—a daughter who might never know that she'd had a mother who loved her as much as Arianna did. The pain of it all was unbearable.

In one motion, she swooped an arm across the shelf, catching everything that she could touch to send it all crashing to the floor. She opened the small cupboards below and began hurling out the papers that had been stored there—looking for what, she didn't even know.

She was pulling out files and books and other papers when something caught her eye. It was a plain manila envelope, but there was something inside that caused a slight bulge. Arianna could hear Gigi calling to her from downstairs, sounding slightly panicked, but she couldn't speak through her sobs as she sat down on the floor to open the envelope.

She tilted the envelope and a small bracelet fell into her lap. It was silver and looked expensive. Arianna's breath caught as she pried the small attached locket open. It was a picture of an infant, and it could have very well been Arianna, similar to the one that Lia had showed her in Tuscany. But she sobbed with recognition because she knew that it wasn't.

She pulled out the papers that lined the inside of the envelope. One was a typewritten document that consisted of a few pages stapled together. The other was a handwritten note on her mother's stationery. As she skimmed the note, tears streaming down her face, she realized that Gigi had quietly entered the room and was kneeling down beside her.

Gigi sat on the plush carpet with her back against the shelf with everything strewn about, and pulled Arianna's head into her lap, stroking her hair.

"Bella, it's okay. Everything's going to be okay," Gigi said in a voice that was both soothing and strong. Exactly what Arianna needed as she tried to focus on Gigi's words and the motion of her comforting fingers running through her hair.

Finally, after several minutes, Arianna felt that she could breath again and held the letter up for Gigi to see. "It's from my mother. I found a letter from my mother. And look." Arianna held the tiny picture up for Gigi to see. "This is my daughter." Arianna started sobbing uncontrollably and wrapped her arms around Gigi's middle.

"There, there, bella. Let's see now." Gigi reached for the picture and held it up to the light shining in from the window. "She's gorgeous, isn't she?" Gigi quickly wiped the tears streaming out of her own eyes.

Arianna opened her hand to release the letter from her mother. "I only skimmed it. Will you read it to me?"

"Let's have a look then." Gigi reached around her neck for her reading glasses.

My Dear Arianna,

I can't tell you how many times I've started this letter to you only to end up throwing it into the fire, never to be found by a soul. Try as I might to be honest with you, I cannot. It's my problem, not yours. I am a weaker woman than you by far.

I look at you, at the woman you've become, and I'm amazed.

Not because we—your father and I—have done anything right; we've done everything wrong. Yet, I marvel at your strength and the courage that you have to be your own woman, to go after what you want.

I fear that one of my deepest regrets in life will be tearing that child—your child—out of your arms. I will never forget that day as long as I live, and I will spend every moment of my life in regret that I could not have been the strong mother that you deserved, Ari.

You could have done it, could have been the mother to your child that you wanted to be, even at your young age. I know that now.

I can only hope that someday you might forgive me, that I'd be able to talk to you and laugh with you and hug you as any mother longs to with her daughter. I fear that I've lost that opportunity forever and I don't blame you. I only blame myself.

When your daughter was born, the nurse gave me the picture that they'd taken of her sleeping so soundly and looking every bit like you. I couldn't bear to get rid of the picture, as much as I'd wanted to erase her from your memory that day.

If I ever find the courage to give you this letter, along with it will come your daughter's picture and the papers that we do have from the birth and adoption that took place that day. I know it's not much to go on and I know it's too late, but maybe one day you'll be able to forgive me for the choices I made. For the choices I made for you. I know that I cannot forgive myself. I only hope that you will not carry a burden of guilt with you for what your father and I made you do.

I do love you Arianna…with all my heart.

Your mother.

Gigi finished reading the letter and silently laid it down on the floor beside her, holding Arianna tightly to her as the exhausted girl wept openly in her arms. Arianna felt so tired. Something had shifted inside her. It was as if a dam had broken and all of the leftover tears that she hadn't wept were now coming. She'd been afraid for a long time to cry at all, to express the rage that she'd felt tonight. And suddenly it was over. With the letter that her mother hadn't had the courage to give her, she finally felt some of the love and sorrow that had been missing since she'd given birth to her daughter.

She peered now at the other documents. In them were the details about the time and birth of the daughter she'd only gotten to hold once in her lifetime —that she would only ever hold that one time. Arianna wiped the tears from her face. There was the name of the adoption agency, so it was possible that her daughter could eventually be found.

Gigi shifted the placement of her hand around Arianna's back to tilt her face up towards her. "Bella, are you okay?"

"Yeah. I think I am, actually. Gi, do you think my mother loved me?"

"I do. I think she loved you as much as she could. I

think your mother was afraid to love you. One day I heard her crying to your father. I think she knew about Lia—that she'd come looking for you. Maybe she'd overheard him on the phone with her. I heard them talking—your parents. She was crying about losing you. That she couldn't bear it—that she needed to make things right with you. And then the accident happened." Gigi looked Arianna in the eyes before continuing. "I think it's best for you if you can forgive your mother—your parents. For as long as I've known them, I think they tried. They really did. That wanted you so desperately, and when you had your struggles—the rough patch and the pregnancy—well, they just weren't prepared for that. But I think they loved you. I do."

Arianna was quiet for a few minutes. "I think they did love me too." She sighed. "I wish they would have trusted me. You know, to make the decision for myself. I think it's not so much the fact that they forced me to give her up—God, the way everything has happened, it really was the best thing for her, wasn't it? I wouldn't have wanted to put her through this now. But I think it's the fact that they made such a big decision for me. I didn't even have a voice in it. And I've hated myself for that." Arianna's voice caught as another sob escaped. "I've hated myself every day since the day I let them take my baby out of my arms."

"I know, bella. I know." Gigi was crying silently too. "Ari, I think it's time to forgive your parents and yourself."

"I'm not sure I know how to do that," Arianna cried. "I want to. I really do. I feel like something has changed in me today though. Finding this letter. God, finding this information about my daughter. And the picture." Arianna held up the locket so that she and Gigi could both see the picture of the infant girl. "I have a picture of my daughter. And she's beautiful, isn't she?"

Gigi nodded her head. "Bellissima." Arianna didn't have to look at her to know that she was grinning as she said it.

It was time for forgiveness.

CHAPTER 37

Arianna woke up the next morning with a dreadful headache. Her body felt hot; she rang Gigi when she discovered that she couldn't make it to the bathroom on her own.

"I think I should take you to the doctor. You're not looking well at all," Gigi said with a worried look on her face.

"No, I think I just need to be in bed. I have a meeting with Doc—later this morning. I really wanted to see her today." Arianna had the strangest feeling and wondered if it would be worth asking Doc to come visit her at home. She knew that she was in no shape to make the trip into the city today and she desperately wanted to talk to her—for one last time.

"Gigi, do you think maybe Doc could come here today? I hate to ask her but—" Arianna could hardly get the words out, her head hurt so bad.

Gigi handed Arianna two pills and her glass of water from the bedside table. "Bella, you take this and rest. I'll call your therapist and tell her you're not well today. Let's see what we can do, shall we?"

Gigi left to make the phone call, leaving Arianna to fall back into a restless sleep. She'd been dreaming a lot lately. Blissful dreams—the kind one didn't want to wake up from. Happy times that she'd had with Lia in Tuscany, surrounded by all of her friends at the villa. There was a dream of her with a child—a young girl whom she thought was Jemma. They were sitting together playing in the garden, the young girl's back to her, when suddenly the little girl turned around and she realized it was her daughter, with her dark brown eyes and long lovely dark tresses of hair. She awoke from that dream with a start, and a longing in her heart that wouldn't go away.

But, oddly, she was beginning to feel a strange sense of calm. It had started last night after Gigi had read her her mother's letter. Her mother had longed for Arianna's forgiveness, and this morning she woke up with the sense that she could and had forgiven her mother. Her parents had wanted her, they'd chosen her, and there were times when they'd shown her the kind of love that she'd longed for later—after the pregnancy. It was as if she was suddenly aware of this wall tumbling down around her heart, and she knew that the timing was right. There wasn't time for bitterness and resentments. Her time was running out now.

Arianna nestled down into her thick blankets as Gigi knocked quietly on her door.

"Bella, are you awake? I brought you some tea and I have some good news for you."

Arianna sat up and rubbed her eyes, then her head. "Did you get hold of Doc?"

"*Sí*, yes. She is coming here in one hour. Don't get dressed. I'll see her in and you can talk to her here in your room."

Arianna smiled at Gigi. "Thank you for that. I think I can make it downstairs. In fact some fresh air would do me some good. Let's have our session in the garden. I'd like that, and I want to show it to Doc. I've told her about it a few times. I'll just be down in a few minutes."

"Do you need some help getting dressed?" Gigi said.

Arianna started to shake her head and then seemed to think better of it. "Yes, I think I do." God, she was so tired, and her head hurt so much that it was hard to think.

Gigi helped Arianna dress in a comfy pair of sweats and an oversized sweatshirt that would help guard her from the early morning chill outside. Arianna asked Gigi to grab her journal and pencil from the bedside table, and they made their way together down the stairs and out into the cool morning sunshine.

Gigi helped Arianna to get set up in her favorite lounge chair outside, bringing her a heavy blanket to wrap around her legs. The sun on her face felt so good. She was going to miss mornings like these. Arianna sighed as she looked out over the view. She hoped that the people whom she loved would continue to meet at this place, in this garden. That there would be happy times and laughter ahead. She loved imagining that here.

Arianna opened her journal and thumbed her way to the last pages, where she was almost finished. She caught herself thinking that it was time to buy a new journal. There would be no more journals for her. She'd just have to end it well. She smiled. She knew how the story—her story—would end, and it was a good ending, a better ending than she ever could have imagined a few short months ago. She was creating a different future. She knew that now.

She had come as far as she could in her own journey, but she could leave a legacy for those she loved. She felt herself getting a little burst of energy even now as she thought and wrote about what her hopes were for the future. She couldn't help but smile as she thought about what she intended to give to Lia, what she wanted for Blu and Jemma, for Gigi—and she still held high hopes that Gigi's future included Douglas. And she hoped to leave a legacy for the daughter who never knew her. She wanted that more than anything, and she would choose to believe that it was possible. That someday this young girl would become a young woman and she would know the love of a mother who'd given birth to her. Arianna had to believe that this was possible. It was what she was holding on to now.

Arianna gave a start as she heard Gigi at the door to the house. "Arianna, Docter Jonas is here." Gigi led Doc out into the sunshine as Arianna looked up from what she was writing.

"Hi, Doc." Arianna grinned widely. "Thanks so much for making the trip out here. It means a lot to me." She tried to get up off her chair, but winced in pain.

"Don't get up, Ari. It's okay." Doc walked over to sit in the chair next to her. "So this is the garden I've heard so much about. The view really *is* lovely." She bent down to give Arianna a little hug. "How are you doing?"

"Oh, you know. I've had better days." Arianna tried to laugh but it came out as a slight grimace. "Do you want something to drink?"

"Yes, Gigi—who does seem lovely, by the way—is getting me some tea, thanks."

Gigi delivered Doc's tea and then excused herself.

Arianna and Doc sat in silence for a few minutes, sipping their tea and taking in the view of the bridge and the bay.

After a few minutes, Arianna stirred.

"What would you like to talk about today, Ari?" Doc said.

"I have a lot to tell you, actually. A lot that happened just last night. I thought I'd need help processing it all, but oddly enough, after writing in my journal before you came, I feel a strange sense of peace about it. About everything."

"That's good, Ari. Very good." Doc leaned in to hear Ari's quiet words.

Arianna recounted the events of the night before to Doc, and in telling it she found herself feeling oddly void of emotion. Not that she didn't feel anything, but it was as if she'd already spent all of her tears and thoughts about it all.

The two sat in silence for several minutes and finally Arianna spoke quietly.

"I think this is it, Doc. I don't have much time now." She wasn't exactly sad or scared. She just felt a certainty about it and about what she wanted now more than ever before. Arianna took a deep breath in and pulled the blanket tight around her legs. "I'll say goodbye to you today." She looked at Doc with the first sign of tears coming to her eyes. "And thank you—for everything."

Doc looked at her, and for the first time Arianna saw emotion on her face as she too wiped at the tears that threatened to stream. "Arianna, it's been my pleasure. You're a dear young woman and my hope for you is that you feel a sense of contentment. Do you?"

Arianna nodded her head and looked thoughtful. "I feel contentment, but more than that, actually. It's a sense of peace that I've never had before. I feel years older— like I have lived a lifetime. I don't know if that makes sense?"

Doc nodded, encouraging her to continue.

"I finally have a sense of how I can make a difference, you know? I've never cared about that before—not even after the accident, my breakdown—or even my diagnosis. It's like that trusting piece was missing in my life, from everything; and all at once—once I learned that it was

okay not to know how things were going to turn out—
everything fell into place and I finally started to live my
life in a way that mattered."

"That's wonderful, Ari. Many people live much longer
lives and can't say as much. I think you should feel proud
of yourself for how far you've come. It seems like you've
gotten closer to the people in your life that you care
about, and I'm sure that it's the greatest gift that you
could ever give to them."

Arianna nodded in agreement, knowing that she could
do more—that she would do more. "Yes, I'm sure you're
right, and they'd probably agree with you on that."

They sat in silence for a few more minutes and
Arianna noticed that Doc wasn't looking at her watch
today. She also noticed that she hadn't brought her
notebook with her. It was a nice. Another relationship
that was coming full circle. She could almost see a
checklist in her mind, although that seemed a bit cold and
she didn't mean for it to be. But there *was* a list, of course.
People that she had to say goodbye to. People that
needed to know how much she loved them.

She stood now, wanting to give Doc the excuse she
needed to get back into the city. "Well, I should let you
go. I'm sure that you have other patients to see today
besides me, although I greatly appreciate the house call."

Doc stood too. "It's okay. I've cleared my schedule
today."

Arianna looked at her curiously.

"I thought maybe I could use a little time to myself after our meeting." Doc seemed to be trying to fight back tears, and there was no mistaking the look on her face. Arianna appreciated it in that moment. It wasn't a lack of professionalism, but an authentic show of who she was as a person. Of who she'd been to Arianna.

Arianna crossed the short distance between them and wrapped her arms around Doc tighter than she'd ever done before, not worrying about how it made either of them feel. "Thank you," Arianna said.

Doc nodded, turned and, led by Gigi, who had appeared during the last minute or so, walked back into the house.

Arianna spent the remainder of the day resting in bed, growing more and more tired, yet determined to get the things done that had to be done. Pictures were put together, letters written, and boxes tucked away to be opened later. She thought to herself how interesting it was that she had this time of preparation when her own mother had not before she died. She couldn't help but wonder how things might have been had her mother had the chance to give her the letter and information herself, rather than for Arianna to have found it the way that she did.

It might have been better for Arianna, she supposed, because she could have forgiven her mother to her face, perhaps giving her that peace that she doubted her mother had had before she died. Her heart broke a little as she thought about the last exchange she'd had with her parents before they left. It was a typical argument and this time they'd been arguing about Arianna's big trip that her father had already paid for, but didn't truly support. She had argued fiercely for what she wanted and she'd gotten her way, probably because of the guilt that they felt and would carry to their grave. She sighed. She couldn't do anything about that now except forgive them for herself. And she had. She truly had. Now it was only about moving forward with the things that she did have control over.

Arianna went to bed that night after a phone conversation with Blu. She'd called her in near hysterics during a moment of fever-induced panic, and poor Blu didn't know what to do on the other end of the line from where she worked behind the bar. Finally, able to take a quick break and calm Arianna down, Blu was able to get a cohesive conversation out of her.

"Blu, I need you," Arianna sobbed on the other end of the line.

"Ari, what's wrong? You're scaring me. Shall I come?" Even in Arianna's state, she could make out the panic in her best friend's voice and immediately felt guilty for it.

"No, I'm sorry. It's—it's just I think I need to spend time with you, Blu. Tomorrow. And Jemma. I need to see J-bean." Arianna sobbed on the other end of the phone, waiting through the silence at what must have been Blu's panic on the other end.

"Yes, Ari. Of course. I'll get off work tomorrow. I'll bring Jemma. We'll spend the day together. Maybe I'll let Jemma go to daycare in the morning so you and I can have a bit of time alone together, okay?" Arianna could hear that Blu was fighting back tears herself.

"Blu, can you help me in the morning? I want to go into the city—one last time. I can't drive. Will you come get me? Take me in the convertible? I need to go to Douglas's to take care of some last things."

"Ari, I'm sure Douglas could come to you. Do you want me to call him? Maybe you should stay at home in bed. Can I talk to Gigi? Is the nurse there?" Blu's voice rose a little higher with each question.

"Yes, Gigi and the nurse are both downstairs. I'm okay. They are checking on me." She heard a slight sigh of what she guessed was relief on Blu's end.

"Okay, and Douglas? Shall I call him to come to you tomorrow? Ari, I'm sure that he would."

"No, I—I really want to go into the city tomorrow." Arianna's voice grew very quiet. "One last time over the bridge in my car, you know?" She couldn't stop the sob that escaped her as she said the words. "I'm sorry, Blu. I don't mean to be so heavy. I don't. I know it's a lot…" she trailed off.

"Ari. Don't you apologize to me." Blu's voice was firm and steady. Arianna imagined the look that she'd seen when Blu seemed determined not to crack under pressure. "Listen, I gotta go now because the boss is giving me a look, but I'll get off all day tomorrow and I'll be over at nine o'clock after I drop Jemma off at daycare, okay? We'll pick her up again after the meeting with Douglas. Does that sound good? Ari, are you there?" Arianna's eyes fluttered open and she realized that it was her turn to speak into the phone.

"I'm sorry, Blu. I'm so tired. It's the medicine. Yeah. That sounds good. I'll see you in the morning."

"Okay, Ari. Get some sleep. See you tomorrow."

"And Blu—I—I love you, Blu."

She had already hung up. Arianna clicked off her phone, rolled over, and went into the deep sleep that her body was craving.

CHAPTER 38

Arianna was still sleeping the next morning when Gigi let Blu into the house and led her up to the bedroom. Gigi knocked lightly on her door before letting herself in, followed by Blu, who went straight to the curtains to open them. The morning sunlight along with Gigi's gentle stirring brought Arianna out of a deep sleep.

She tried to sit up, and Blu went to help her while Gigi left to fill her water glass and let the nurse know that she was awake.

"Wake up, sleepy head." Blu gently rubbed Arianna's back. "How are you feeling?"

Arianna wiped her hands across her eyes as if doing so would bring her to a new level of being awake that she didn't feel. "What time is it? God, I've slept too late. And man, I feel like I've been hit by a truck. Or a tornado. Wow, worse than any hangover I've ever had." She tried to laugh but doing so hurt too much. "In my dreams, this would only be a hangover that some food and a long sleep would cure, right?"

Blu nodded and moved her hand to hold Arianna's in her own. "Do you still want to go into the city? We don't have to, you know. Gigi said that she'd talked to Douglas earlier and he's happy to come over here." Blu grinned and whispered so that Gigi wouldn't hear. "Between you and me, I think she'd love to have his company here this afternoon too."

"I heard that." Gigi said in what sounded like a stern voice, but one not hidden beneath an undercurrent of laughter. "Douglas is welcome here, of course. It's whatever is best for Arianna, though. He is waiting for my call to let him know."

"I do want to go in, Blu. I think I need to. Will you help me to the bathroom, please?"

Arianna was getting weaker, and she hated asking for the help that she now knew she needed. Maybe she should ask for the nurse this morning and clear her room while she got ready to go out. But Blu was there, offering her arm and her support. Just like she always had done. And Gigi too. She felt so much love for them. Yes, she knew what she had to do today, and she needed that final trip across the bridge. It was the one thing she'd known this morning as she awoke. The thought of it made her happy, made her feel that contentment that Doc had talked about yesterday. So she'd just keep putting one foot in front of the other this morning with the help of the others.

Blu helped her to get dressed, and she chose her favorite pair of jeans and a nice top, short heels, and a jacket that she'd bought a few weeks ago. She couldn't bear to stay in her sweats or track suit another minute, and she wanted this morning to be as normal as possible. She was craving normalcy.

Once she'd gathered the papers and things she needed for the meeting, she had the light breakfast that Gigi had prepared for her. It was a small cup of tea; the taste of the coffee seemed to be bothering her lately—she suspected it was a side effect of all the medication she was on. She and Blu sat in the garden drinking tea and eating one of Gigi's delicious scones that Arianna loved so much. God, these were heavenly. She'd have to remember to be sure that Lia tried them. They'd be perfect—her mind started to wander to conversations that she wasn't quite ready to have.

"You ready to go, rock star?" said Blu when Arianna hadn't touched her scone for a few minutes. "Did you get enough to eat?"

"Yes. Let's hit it."

The two walked back into the house. Arianna gave Gigi a quick kiss on the cheek, took the two pills that the nurse handed her, and waited for a minute as the nurse popped a thermometer in her mouth.

"Arianna, you do have a temperature." The nurse looked worried as she delivered the news. "It's against my better judgment that you are going out."

"We won't be long. I promise. And Blu here will look after me. Won't you, Blu?"

Blu nodded towards the nurse, not looking at all

confident as she did so.

"As long as you tell me—as long as you're honest with me if you are feeling really bad. Deal?"

"Deal," Arianna said as she picked up the keys from the foyer table, tossing them to Blu. "I call shotgun." Arianna laughed as she headed towards the passenger side of the convertible.

"I call music choice," Blu bantered back, and Arianna thought she'd never felt anything more lovely and normal than the conversation that was taking place in that moment.

Arianna laughed. "How 'bout your choice on the way over, mine on the way back?"

"Deal," Blu said as she turned the dial to her favorite rock station and they pulled out of Arianna's driveway.

"Blu."

"Yeah?"

"I don't hate your music."

Blu looked at Arianna over the top of her sunglasses as the traffic stalled for a minute. "Yeah, well, I do really hate *your* music." Blu smiled and they continued into the city in silence.

They pulled up to the parking lot at Douglas's office and Blu shut off the car. "So do you want me to come inside with you?" Blu glanced at the papers Arianna held in her hand.

"No, I need to do this one on my own. Would you

mind just helping me inside?"

"Of course. I'll go round the corner to get a coffee and you can text me when you're ready to meet back here. Sound good?"

"Perfecto."

Arianna let Blu help lead her to Douglas's floor, and his receptionist told them to go straight back. Blu said a quick hello to Douglas and gave Arianna a hug before turning to go back to the parking lot, where she'd left her wallet in the car.

Douglas kissed Arianna on the cheek warmly, but not before she saw the concerned look in his eyes. He led her to the chair on one side of his desk and sat down across from her.

"I could have come to your house, you know. Gigi told me that you weren't feeling very well and I should have insisted."

Arianna shook her head. "No, I needed to come here. To come into the city—one last time." Arianna looked down as she spoke, not completely trusting her emotions and not wanting to make Douglas uncomfortable either. But who was she kidding? She knew that she could be herself with Douglas. She owed him that. He'd been so amazing to her and had become more than her father's best friend; he was her good friend and she trusted him completely.

"But Douglas—will you come later? This evening. I'm having a little party—in the garden. Just us. Blu and

Jemma. Lia. And Gigi, of course." Arianna winked, true to form even in her current state of health.

Douglas laughed. "Yes, Gigi invited me already, and of course I'll be there. It sounds lovely."

Arianna nodded, looking pleased. "So, everything we talked about on the phone—I brought everything with me that you asked for. Are the documents ready for me to sign?"

"Yes, after several phone calls, video chats, and faxes, everything is in order. Just how we discussed, and rock solid, so you've nothing to worry about. I just need your signatures."

Douglas slid the documents over towards Arianna across his desk, showing her where her signature was needed. "Arianna, I'm proud of you." There were tears in his eyes as he spoke. "Your father—your parents would be too."

Arianna looked up from the paper that she was signing. "Thank you. Thank you, Douglas, for everything. You didn't play a small part, you know. In my growing up a bit. Making these decisions. You've been a strong support and mentor to me, and I'm so grateful for that." Arianna signed the signature field before her.

She continued. "No, you're more that that. You've truly become a friend to me. I only wish I'd be here to see what happens with you and Gigi." Arianna laughed, trying to make the conversation a little less intense.

Douglas laughed too. "Well, if I'm being honest—and

with you I will be..." He grinned. "I think you might have been on to something there, suggesting I ask Gigi out a few months ago. She sure does seem to keep me on my toes, and I'm enjoying that." He winked. "So far, at least."

Arianna laughed and finished signing the papers. "So is there anything else that needs to be done with this?"

"Nope, that's everything. It's all in order."

"Good. Very good." Arianna sat back feeling the most peaceful that she'd felt in days. Everything was going to be okay. It really was. "I should text Blu then and start thinking about heading back home. We'll see you in a little while at the house?"

"I wouldn't miss it," Douglas said as he helped Arianna out of the chair and out to the parking lot, where Blu was waiting in the car. He gave Arianna a big hug and vowed to see her in a few hours.

"So how was it? Everything good?" Blu said as she helped Arianna into the passenger seat.

"Yes, everything is perfect. Just exactly the way it's supposed to be, I think." Arianna leaned her head back and closed her eyes, letting the sun warm her face as she breathed in deeply.

"Blu?"

"Yes?"

"Can you call Lia for me? See if she's ready to come over now? Maybe we can go pick her up before we get Jemma?"

Blu nodded, reaching for Arianna's phone. "Of course we can. It's gonna be a nice day, Ari."

Arianna glimpsed the look of Blu's holding something back, but she wouldn't press it today. There would be time for talking later. Today was just about being together, and she wanted everyone with her.

Blu got hold of Lia, who agreed to be ready for pick-up in twenty minutes. When they stopped by her apartment, the sight of her took Arianna's breath away. She still couldn't believe that she was spending time with this woman who was her mother. And that they adored one another.

"Don't get up." Lia said as Arianna made a move to let her in. "I can sit in the back seat and I don't mind climbing over." She laughed. "It's good for my old bones."

Blu laughed. "Lia, there's nothing old about you, girl."

Arianna nodded. "Thanks for coming over early. What's in the bag?" she smiled, hoping it was an amazing Italian dessert of some type.

"Oh, you'll see." Lia winked. "Only one of your favorites."

"Well, remind me that I want you to taste Gigi's scones. She's just made a new batch this morning and they are delicious. We're gonna pick up Jemma from daycare and then we'll head over."

"Sounds great," said Lia.

"And then I may excuse myself for the tiniest of naps

when we arrive—if you all don't mind. I want to be ready to party later." Arianna laughed, and Blu and Lia exchanged a serious look between them.

"Whatever you need, honey," Lia said.

CHAPTER 39

Blu went by her house to pick up the car seat and then pick Jemma up from daycare. Arianna traded seats with Lia so that she could sit by an excited Jemma in the back seat of the convertible.

Jemma let go of Blu's hand as soon as she saw Arianna standing by the convertible in the daycare parking lot. "Ari, am I gonna ride in your red car?" she said as she ran up to Arianna, nearly knocking her down with a big hug.

"Hey, J-bean. You're getting fast. You nearly knocked me down." Arianna tried not to show the pain that she was feeling, instead crouching down to eye level with the little girl. "You want to come over to my house and play for a little while?"

Jemma nodded her head yes. "I love you, Ari. I love to go to your house."

Arianna's heart melted as it always did during these moments with the little girl. "I love you too, bean. More than this much." She stretched her arms out wide.

Jemma stretched her little arms out as wide as they would go. "Oh yeah, well, I love *you* this much, Arianna."

She grinned and laughed.

"Okay, squirt. Hop in the car seat. I'm gonna sit in back with you while Mommy drives today."

They all piled back in the car and, with the top down and the gorgeous San Francisco sun beaming down on them, made their way to the bridge.

At the stoplight, Blu turned to Ari. "You want your music, opera girl?" she teased.

"Play yours. It's fine. Maybe until we get to the bridge." Arianna stared out at the bay and then turned to give Jemma a big smile. "Jemma, do you like Mommy's rock music or Arianna's beautiful opera music?"

Jemma thought about it for a moment and replied. "I like to listen to you sing, Arianna. Sing a song with me."

Arianna and Jemma sang the nursery rhymes and silly songs that delighted children, Jemma laughing and clapping her hands. Arianna was having the best time that she'd thought she'd possibly ever had. Perhaps this was going to be the best moment of her life. The thought wasn't lost on her. Her life these past months had been a string of the very best moments of her life…with Jemma, with Blu, with Gigi, and with Lia. How thankful she was that she'd had these last moments with her mother and the people that she loved.

As if in sync with the sentimentality of how Arianna was feeling in the instant, Blu turned Arianna's Italian opera on, and then Lia reached over and turned it up loud as they began making their way across the bridge.

Arianna looked around her. Jemma laughing and so lovely sitting beside her. Her best friend and her mother in front of her. And for as far as she could see, the beauty of this home she'd come to love so much. Her hair whipped back behind her as the music filled her heart as it had done so many times before…just like any other ordinary day—but it wasn't an ordinary day at all.

Arianna knew deep down that this would be the last time she'd make this drive and feel the sun beating down on her in this exact place. And in that moment, she was okay. Everything was in order and everything was going to be okay.

Everyone, even Jemma, was quiet during the remainder of the car ride home, as if they could feel the importance of the moment. Gigi came out to greet them when they pulled into the driveway, treat in hand for Jemma.. She took the little girl by the hand while Lia and Blu helped Arianna out of the car and into the house, where the nurse was waiting for her.

"How are you feeling, Arianna? You look pretty worn out." The nurse reached out to feel Arianna's forehead and then hand her a glass of water and some pills. "I think it's best if you lie down for awhile, don't you?"

Arianna nodded in agreement, turning to Blu and Lia. "Do you mind? Please make yourselves at home. Gigi will get you whatever you like, and when I wake up, we'll have a little party in the garden." Arianna tried to smile, but the pain that filled her body betrayed her and all she managed was a slight wince.

Lia went to hug her gently. "*Sì*, bella. We'll be fine. Can I help you up to your room?"

"Sheila will help me to bed. You two go on and have Gigi give you one of her delicious scones to try. I promise, Lia—you're really going to love it." Arianna made her way upstairs with the help of the nurse, who left her tucked into her comfortable bed.

Arianna woke up feeling a bit better and ready to tackle the last thing that she had to do before she'd see the others later. She carefully pulled out her notebook that contained the letters that she'd written right before she got so sick in Italy.

She felt a strange comfort in reading the letters back. She had, oddly, discovered so much about herself these past months. It was amazing the clarity that she'd come to and also the sense of peace that she now had. Her life had more meaning now than it ever had before. She knew now that the things she had decided, the people that she had chosen to spend time with, had meant everything to her. Her decisions these past few months had been wise. The most grown-up decisions that she'd ever made.

She folded each of the letters, placing them in individual envelopes and carefully writing the name on each before closing them. Then she pulled the small leather box that she'd gotten in Florence out from under her bed. She smiled at the memory of that day, shopping there with Lia and enjoying her first days in Italy.

She opened the box, pulling out her modeling portfolio, taking out all of the carefully posed pictures from her various modeling gigs. She reached for the stack of fun pictures she'd taken and had Gigi get printed of herself, alone and with the others. She'd never been one to plaster social media with selfies, and that wasn't why she'd been taking them. She smiled as she thumbed through the carefree, silly poses and then glanced over to the model pictures she'd set aside. Yes, this was her. These quick pictures capturing those moments of fun and pure happiness. This was the woman she wanted her daughter to see one day, not the made-up model in the posed pictures. She pulled out the photos of her with Jemma, with Blu, with Gigi, and with Lia, leaving the copies that she'd had made of each in the pile.

Looking at the one of her and Lia, she was flooded with the memory of them standing at the viewpoint in Florence, with the beautiful view of the bridges along the river winding its way through the city behind them. But all she saw in the picture was their wide smiles and the light in their eyes. *We look alike. My mother and I.* Arianna smiled.

She had a lot to be thankful for. She'd known a lot of pain, but she'd known a lot of happiness too. And she had the party to look forward to later. There'd be one last party in the garden with everyone. She smiled. There'd be music and good food. And her friends. All of them together, admiring the view of the city, smiling and laughing as they talked about their times together in Italy. Arianna knew that she was getting ready to say goodbye. And she finally felt ready for it.

She put the lid back on the leather box and left it just out from under her bed. She picked up the modeling photos and put them aside on the bedside table. She'd make Blu promise to throw them away. She knew she could count on her, where Lia or Gigi, she felt, might be more likely to want to keep the pictures. Blu would destroy them. Blu would understand. Arianna smiled.

CHAPTER 40

Arianna awoke with a start to the sounds of opera music and Jemma's laughter down in the garden. She glanced at the clock by her bed and couldn't believe that she'd been asleep for nearly two hours. She wondered if she could manage to get herself the short distance to the window where the curtains were drawn without having to call for the nurse.

She slowly sat up in bed, rubbing her head and taking a drink of the water that had been left beside her. She hoisted her legs over the edge of the bed and willed herself to be able to take the weight of her body just the short distance to the chair by the window. God, how was it that she'd gotten so weak, so fast. She hadn't been prepared for it, really. It wasn't even so much just the physical toll it was taking, but the emotional one as well. And maybe even more so in that regard. She pulled back the curtain and cracked the window open a bit so that she could hear her friends below.

She'd lived a good life. As much as she'd complained these past months, she knew the privileges that she'd had, not the least of which was being surrounded by these people that loved her. She had come full circle and she finally felt no anger; and with the anger, the guilt had vanished. She had even allowed herself to feel full forgiveness for her own transgressions. It was time. She'd hated herself enough since the birth of her daughter to last a lifetime. And it almost had lasted her lifetime. But no more. She'd not leave this earth with one more ounce of regret if she could help it.

She watched Lia playing frisbee with Jemma outside as Blu relaxed in the lounge chair beside them, something her best friend rarely allowed herself time for these days. Arianna loved to see Blu like that—looking happy and content to just be in the moment, watching her daughter laugh and play and have a good time.

Not far from the others sat Gigi and Douglas. They looked deep in conversation, and Arianna smiled as she noticed Douglas's hand casually around Gigi's shoulder. She knew they were going to end up together. If only she'd be here to witness the wedding. That would be a lovely day.

She could smell something Italian and delicious, and suddenly she was extremely hungry.

She hobbled back over to her bed and reached for the monitor, used to call the nurse who was standing by while she slept. Sheila came right away to help her downstairs.

"You're looking better, Arianna. Rested. How do you feel?"

"I'm okay." Arianna smiled. "I think some time in the garden with my friends and some of the delicious food I'm smelling is what I need." Arianna leaned on Sheila for support while they made their way down the stairs.

When Arianna and Sheila entered the garden, Jemma made a beeline for her legs, with Blu scooping her up just before impact.

"Jemma—honey, Arianna's not feeling so well, so let's play gentle, okay?"

Jemma looked at Arianna with the expression of a little girl who knew way more than one gives little girls credit for. "Ari, does your tummy hurt?" she asked, walking over to where Arianna now lay on the lounge chair and gently patting Ari's stomach with her sweet little hand.

Arianna motioned beside her. "Jemma, come up here and sit by me for a minute, okay?"

Jemma nestled in the chair beside Arianna, laying her head on Arianna's arm as she patted her leg. "I'll stay with you until you feel better."

Arianna's eyes filled with tears as she pulled Jemma close, kissing the top of her head and whispering to the child. "Jemma, I love you very much. Promise me that you will always remember that, okay?"

"Okay, Ari. I will."

Out of the corner of her eye, Arianna noticed Blu, tears streaming down her face, and motioned for her to come take her hand. She squeezed Blu's tightly, just enjoying being with them—loving them and allowing them to love her back.

Lia had come back outside from the kitchen, and Arianna smiled at her when she saw her. "Are you the one responsible for those delicious smells? I'm getting hungry."

Lia smiled back at her. "*Si*, just some nice appetizers and a bit of the pasta that you seem to enjoy so much. Would you like some now? I can bring it out here for you."

"In a bit. I'm not quite ready yet. Come sit with me, will you?"

At that, Blu knelt down to give Arianna a quick kiss on the forehead, scooping a reluctant Jemma up out of her chair. "Jemma, give Ari a hug and let's go see if we can help Gigi in the kitchen."

Jemma kissed Arianna quickly and patted her on the head. "See ya later, Arigator." Jemma giggled at her own joke and Arianna's laughter.

"She's a doll," Lia said as she pulled a chair up close beside Arianna. "They all are. This lovely little family you have here." Arianna thought she saw a look pass across Lia's face that she'd not seen before.

"Lia, they all adore you too, you know." She smiled broadly to try to cover up the pain she was suddenly feeling in her head. "Lia—I hope that you will all come together sometimes. That would make me very happy— to know that. I like having you all here. I'd love to think that you would grow close with them and someday maybe…" Arianna's voice trailed off as she was overcome with another shooting pain in her skull.

"Lia, I think—I think I need the nurse. Could you get her for me, please?"

Arianna was taking deep breaths and trying to think of peaceful things as she looked out at the view and the garden. She tried to freeze this moment, right now. This was the best moment yet of her life. Or the best of the series of moments she'd remembered earlier that day. Was it today that she'd had that thought? Every thought was starting to jumble together, and she couldn't seem to get a clear picture of what it was she had just been thinking.

Sheila came to her, with Lia right behind her, to check her vital signs. Gigi and Douglas watched from nearby, and Blu was by her side just as soon as she'd noticed the nurse.

Sheila looked at the small group gathered, saying, "I'm sorry, but I think that Arianna has had enough for today." Arianna looked at her with a question in her eyes, knowing the answer, but not wanting to know at the same time.

Finally she didn't fight it, and let the nurse lead her upstairs half carrying the weight of her. Once tucked in her bed, she whispered to her the question that she'd wanted to say before. "It's almost time now, isn't it?"

When the nurse nodded, Arianna asked her to tell Blu

to take Jemma away to the sitter and come back. And for everyone to stay—to spend the night if they were able. She felt in her heart that the time was getting close and she had things that she needed to say to each of them. But for now, she'd sleep. And hang on for just a little longer.

CHAPTER 41

Arianna seemed to be having a hard time getting comfortable. Gigi called for the nurse, who came right away, asking Gigi to give her a moment to check on Arianna. Gigi made her way down to the kitchen where Blu, Lia, and Douglas sat quietly waiting to hear when they might be able to visit.

The nurse came in looking somber and asked Gigi if she could speak with her for a minute.

"It's time now. I'm sorry. It's time to say your goodbyes. She's waiting for you," the nurse said.

Gigi cried out loudly and the others rushed to her side. "The nurse said it's time to say goodbye," she said through her tears.

Douglas put his arm around Gigi and her body gave way to the strength that he offered her as he led her over to a chair.

"Blu, you go." Douglas said, seeing the look of panic on Blu's face.

Blu left the room quickly to make her way upstairs to Arianna's bedroom. She knocked quietly on the door and entered without waiting for a response. The curtains were open and the sun was shining down on Arianna as she lay so quietly on the bed, barely moving. Blu rushed to the chair beside her best friend, taking her hand in her own and talking in a quiet voice.

"Hey there, rock star." She reached out to smooth Arianna's damp hair off her forehead as her eyes fluttered open.

"Hey yourself, Bluesy." Ari winced a bit, but then smiled. "You didn't bring J-bean, did you? I don't want her to see me like this."

"No, sweetie. She's at daycare." Blu gulped back a sob. "Ari—" Blu broke down, sobbing, before she could stop herself. "There's so much I wanna say to you."

"Shhh. Shhh. It's okay. Blu, listen to me for a minute. Alright?" Arianna took a deep breath and Blu nodded.

"I want you to give Jemma the biggest hug for me. You tell her that I love her so much and that I know she's going to grow up to be the most amazing woman. Ask Gigi to give you the jellies that I bought the other day for her. They're in the kitchen." Arianna coughed and tried unsuccessfully to sit up a bit.

Blu reached for the water on the nightstand, helping Arianna to raise her head just enough to take a sip.

"I will. Jemma loves you so much. She won't forget you. Ever." Blu couldn't hold back the tears; they were falling freely now as she reached for the tissue beside Arianna's bed. "Ari, there's so much I want to tell you." More sobs. "I'm not ready for you to go."

Arianna looked Blu in the eyes, willing the strength not to leave her body before she finished saying everything that she needed to say.

"Blu, listen to me. I need you to promise me something, okay?"

Blu nodded at her best friend as she spoke the final words that Blu would hear from her.

"I've got everything arranged with Douglas, and he'll help you sort out anything that you need. I'm leaving you the house in San Diego—it's for you and Jemma. There's room there for your workspace, and there's plenty of money for whatever you need to get your clothing line going. Your life will be easier there. And there's a trust fund set up for Jemma. For college—or for whatever she needs...for whatever she wants." Arianna stopped for a moment to catch her breath.

Blu was sobbing uncontrollably, and Arianna wondered if she'd heard her at all.

"Blu, it's gonna be okay." Arianna smiled through her pain. "Do you know how happy it makes me that you're finally gonna accept something from me? You are one stubborn girl, but I am not giving you a choice here." Arianna winced and did manage to pull herself up a bit.

Blu took a deep breath as she looked at her friend lying in bed. "Ari, you're the best friend I've ever had. I love you so much. You know that, don't you?"

Arianna nodded and smiled. "I love you too, Blu. I do." She waited for Blu to continue, as she looked like she had more to say.

"Ari, there's something I need to tell you. It's about my past, about—"

"I know." Arianna interrupted Blu. "Well, I don't know, but I know that you have your past—your secrets—and nothing you could say would change how I feel about you. Okay?"

Blu nodded, tears streaming down her face as Arianna continued.

"I want you to have the best life. And work it out if you have stuff to work out. I trust you. I've always trusted you more than anyone else." Arianna started coughing again and her eyes closed for a few minutes.

"Ari? Arianna?" Blu started to cry again.

"Blu?" Ari's eyes fluttered open. "I think I should see Lia now." Her eyes closed again for a moment.

"Of course." Blu reached over to Ari, giving her a kiss on the cheek and smoothing out her hair. "I'll send her in now."

Blu turned to walk out of the room, tears streaming down her face.

"Blu?"

Blu turned around at the sound of Arianna's quiet voice.

"One last thing."

Blu nodded. "Anything. What is it?"

"My car keys are downstairs in the kitchen. Douglas should have the title for you. Promise me that you're going to leave here today in that convertible." Arianna laughed lightly.

Blu grinned at Ari for the last time through her tears. "I promise." She turned to walk downstairs, calling for Lia as she reached the bottom and started to sob uncontrollably again.

It was Lia's turn now to go upstairs, and she wasted no time when she heard Blu calling for her. Arianna heard her enter the room quietly as she moved to the chair next to her bed, and felt her fingers gently stroking her hair.

Arianna willed her eyes to open.

"Lia—Mom." Arianna gave a weak smile and watched the silent tears slide down Lia's cheek.

"Bella, my sweet daughter. Time has been at the same time cruel and lovely for us. I will treasure these past months—our time in Italia, getting to know you…it has truly been an undeserved gift from a God that brought us back together just in time. Lia looked at her and Arianna saw her catch her breath as sobs seemed to overtake the words she had yet to speak.

Arianna struggled to open her eyes and raise herself a little. It was her turn to talk now—to the mother she had only just begun to know, but a woman she loved nonetheless. She cleared her throat and asked Lia for her hand.

Lia reached out to hold her daughter and brought her chair as close as possible to Arianna's bed.

"I want you to know how incredible these past months have been for me. To have the chance to get to know you, to spend time in Italy with you. It was truly the dream that has made all of this pain worthwhile." Ari winced and struggled to continue as she reached next to her to pull her journal onto her lap. "There wasn't enough time, not near enough, but every moment I spent with you was treasured. I want you to have this." She placed the thick leather-bound journal in Lia's hand. "From the moment you called me, I knew we wouldn't have near the time to spend with one another that you'd imagined. But I wanted you to know my thoughts and everything I was afraid and excited about back then. I wrote them all here for you."

Lia took the journal from Arianna and stroked the leather lovingly with her finger. "Bella, I will treasure every word." Lia could no longer hold back the tears, and Arianna took the moment to close her eyes and collect another deep breath.

God, it was getting very hard to breath now. But she still had things to say.

"Arianna, I need you to know how much I love you. That I never stopped loving you from the moment they placed you in my arms when you were born," Lia said.

"I do know that." Arianna's eyes met Lia's and she held her gaze for a beat. "And I love you too. I never imagined I could love so much that I feel my heart would burst for it. But I do. I really do, and it's as if something that was missing all my life is suddenly in front of me. And for the first time, I'm grabbing for it. That's what knowing you these past few months has been like for me. So thank you for that—for calling me." Arianna smiled.

Lia sobbed quietly next to Arianna, holding her hand and stroking her hair for several minutes while Arianna rested a bit. At her stirring, Lia reached for a tissue and dried her eyes.

"There's something else that I have for you. Douglas has everything and he will sort it all out after—" Arianna's voice trailed off for a moment and she seemed to be mustering up the strength needed to continue. "I bought you Thyme." She smiled at the confusion that she saw on Lia's face. "Our little restaurant in Tuscany. The one that you loved so much." A single tear slid down Arianna's cheek. "The one that *we* loved so much." Arianna was crying now, without shame. "Lia—Mom. Make it special. Be happy there. It's a time for forgiveness. For both of us. Too many years have passed and I want you to live your dream. There's money too. Enough to buy a villa nearby and—"

"Ari, no. It's not what I wanted. I only wanted you. I—"

"Shh. I know." Arianna reached to pull Lia to her. "It's not just for you. It's for me too. Giving you this— your dream—is making me so happy. You have to know that."

Lia looked at Arianna in disbelief, overcome with

emotion and the sadness of knowing these were the last words she'd speak to her daughter. "Arianna, I don't know what to say. I'm not ready to say goodbye to you. I don't want you to leave me now." Lia hugged Arianna tightly and their tears mingled together in an abandoned river of grief.

Finally, Arianna pulled away slightly, putting some distance between them. "There's something I'd like to ask of you."

"What is it, bella? I'll do anything for you."

"Douglas has hired someone to find my daughter. To contact the parents." Arianna took the deep breath that she needed to continue. "Not now, but when she's older. When her parents feel comfortable or when she's eighteen, I want her to know that her mother loved her. I've left a lot of money to her in a trust fund, and Douglas will be sure that she's taken care of, but I wanted to be sure…" Arianna's voice trailed off and her eyes fluttered shut. "That you will all tell her that I loved her. You and Blu and Jemma and Gigi and Douglas. I wish that she could know you all. That she could be loved by you all." Arianna got very quiet and whispered, "You'll give her the box in my closet, won't you? It's for her. And the locket? And you'll tell her that her mother loved her very much?"

Lia, with tears streaming down her face, looked at Arianna and nodded. "I promise, Arianna. Your daughter will know that you loved her. We'll find her."

"Okay, that's-s-s good. I'm so tired now. I love you. I

think it's t-t-time to play some music."

"I love you too, Arianna. So much." Lia sobbed, then took her hand. "Okay, shall I get Gigi and Douglas? They'll want to say goodbye too."

Arianna nodded with her eyes closed. "Yes, it's time—for the party. Have them all come up. And tell Blu to b-bring the music. Please." She smiled faintly, content to wait a few more minutes.

Lia crossed over to the intercom to buzz the others upstairs, asking Blu to be in charge of the music that Arianna had instructed her about earlier that week. They entered led by Gigi, who rushed to Arianna's side, with Douglas holding back just a bit to give them a moment.

Arianna's eyes fluttered open when she smelled Gigi's perfume and felt her arms around her neck, squeezing her tightly to her chest. "Bella, bella. What will I do without you my darling girl?" Gigi sobbed uncontrollably and Douglas stepped nearer to place his hand lovingly on her back.

"Gi, I have the feeling this man behind you wants to make an honest woman out of you." Arianna winked at Douglas, who smiled at her behind Gigi.

Gigi laughed lightly in spite of her tears. "Arianna, you've become such the little matchmaker. We'll see how everything goes, but yes. We are happy together. You did very well, bella."

Arianna smiled.

PAULA KAY

"Blu, I think it's time to fire up that playlist for me. Do you have it?"

As Ari's favorite opera songs began to fill the room, she smiled and reached for Douglas, motioning for him to come closer so that she could whisper to him.

"Thank you, Douglas." She looked into his eyes and tried her best to give him one of her biggest smiles. "For everything. You did good by me. And I know you'll see to it that everything I've left is carried out, including the plans for the garden wedding." She couldn't help making another joke, and Douglas laughed in spite of himself.

Douglas leaned over and whispered in Arianna's ear. "She's lovely, Ari. I think I love her."

Arianna smiled and squeezed his hand.

"I love you too, Ari." One last squeeze from Douglas.

Now only Gigi was left. One last hug, and then she was ready to listen to the music.

She pulled Gigi close to give her the biggest hug her waning strength would allow. "I adore you, Gi. You've meant everything to me."

Gigi sobbed and just hugged Arianna closer.

"Now, I know you're not going to argue with me about everything that I've got set up for you. Douglas has it all. You'll have this house, and Gi—" Arianna pushed her back a bit so that she could look her in the eye. "Fill it with love and music and parties…" Gigi nodded, unable to speak.

Arianna propped herself up in bed one last time as

Gigi walked over to be near Douglas. She looked around at the small group of people that she loved so much, smiled as her eyes settled on Blu. "Could you turn it up just a bit, please?" She let the music fill the space as her head sank back into the pillow and her eyes closed for one last time.

CHAPTER 42

Blu and Lia stood outside in the law office parking lot, quietly talking as they waited for Gigi.

The women looked over at Gigi and both smiled at the same time. She'd come out of the building with Douglas. With his arm lightly around her waist, they seemed lost in conversation before they finally noticed Blu and Lia by the car. Douglas leaned down to give Gigi a quick peck on the lips as they said their goodbyes, and Gigi made her way to where Blu and Lia were talking near Arianna's convertible.

There was a comfortable silence as they waited for a moment, each lost in their own thoughts about everything that had transpired in Douglas's office that morning, how much each of their lives would be changing. In good ways, but bringing with it the reminder of such great loss.

Finally Blu broke the silence. "Lia, can I give you a lift? Do you have plans for the rest of the day?"

"No, no plans today." Lia wiped a tear and seemed to struggle for a moment. There was more to say, but a lot had already been said too. Arianna had only been gone for two months and their grieving had only really just begun.

"Well, I have an idea that I think Ari would have loved," Gigi said.

Blu and Lia looked at her in expectation.

"It's such a lovely day. I say we all head back to the house and share a bottle of Arianna's favorite Chianti in the garden."

Blu and Lia looked at one another and grinned.

"That sounds like a perfect plan to me. Do you want to invite Douglas?" said Blu.

"Yes, he'll be along in a little while." Gigi winked and smiled.

"Okay, then. Shall we?" Blu said, gesturing towards the car.

As Blu started up the car she turned to Lia in the back seat. "Any objections to the top being down?"

"None on my part." Lia smiled in anticipation of feeling the sun on her face and the wind in her hair.

As they made their way across the bridge, each lost in their own thoughts, Gigi reached over to the volume, turning it as loud as could be as the first notes of Arianna's favorite opera began to play.

ABOUT THE AUTHOR

Paula Kay spent her childhood in a small town alongside the Mississippi River in Wisconsin. (Go Packers!) As a child, she used to climb the bluffs and stare out across the mighty river—dreaming of far away lands and adventures.

Today, by some great miracle (and a lot of determination) she is able to travel, write and live in multiple locations, always grateful for the opportunity to meet new people and experience new cultures.

She enjoys Christian music, long chats with friends, reading (and writing) books that make her cry and just a tad too much reality TV.

Paula loves to hear from her readers and can be contacted via her website where you can also download a complimentary book of short stories.

PaulaKayBooks.com

ALL TITLES BY PAULA KAY

http://Amazon.com/author/paulakay

The Complete Legacy Series

Buying Time
In Her Own Time
Matter of Time
Taking Time
Just in Time
All in Good Time

Visit the author website at PaulaKayBooks.com to get on the notification list for new releases and special offers—and to also receive the complimentary download of "The Bridge: A Collection of Short Stories."

Made in the USA
Las Vegas, NV
30 May 2022